ALFALFA GIRL

ALFALFA GIRL

THE PATH FROM CHILDHOOD
MOLESTATION TO SOUL

EDNA SAILOR

To order additional copies of this book, contact:
Xlibris
1-888-795-4274
www.Xlibris.com
Orders@Xlibris.com
782893

DEDICATION

This book is dedicated to my dearest children and grand children. To Robbie and Cheri. Thank you for your stalwart support of my writing efforts over the years. You first saw me write as children playing around me in our living room. You were always the wind beneath my wings even though I may not have said it often enough. And to Jamie, I dedicate this to you in your absence from our lives. You were gone too soon in life, but you inspired me in so many ways and I will never forget that long winter phone conversation about your cancer and life in general. We shared the beautiful snowfall together that day and a passage in the book recalls some of that conversation about the gentle snow fall.

And to my beautiful grandchildren, Dominique and Desiree, Costas, Jersey and Dylan and little Journey Elizabeth, I dedicate a part of this book to all of you. You all inspire in ways you will never know. You are my heart.

ACKNOWLEDGEMENTS

Thank you to Jan Witkin and Cedric Red Feather who helped me so much with readings and suggestions. Your contributions were invaluable.

Thank you to Irene Van Eeckhout who painstakingly threaded through a very early draft to help with the grammar and punctuation corrections that my old eyes kept missing. And finally, thank you to my friend and Editor, Jerry Kram for your encouragement and finally to Sue Stein whose expertise and encouragement brought the book to a publishable final product. I owe you all. Thank you to my dear friend Willliam Wilber who offered his technical computer expertise more times than I can count.

CONTENTS

Chapter 1   Jenny..1

Chapter 2   The Assault..48

Chapter 3   Alfalfa Girl 67

Chapter 4   "Girlie" 119

Chapter 5   Cally 148

Chapter 6   The Crawford Family 183

Chapter One

JENNY

She stumbled her way into my office that day as if her world had just ended. She was crying and it looked like she cried her insides out for a long time. She kept her head down being careful not to make eye contact with me. She verged on hysteria but thwarted all of her energy into wiping and wiping at tears on her face until her face was red from it. She looked empty. She was. I could tell. Jenny was trying to find her way back to a life…just some kind of life. At this point any kind of life that did not include sexual assault, death, rejection or any other inhumane twist life could throw at her would be helpful. She moved through the motions…sometimes. Jenny did the right thing… sometimes. Jenny studied her lessons…sometimes. Jenny faced those who were more than cruel to her…sometimes.

But sometimes she simply could not. Most of the time, she could not access that corner of the soul that harbors and protects innocence, dignity and confidence. She hasn't found it yet and cannot find it when she needs it. Few victims can at first. Jenny was no exception. She bore the pain deep within herself, moment by moment, day by day, week by week and year by year. She felt fragile all the time. She felt like delicate china many times. She felt scattered more often than not. I know the feeling of fragility well. In my own childhood feeling like glass or a cracked egg was commonplace. It might be that

1

certain look from a man. It could also be the "look down your nose" rejection from Mother or some other woman. No telling what state of brokenness was happening. It did not matter just now. She shattered slowly in front of my eyes. Once the horrors of sexual molestation find a victim, there is a special part of the soul that never ever feels the same again. We cry and grieve but we rarely understand why. Jenny is one of those girls. Jenny carries her fragility as best she can. But it is obvious this day she could not. She hung just at the door to my office briefly. Her eyes were swollen and she looked hunched over like a very old woman. One curl of her auburn orange hair hung just over her right eye. She blew it out of her lightly freckled face. It dropped back just as fast. She choked back sobs and tears. She rubbed her eyes vigorously again. No amount of rubbing wiped away the pain.

I knew from the dour look on her troubled face something bad must have happened. Something serious was afoot. There always was when she came to me looking like the distraught waif who now stood in front of me.

"What happened?" I asked, in the gentlest voice I could muster. She would need more than a little gentleness right now. She always did.

Jenny moved more deliberately toward me as she labored to embrace me emotionally, just as she had so many times in the past. We met in the middle of my Work Placement office. She spiked her book bag to the floor as if she could dispel all her bad feelings away from herself. It reminded me of her first day at Rutledge Training Center just under a year ago. She arrived with a social worker and all of her belongings stuffed into a garbage sack. She admitted to the admissions counselor back then that she that felt like someone's garbage.

Today she burst into tears again and clung to me for dear life. She sobbed until there seemed to be nothing left inside to spill out. I pulled up one of the soft chairs and motioned for her to sit by me. She did not. She was more shaken than I had ever seen her. I sensed that sitting down was something she could not grapple with just now. Planting herself might feel confining in her current state. She needed

2

to seize her own power as best she could before the fragility broke her into emotional little pieces too small to put back together again. I knew that from experience.

Mucus dripped down her chin. I grabbed a tissue from my desk and handed it to her. She waved it away and wiped her nose on her sleeve. Yes, she needed to take back her power. It seemed to compose her temporarily as she did. I welcomed her need to address her issues on her terms. OK with me! And certainly it was the best thing for her.

She drew several shaky breaths, raised her head looking for a way to focus. She plopped herself into the soft chair pulling one leg up beside her and let the other one just dangle as if to demonstrate she did not care. She paused and I decided to allow the silence to envelope the room for as long as she needed.

She drummed her fingers on the arm of the chair and kept looking down at the floor. It seemed like hours. Her introspection might serve her well I hoped. So I waited in the silence she seemed to need at this crucial moment.

She was a lovely, fifteen year old girl who looked much younger than her true age. She looked up and her eyes seemed to flutter uncontrollably. She wiped her nose again with her other sleeve, raised her head slowly and looked me square in the eyes. It took every bit of that small vestige of strength for her to find voice.

"Miss Emily," she said and paused, struggling for breath or words or both. "I am going to die! I am going to die! I am going to die!" Each exclamation grew louder. There it was out in the open and she could not take it back if she wanted to.

Now she studied my face. I could feel her intensity as she searched my face for a response. I was careful not to express shock on my face. I looked back at her warmly to let her know she found safety here at least for this moment. I found a smile hoping it would help her find her words. I took a chance that she was ready and cupped her hand in mine.

"Tell me why you are feeling so sad today." I prodded lightly.

She uttered a couple more sighs. Slowly, she managed a couple of deep breaths which seemed to spare her only moments to delve deep into herself. Hopefully she could pull forward whatever horrible news she wanted to share.

Then she just suddenly blurted it out. "They are coming! Coming here to Rutledge! Here! In two days they are coming here! If he comes along I will die! I will just die!" she spit out the words in explosive, angry bursts. She seemed to sink deeper into desperation each time she blurted out the words uttered with such desperation and ugliness.

I knew her story well. She did not have to explain. Her maternal Grandmother, Gloria Nelson and Grandma's live in boyfriend of two decades, Alex Turner, must have arranged to make one of their self-satisfactory, self-aggrandizing, obligatory visits to Rutledge training center. The center was complete with dorm facilities. Students lived and studied at the center around the clock. It is a holistic approach to training students for the workforce. Grandma and Alex appeared to want to move Jenny out of their way. Most students need the discipline provided by this training environment. For Jenny it also meant safety from her abuser and his unwitting supporter.

Jenny lived with Grandma since her Mother died of cancer when Jenny was just five years old. Jenny built a small shrine in her bedroom at Grandma's house. It held precious memories of her Mother. There was a photo of them both with bald heads during the cancer. Jenny shaved her head. Jenny kept the handkerchief that her Mother used to wipe both their faces often. She protected a withered and disintegrating rose from her Mother, Annie's casket. She kept the brush and comb used when she combed her Mother's chemo thinning hair. And there was the blue blanket Mother wrapped her in when she was born. She laid the drawings of Mother and the rose on top. She tried to cry about all of those things. She cried about the place in her heart that her Mother left unfilled at her death. Her father, Karl, was angry and he screamed at her repeatedly to stop her useless sniveling.

Karl could barely handle his own grief and arrived at this paralyzing grief with no way to help Jenny with hers. Her brothers simply slinked away outside or to the back shed. They never shared what they were thinking with Jenny or her Father. Jenny did not know where to put the feelings when he yelled about it. But in her child's heart she seemed to understand how much he hurt too. She could not help him either. The anger built a wall far too great for a hurting child to scale.

Karl stayed in the picture for a few years, but alcohol soothed the devastating loss of his beloved wife. More and more often during that time he sought comfort in a bottle. He lashed out often at Jenny and her brothers and many times they bore the bruises inside and out. He refused to attend any grief counseling although it had been suggested by many friends and family clergy at the time. His grief completely overcame him over weeks and months. Despondent and isolated he lashed out every day.

Life lashed back at one of his lowest points. He walked down the sidewalk and never returned. He simply abandoned the children.

The three children survived on their own alone in the house for a few weeks before a curious neighbor alerted authorities. A week later the Highway Patrol found Karl dead in his car. It rolled over an embankment and landed in a gully after one of his daily trips to the bottom of a bottle.

Jenny loved her family and her life. The loss of first her Mother and the loss of her Father not long after was debilitating. She lost her bowels often and wet the bed many nights. She kept a tattered picture of her parents under her pillow. She hoped they could come back together as a family and she fretted about how that could happen. No one was there to reassure the dismal fretting.

Jenny's two brothers were placed in foster care after that. Jenny found herself living at Grandma Gloria's house, which she found uncomfortable for many reasons. Grandma wasn't very friendly to Jenny and she did not understand what she did to deserve that. Grandma did not know how to deal with the situation. Just having Jenny in the house challenged her daily.

Jenny did not know that Grandma Gloria was once a throw away child from a family of thirteen children. The siblings all got away from that home as soon as they could. Grandma lived with an older cousin, Gertie, who found Gloria quite ugly. Grandma owns 28 mirrors, all to make sure she looks perfect as Gertie said so "some damn good man can take you off our hands."

Grandma and her partner occasionally showed up at center for ceremonious visits. Jenny always struggled past the chill of the meetings between them. She beat it out the door as soon as she could after each visit. Even with the passage of time, Jenny's scars sliced deep. Her journey day by day included trying to heal the wounds with the help of several counselors in the training program.

At the center meetings, Grandma and friend said all kinds of meaningless words about loving Jenny and wanting the best for her, but their words felt phony to all of the staff when they spoke about Jenny. Their cold attitudes and their discounting of her needs made the room feel frigid with every word.

"I... I... I think I could handle it if just Grandma Gloria came," Jenny said as she tried her best to explain the situation to me. "Sometimes Grandma was actually nice to me. She didn't hurt me like he always did."

"But HE is coming too. Why does she have to bring him? She knows what happened and she still brings him! She STILL brings him!" she half wailed, half whimpered like a small child. I expected this type of regression when she was forced backward into the disturbing memories of her childhood sexual molestations.

She repeated it another time as if repetition might make the bad feelings spew out of her body. She yearned to feel better about herself. She didn't and that reality was written all over her face in pure anguish just now. The agonizingly twisted face said it all.

I watched her face grow paler. I could imagine her rerunning the memories of the repeated molestations through her mind. Those memories are encased forever in her psyche somewhere to be splashed forward into consciousness at frequently inopportune times in life like they were today. I empathized easily because mine still do too. It is far less devastating to me over years of work with counselors and healing.

Jenny's brows furrowed. I knew that she was digging deeper and deeper to try to find a safe place inside herself. She looked for that safe place to rest or feel better or find even a shred of decency that would allow her to go on! To just go on! That basic! Just go on! She drew a long labored breath.

She could not be looking for answers right now. She was emotionally incapable of bringing herself to that point. That would take a lot more time. Organizing thoughts was difficult for her at this stage. She finally found some words to speak again. I mentally gave her great credit for trying.

"I asked her not to bring him! She said it was all in my imagination! She said I need to learn to deal with things now that I am grown up! I don't feel grown up! I don't know how that feels at all!" she half angrily whimpered like an injured toddler again.

I felt my own hand go limp. I managed a friendly squeeze. She squeezed my hand back. That encouraged my heart.

This time I was the one who needed a breath. I took a long one. In reality it was too short for complete composure, but it was all I had and it damn well has to be enough right now. This journey belongs to Jenny. I would do my best to help her through it. I had no one back in the days when it was my journey. That kind of isolated loneliness was bone chilling. I did not want that for Jenny and I did my best to help her. So I hoped for at least a little step forward.

"How did you find out they are coming?" I asked, fearing I already knew the answer. But I wanted to hear it from her and give her one more platform to express herself. From my experience that is something many victims never get a chance to do. Victims are many times relegated to the back of a pile of paperwork in some office somewhere, or they wind up being shut down by the perpetrators and never fully get the opportunity to divulge the crimes committed against them. And even if they do there is always someone standing by to discredit or discount the crime.

I wanted to scoop her up and help her know it would be ok. I wanted to protect her from all of it. But I could not and I knew it. Too much push and I was afraid I would lose her and not be able to help at all. So I pushed cautiously forward one step at a time with what it seemed she could handle for the moment. Her tears started to roll again. They splashed down her cheek and she rubbed them away.

"It's ok to cry. Just let it all out. I understand," I said.

"They… They…" she stuttered a bit. "They sent me a letter," she said finding faint voice. She stopped abruptly with that.

She withdrew a wrinkled ball of note paper from her pocket and launched it on my desk. I picked it up and just held it. I wanted her to take the lead. Now she chewed on a lock of hair as she kept bumping her toe against the leg of my desk in a little rhythm only she understood. Anger? Confusion? I couldn't tell. It did not matter. It seemed to be helping her. The rhythm gradually slowed.

Rutledge Training Center, where I have worked for the past eight years, encourages family visits. Jenny is in her last year of culinary arts training. For most kids, family visits are good for them. For some not so good and Jenny was one of those kids. Unhealthy existing family dynamics do not go away for many students during the visits. Jenny struggled in her efforts to change things about her life. Despite those struggles, she did well academically and showed progress in her cooking skills. She didn't like culinary well enough to seek it to a professional level and go into advanced training as some students did.

She was really incapable of looking at long term options during that time. But she could learn enough skill to get out on her own and she relished the thought of independence. It was doubtful she completely comprehended all that means yet.

Jenny carried so much to overcome. Staff always noticed a downward slide in her attitude and training performance after a Grandma and Alex visit. The visits were always followed by crying spells, confusion and anxiety all mixed together. For days Jenny seemed to sleepwalk in a non productive fog. Veteran staff observed that she arrived from home in a much worse condition less than a year before, however. Staff all understood and welcomed small steps of improvement in each student. In Jenny's case progress went up and down, and to her credit she did not give up.

The term Grandma does not really fit Jenny's Grandma Gloria. She gave birth to Jenny's Mom very young and now in her early fifties, she is still attractive, having never let go of that being perfectionist thing. She was out for a good time. She had bottle dyed blonde hair drawn up in a twist on top of her head. She was very attractive with a pencil thin body and dressed far too young for her years. Spike heel boots, short skirts, leggings and huge hoop earrings completed the faux youth impression she sought. She splashed phoniness in every direction no matter what she was doing. Her self-absorption bordered on narcissism. I once saw a picture of her Face book with come hither expressions and seventh grade hair wraps on this so called adult. She pranced more than walked and always held her head like she expected someone to install a crown on it. She did not deserve to be anywhere near a child, let alone raise one. And yet there was something very sympathetic about her from too many sessions in front of a mirror and guardian urging her to be the perfect catch for her man. I felt sad watching her.

Grandpa was not a typical Grandpa either. Alex Turner was younger than his Grandma roommate by a good eight years at least. He was one of a number of live in partners over time and saw himself as Jenny's "keeper." He said so in a meeting with staff earlier in the year. I had no idea what that meant then. When I pushed him to describe what that meant, he lost no time in trying to put me in my place.

"Jenny needs a firm hand. She needs someone to show her things. Damn girl will waste all this time in school and then go out and get pregnant and it will all be for nothing. Nothing I tell you," He ranted. He wasn't done yet as he turned his attitude on me.

"You educated women are all the same. You always think you know so much and you know nothing. Most of you just need to go out and get yourselves laid. I know what is best for Jenny. She needs a man's hand. That's all. She thinks she is so high and mighty because she is going to school now," he sermonized.

"Men like me have to stand up to all of you," he accused forcefully. He grimaced and his voice grew louder into such a tirade he spit on himself while he ranted. He wore his misogyny and disdain for women like phony armor.

I know his type well and have run into them many times in my life. He once told me "All you educated women are just a bunch of dumb ass dykes. You all just need a real man. A couple of rolls in the hay with a good man is what you need."

If I ever thought misogyny was an isolated viewpoint, my perception was totally out of step. His attitude reflected the mindsets of many corporate and government environments at this time in our country, unfortunately. There doesn't seem to be an end season on pejorative and condoned attacks on women. The election cycle news was full of it these days, sadly.

Jenny is scared of Alex Turner. She has good reason. His attitude alienates many of the staff who encountered him. Several times the meetings were abruptly curtailed to protect everyone from his bully ranting.

Jenny carries all the weight of the two dysfunctional adults in her life on her frail little shoulders. And more than once she looked like the fragile as glass girl who could break. I stopped looking for fairness a long time ago. It was a fool's errand and I had to admit it to myself after more than a few hard knocks.

"I wish my Momma had not died. It would be different. It would be so different," Jenny sobbed. I held her in my arms again and just let years and years of bottled up grief pour out onto my shoulder. My own counselor did that for me many years ago. Jenny needed understanding at this moment. I understood.

Sympathy alone could paralyze her in her fears. I have known many females who never even got through that stage. I hoped for more for Jenny. Our program worked hard to provide her with life skills to succeed.

Jenny's mom died very young at the age of 36. She suffered from brain cancer and spent her last month's fighting pain, taking chemo, watching her hair fall out and trying to make a life with Jenny as best she could. Jenny's father was supportive and loving yet during those years. Family meant everything to him. He deeply loved his wife and family. Jenny spoke of him lovingly, but knew her Mother's death set him off in a grief stricken direction from which he never recovered. The loss destroyed him. Jenny stood sidelined watching it unfold and rip her heart out.

Despite the weeks, months and years of cancer, Jenny held those last years and hours with her Mother close to her heart. She told me one of her most treasured memories once.

"We used to make drawings together. We used thick pads of paper and we painted and drew all the time. She asked me to draw life one time," Jenny said. "I tried to draw her and we laughed at how funny she looked on paper. My mother kept that paper next to her heart until she died," Jenny said.

"She loved pink roses and drew me one. I still have both of our drawings hanging in my room in the dorm. Mom always hugged me next to her and we laughed and drank mint tea. She said the mint made her feel better. We ate butter cookies from the store. She could not bake cookies for me anymore," Jenny added with an intimate understanding of her mother's cancer limitations. The last weeks and months of their relationship were spent on or near the living room sofa. Items nested around it so they could be close at hand when needed.

Once one of Jenny's dorm mates saw the two childlike drawings and made fun of Jenny. The poorly adjusted roommate took the framed drawings down from the wall and threw them on Jenny's bed.

"Those are just stupid," she sneered at Jenny. One of the frames cracked and later had to be repaired. Staff dealt with the cruel issue and the roommate, but it was an emotional setback for Jenny and took her some time to recover from it. The drawings were nearly sacred to her.

The Grandma visit still loomed in Jenny's mind. But little by little as we sit together in my office, she stopped shaking and again she searched my face for answers. I had none. But she always tried. I searched for my own voice. It took me a few moments to find it. "Let's talk about what we know for sure right now and not worry about everything at once," I said.

Because of my own trauma and years in counseling, I sensed the weight of her degradation right through her skin. I know Jenny's story well. It is my story and millions of other girls' stories.

"We will see what we can do here. We have some options. We will not let you be alone with him," I reassured her.

She stiffened at the comment. Jenny reacted like so many other abused girls and women I had met over time. The wall of insincerity and posturing by grown-ups is one we all suspect. Jenny bears her mantle of distrust very heavily. She always would unless some competent help could help free her from it. Her troubled facial expression and bent over posture betrayed painful and confusing thoughts mulling around in her head.

"They told me that in my high school before I dropped out." she said. "When no one was looking he followed me into the bathroom at school. He said if I screamed he would kill me," She half declared and half accused as she unknowingly laid the heavy bricks of non trust right at my feet.

"I know what happened then, Jenny. I promise you. We will not let that happen this time. No one will follow you anywhere. I promise you. Let me talk with staff to see what we can do."

I knew better than to promise more than I could deliver for her, but I read the ache she was feeling. She bore the posture of a very old woman. For now the best I can do is offer encouragement to go on! Just to go on! One foot in front of the other! Just go on! Most people don't get it. Just go on! One foot in front of the other! Just go on! It is just that simple and that complex for victims.

She tried to reach deep and it seemed she could not do that right now. This is not the right time for scratching open the many wounds on the inside.

Jenny's blue eyes lost a little of her dread but only a little. They signaled a lot of pain yet. I was sorry to see so much pain in a little girl's eyes. We must go on...one footstep at a time. I tried to encourage some small steps.

"When are they coming?" I asked.

"Wednesday," she blurted out in a panicky voice eyeing the window. Fright wrote itself all over her face. It is time to do something if she can. I tested the waters.

"Let's make a plan. We will talk to your counselor and put together a plan that you are ok with."

"Ms. Emily, do I have to see him?"

I didn't want her to start fretting all over again. "I will check into that for you. Don't worry about that right now. One thing at a time! Tell me more about the part where you think you will die."

"If he does that again, I will die! I will die! I promise you I will die!" she sobbed again. She rubbed her eyes until they were red again.

The tolerance threshold of the physical violence to her body and soul evaporated for her right now. It has been evaporating for a long time. Something would need to change and soon I hoped. I feared her whole life hung in these few minutes. I felt more deeply sad than I had for a good long time. We needed to find a sprig of hope yet today. In a brief moment my mind percolated through what she said again. In a stark moment of self realization I reeled inside with the self stupidity I suddenly felt.

Is she trying to say she will kill herself? I wondered to myself. I was in over my head. And I knew it. I must call in a professional for her. And now! "I want you to do something for me. Here are some of those anise mints you like so much. I have some cold water." I pulled a bottle out of my small office frig and give it to her. "Let's make a phone call to Ms. Connie for us." I deliberately kept my sentence inclusive. I wanted to act with her not for her.

She stuffed a couple of the mints in her mouth, blew the hair curl out of her face again and shook her head to confirm her willingness. She pulled both knees up to her chest and wrapped her arms around them. It struck me as a symbolic sitting fetal position.

"She's nice. I like her a lot," Jenny offered. She makes me feel better," she mumbled slowly under her breath, unwinding her body as she spoke.

I handed Jenny the phone and told her to press extension 234, the center counselor number. When Connie picked up Jenny handed the phone back to me. I motioned her to go ahead and talk but it was a leap too far for her and she pushed the cell back to me.

"Connie, this is Ms. Emily. I have Jenny Nelson in my office. She really needs to talk to you as soon as possible," I said with as much urgency as possible without alarming Jenny. I handed her the phone again, but she pushed it away and indicated I should do the talking. I was disappointed and wanted her to self assert. I knew it was ok if she was not ready just yet. I understood how important it was not to push her into something she wasn't ready for.

It was the end of the training day. Even though it was a little after 4 p.m. Ms. Connie knew the situation with Jenny very well from many past sessions with her. After much collaboration about many students we both worked with, she trusted my judgment.

"Now?" she asked.

"Right now, if you can!" I answered with an edge to my voice to note the importance. "I will walk her over there. I don't think she should be alone right now," I emphasized. Connie agreed to see Jenny.

It was a short walk across the campus. It was a beautiful fall day in North Dakota. The trees throughout the Souris River valley fired up their gold, bronze and orange. Leaves crunched under our feet. Jenny moved at a slow pace which worked out well for me after my recent back surgery. I couldn't help wondering what was going through her mind just now.

Do you want to talk?" I asked

"No. I like the way the leaves crunch."

"Me too! Let's stop at that bench for a minute," I suggested.

She nodded.

"I want you to take a deep breath of this fresh, cool air."

We stopped. We both took deep breaths. She seemed to breathe in the air to buoy her courage.

Breathe in. Breathe out. Breathe in, breathe out. The fall air was cool and fresh.

"Can we just sit here a minute, Ms. Emily?" she asked.

I nodded and looked at her just in time to catch a brief look of awareness spread across her face.

"Miss Emily, why does Alex hurt me like that? He says it is my fault, that I just make him want to do it. He says that all the time. I don't do anything to make him do those things. I don't! I don't." she disclosed with a straight face and a tone far too emotionally distanced for my liking. But I understood her need for distance at this point. She was protecting herself from the inside out. I rejoiced in my heart.

"I do not know the complete answer to your question, but I do know this much. He lies when he says it is your fault. That is just a lie he tells himself. I think you should talk to Miss Connie about that," I said. We sat for several more breaths and then I knew we had to go. Gradually she calmed. It was certainly contagious. I calmed with her.

I rose without saying anything. She clasped my hand, which surprised me. I knew it was little Jenny who held my hand. Teenage Jenny would not do that and take a chance on other students seeing her.

We moved toward the Franks building. It was named after a former counselor who developed the quality counseling program when the building was first built during the nineties.

"Can you go in with me?" She asked with great trepidation in her voice.

"I think Ms. Connie will want to talk with you alone," I said. "But I will wait outside for you until you are done."

We arrived at the door. The door plaque read Connie Williams, MA. Social Work. That's what it said, but over the years Connie took more coursework in her PhD program and spent hours and hours in advanced training and earned certifications in sexual abuse and assault. Her expertise was known everywhere and she enjoyed a stellar reputation in her field. Ms. Connie greeted us at the door. Lavender scent bloomed out the door around her. She raised the lavender in her own herb garden and it felt calming to me. Jenny told me many times she liked it too.

Connie Williams was a short pleasant woman with dry flaxen like hair pushed back behind her ears. Her blond graying hair suited her well. She wore skinny, rimless glasses which she peered over most of the time. She did not bother with makeup, telling me once that "she damn well did not have anyone she wanted to impress that badly." I enjoyed that about her.

She smiled at both of us and welcomed Jenny into her room.

"I will wait right here," I told Jenny and included Ms. Connie in the reassurance.

I sat down on the soft blue chair by the office to wait. My mind spiraled as I thought about Jenny and her situation. She has so much potential. She has never really had much of a chance in life. The stuff of her life is her fate but not her fault. Her youth was squandered by losses and by the adults around her. Her father began to drink and use drugs after his wife died. Prior to that time he lived his life as a devoted, committed family man. He was kind and gentle, but the loss of his wife ate holes in his soul and over time it destroyed him. Jenny and her brothers spent their time learning how to avoid sticks and straps and any other weapon of opportunity as they grew older. Dad spiraled more and more downward into despair. Many people knew the beatings were happening, but it is a small town and no one reported anything of that nature then. It was a "mind your own business" community like so many others. Blue Trousers and Blue Skirts lived in every single one.

Once, Jenny disobeyed her Dad and sneaked away with some other kids to a pond just outside of town. She fell off the makeshift raft and went home drenched knowing that punishment would be swift. It was and it was more brutal than usual.

Her father stripped her down to her wet panties and bra. She could hardly bear the humiliation of her budding breasts and pubic hair clearly outlined through her wet underwear. Her Dad beat her in front of her two brothers gathered around the supper table. She was late for supper on top of it, another infringement of the rules.

Jenny bore the beating as best she could, making no sound or crying out. But what she remembered most about it was seeing her own body float above the scene actually watching her father take the thick leather belt to her butt and back for what seemed like an eternity.

After a bit numbness protected her from the blistering stinging and slashing of the skin. The growing muscle numbness allowed her to feel the blow but not the biting pain. She looked down on the brutality and grieved for the humiliation of the little girl below. She finally let those tears roll out. She was too young to know or understand that the out of body experience saved her emotionally. Her brain protected her from pain no girl should ever have to suffer.

Then it was over. He put the strap on the back of the chair. She steadied herself as she stood up, flesh still burning from the beating. Jenny's descent from the overhead out of body experience was foreign to her. Then she found herself standing right in front of the dining table never understanding how she got there or anything about the experience, except for the burning pain up and down her backside.

The two male siblings were laughing at her. The beatings were common to them as well. It was the half naked sister in front of them they found funny as they laughed and poked each other and hooted little cat calls to her. Her Dad did not stop them and that stung too. She might have felt humiliated, but that would have been a step up. Instead, she felt like nothing inside and out. She would not feel anything again for a very long time in her life. She told me that one of her counselors said that the laughing boys were probably nervous for her. She said that made her feel better about it. The incident was never mentioned in the household again. Jenny still carried the emotional scars of the inhumanity of it all.

"Now don't be going down to that pond again, ya hear?" her father barked at her.

She missed her Mother more than ever at times like this. She missed drawing life and roses on slips of paper that would keep forever. It seemed nothing else would or should last forever in the strange world that life handed her.

She nodded in compliance and went to the bedroom for some dry clothing, grateful for the temporary reprieve and solitude. The boys stopped laughing. She ate no food that night. In the mirror she could see the black and blue and purple marks down her back. Food was the last thing on her mind. The laughing did not stop in her mind for a long time. The laughing was almost harder to bear than the beating. She did not really cry until then. Her back still smarted from the beating and a river of grief poured from her frail body as she found sanctuary under her stiff quilt on her bed. She pulled it over her head and only let her nose and mouth stick out. She needed to hide then and long after that.

Jenny's stories played over and over in my mind as I waited. They were my stories too in many ways. I felt her fear. It was so familiar to me. Thousands of hours and dollars of mental health therapy helped me find a safe center for myself. But I felt the pain ripping open again ever so slightly as I watched Jenny go through her pain.

I tried to distract myself. I needed to focus more on what we could do to help her.

The TV was on in the corner. An announcer was talking about the 2016 presidential campaign. They played the ugly tape of the so called locker room talk. Every muscle in my body tightened. My stomach turned and I grabbed a tissue out of my pocket fearing I would puke right there. I felt claustrophobic like the day I stopped by the shoe store to look at some new penny loafers I was eyeing. I was ten years old. On that day Mr. Benson, with putrid cigarette and whiskey breath took me behind the counter at his shoe store and forced his hand into my panties and fingers into my genitals. I wasn't even a Miss America contestant or friends with a once beloved movie star. I was just a little girl with braids and a plaid dress who wanted to look at the shiny new penny loafers on the shelf. Little Plaid dress girl could not object. No one would listen. Power always gets what it wants. I learned that as a very little girl. Those hands just "grab" what they want whenever they want it.

I wanted to scream at the television, but refrained from letting myself get that emotionally caught up in it. I felt frozen in time on my comfortable chair outside the counseling office. I had no idea how much time passed. It was a blur. I read over some files that I brought to work on. I must have dozed a bit as well.

Michelin Tires were rolling across the TV screen when I looked up. I looked out the side window and noticed it was starting to get dark.

I looked toward Connie's door as I heard the knob turn. Lavender scent whooshed toward me and Jenny came out first. I smiled. She did too, but it was forced smile and I waited for them to take the lead.

Miss Connie took a breath and said, "Look, it is time for her to go to the cafeteria now. I have another student in five minutes, can you go with her?"

I agreed but I had so many questions. Connie read my mind. "I know you have questions, I will call you in a few minutes," she said. "I have your number in my cell." She patted Jenny on the back and squeezed my arm affectionately. We headed down the hall to the door.

Jenny and I headed over to the cafeteria. They did not like it if students came late, but I knew I could pave the way for her since she was with staff. She chose the lasagna and I had the vegetable beef soup.

Jenny picked at her food. "I guess I am not hungry," she said.

"Would you rather have this soup?"

She brightened a bit. "Yup!"

I had not eaten any yet so we just switched the dishes.

My cell rang. It was Miss Connie. "She does not seem to present as suicidal, right now, anyway, but I am sharing my notes with Dr. Bennington just to make sure. I know you had those concerns. I think we are dealing with a sort of PTSD here and she just keeps reliving her pedophile's abuse when it is triggered by something."

Dr. Bennington was the consulting psychiatrist for our training center. His office was not on center, but he made regular visits and worked with groups as well as individual students. He also held staff trainings. Recently he held a workshop on bullying. It was starting to become more of a problem and on center. We wanted to nip it as soon as we could. Silly me for letting my mind wander. I apologized to Connie and we resumed our conversation.

"I am not surprised that the seriousness of Jenny's condition has gone unaddressed. The previous counselor did not have much experience with molestation and sexual assault, so I am going to meet with Jenny regularly and work with another therapy that will be a better fit for her. If you can stop by before you go home, I can share some new research that is being done. It is promising a new way to work with sexual assault victims. Also, I checked with security and her Grandmother and the boyfriend have cancelled the visit. They have some business deal that came up. That will give us some time," she said and paused. "I am also going to file a formal report as a mandated reporter. I am learning the boyfriend had community connections. He pulled some strings last time a school counselor raised allegations. He tapped his friends at city hall in their town back home. The report was never made. I looked back in the records and he manipulated the last counselor here on center. She was new. I heard she does not have her license to practice anymore. None of it should have ever happened. Sadly, the proper reporting has never been done either," Connie said.

"I hear balls dropping everywhere," I quipped cynically. "Is she cleared to go back to the dorm?" I asked.

"Yes, if she wants to. I called her night resident and she knows Jenny's story, so she will keep a close eye on things for tonight," Connie said.

I appreciated her thorough approach to our students. Jenny frequently cried or emotionally broke down at the dorm. She frequently had trouble organizing herself. They were typical symptoms of abused girls. Most people failed to understand what was happening. The other girls in the dorm made fun of her. Some even bullied her despite staff efforts to quash bullying in our program.

To other students Jenny was a 'cry baby.' It only made her confusion worse and helped drive her self esteem into the basement. At those times she was barely coherent and even if campus security tried to help out, she was too lost in herself to tell them much or understand what was happening internally. It was impossible for her to find her own voice during that much duress.

Jenny and I wolfed down an extra large brownie with ice cream to top off our dinner. Her eyes had a bit more clarity that had not been there earlier. I was glad to see it. But she faced a long road ahead of her. We all knew it. We saw that she tried to reach inside herself to find some strength. There was no way to tell if it worked or not. But she could put one foot in front of the other for the moment and sometimes that's all that could be expected of Jenny or any other victim for that matter.

"Do you feel safe enough to go back to the dorm?" I asked. "The Residential Assistant is there and knows you are coming. Ms. Connie checked," I told Jenny.

She nodded. "I like Ms. Barbara. She is good to me," Jenny said. "She told me her father used to do those things to her too," Jenny added, more matter of fact than I would have anticipated.

I swallowed hard, I did not know that. It felt good that Jenny was willing to trust me with that shared information. Or trust anyone for that matter. Trust building would be a long road for her. We exchanged knowing looks. She wiped a bit of chocolate off her mouth and picked up her dishes. We put them in the dirty dish window.

Predators do not know the long range damage they do to their victims. They don't care. Whether it is rape or molestation a little at a time they do not care. Girls and women bear those scars for a long time. Advocates and professionals are moving the ball forward all the time but there is still isolation such as in Jenny's case. Many times the crimes go unanswered due to denial and cover ups. Sadly, no victim is immune. Public education is the key I told myself.

The public barely understands that many of us who are among those legions of women who have been through sexual assault on any level see through them and their antics. Many of us see the Emperors with no clothes. We recognize the insulated and protected vibrato of those men. We recognize their feeble denials and their flicking accusations off like one more bad business deal to be discarded. We spot and hone in on the betrayals often spoken in public or during adjudication processes. We see right through them. They are straw men, sometimes even straw women. Blue Skirts and Blue Trousers! They insulate themselves in safe and protected cocoons with money, power, prestige, religion or lawyers. Their guilt goes unpunished as does that of their protectors. The victims pay every time.

I call perpetrators and their protectors the Blue Trousers. I call the women protectors the Blue Skirts. I personally hold those women in the worst contempt. They helped perpetuate the myths about assault, rape or molestation and slam bible verses and meaningless platitudes at it sometimes. They have created significant contributions to victim suffering for decades.

Blue Trousers

Blue trousers all sizes and ages
Troll for the innocent
Sport smug faces
Superior in their minds
Blue Trousers everywhere
Run corporations
Are rich
Are poor
Everyday workers
Politicians
Blue trousers wear a badge
Blue trousers wear a uniform
Some clergy
Some teachers
Blue trousers wander
Find easy access
Wear suit of power
Troll for girls
Troll for teens
Troll for women
Troll to hurt females
Troll for the weak
Troll for venerable
Troll for anguished

Troll and troll and troll
Blue trousers weapons
Vicious hands and fingers
Charm that curdles like sour milk
Power penis invade, damage and destroy
Blue trousers ugly tools
Tools betray, fool, disguise
Blue trousers many and everywhere
Go undetected, unsuspected, free
Victims cower, cry, bleed inside
Feel dirty, untouchable forever
Yearn to feel clean, whole if ever.
Blue trousers clueless
Do not care, do not pay
Ever.

The Blue Skirts

Blue skirts do not lead
Cower beside, behind their men
Blue skirts spout platitudes and bible verses
Blue skirts clean kitchens in comfy homes
Blue skirts accomplices
Blue skirts most harmful
Are women too? How?
Are tramp callers
Are the front row deniers
Blue skirt voices lie from shameful safety
Blue skirts assail victims
Are the lie keepers, deceit protectors
Blue skirts accuse, retaliate
Blue skirts live blind
Inflict pain from suburbia
Blue skirts bereft of penis pain.

Denials denials denials denials denials
Blue skirts smile false sunshine.
Own no tears for their crimes.
—*Emily Sorenson 1980*

Part or sometimes all of an emotionally healthy life has been stolen from girls and women in these acts. What part of that don't they get? I kept asking myself that question. I never found an answer for it and decided to refocus on things I could actually do something about instead.

Just recently I ran into a woman that I have known for years. She was all up in the air about a co-worker who had been dismissed from the worksite for making lewd and inappropriate comments to the clients.

She could not wrap her mind around the accountability of the perpetrator. Instead she threw it back on the clients. It felt like a 1935 moment to me. "If they would not wear the tight clothes and low blouses, this would not happen," she proclaimed in her sanctimony. Oh, yes it would. Most assault is pre-meditated. It was the age old, uniformed, hackneyed response I grew to despise so much over the years.

Not to be outdone a pastor from the south announced proudly that "rape and incest were gifts from God and incest is consensual."

I was stunned at the ignorance of the positions. They were educated people with children of their own and I was surprised at the outrageous stances they took. That was one of many I heard over the years. The Blue Skirts were everywhere, practicing their self elevating attitudes. And for reasons I have never understood, they talk and think to protect the abusers. I could never understand why.

Unfortunately, the high profile televangelist was one more of the chilling voices during an election campaign that seemed to spiral in all the wrong directions.

For self preservation I told myself to stop thinking about it. I shook all of those ideas from my head. I had to focus. Now!

It was already too late for Jenny from a prevention standpoint. She was a slender girl, about five feet tall. She chose baggy clothes most of the time. I remember the days when I did not want anyone to see my body either. It is the heavy cloak of shame that some victims wear.

Today she wore a bulky flowing skirt, long over shirt and a sweatshirt over that. She had a rose tattoo on her right hand. She said it was a rose for her Mom. The family put pink roses on her Mother's coffin. Jenny was five years old at the time. For years she hung on to the withered pink rose from the funeral. The nice funeral director gave it to her. But it didn't last and she vowed to get one someday that she could see all the time.

"I had this tattoo done a couple of years ago." She pointed to a faint pink rose tattoo on her right wrist. "I can see it all the time. Grandma was mad as hell." She realized the word slipped out and quickly cupped her hand over her mouth.

I dismissed it as an honest slip with an "I get it look" to her. She should have had a write up for swearing, but it damn well wasn't going to come from me.

I walked in the direction of my car. I waved and she tossed a wave back to me. I waited until I saw her enter the building safely. I called the Residential Assistant to ensure Jenny was in her room. I said a quiet prayer for her. I am not much of a church person, but I knew how to pray, so hoping for the best, I prayed. I just hoped she could get some sleep.

My dusty gold home with its green shutters welcomed me. I was exhausted beyond measure. The house was on the historic register. I diligently honed every part of its delicate features to create my own safe haven. The lead glass windows, hardwood floors and the beautiful wood banister comforted me. It was my intimate sanctuary in every way. I tended my rose garden in the summer. I surrounded myself with nature and beauty. I did not have an alfalfa field anymore, so I created my safety net in the best way I could.

I was single again. Marriage just did not seem to work for me or me for it, I guess. Two divorces and I was done with it.

I turned on my Pachelbel Cannon CD and headed for my recliner for a few hours. But I felt restless and went to the refrigerator for a glass of Cabernet Sauvignon.

The music finished and I turned on the television to catch the news. A coach of a well known football team in our state just finished speaking on his position about "locker room talk."

"We discourage this type of disregard for women. I have a wife, daughters and granddaughters. I do not want any of my players talking like that about women. It demeans us all. It is not fit conversation for anyone. We need to teach that and learn and live those values right now," he said.

I thought about Jenny. I thought about me. I felt temporarily encouraged for the first time in a long time. I headed for the shower. I settled myself to attempt a restful night of sleep. I turned on my diffuser with its lavender and natural blend aromas. It reminded me of wild alfalfa, so comforting to me.

But, sleep was elusive. My mind would not unfurl the events of the day. Dreams came and went.

I was back in the alfalfa field where the plaid dress girl with the braids used to go to feel clean again. Alfalfa had a very cleansing fragrant aroma memory for me. I nestled down into a small patch of it. The wispy plant with its purple flowers followed the shape of my body and I snuggled in until I was completely hidden. I could escape there. Nature caressed my heart and mind. Sometimes hiding was all I could do. I wondered what it felt like to be a whole girl. I longed to feel like those girls where nobody made you feel dirty. I would never know. I gazed up at the blue sky. "That must be where God is," I thought. I wondered about that God all the time. I wondered why he hated me.

My minister said boys and girls who touched each other before marriage were "dirty kids and would go to hell." For him it was simple. Life was simple for him. You stick to the platitudes and the passages and it's all simple. For him it was. For me it was not. For Jenny it was not. For many girls and women it was not. My parents made me go to church and Sunday school. I even taught Sunday school but I always felt like I was living a lie. I always felt like the dirty little girl, even inside church.

Reports of sexual abuse and rape cases were hitting the news nearly nightly these days. In North Dakota three such men were prosecuted in the past month. Another school administrator was prosecuted for child abuse and child pornography. Law enforcement seemed to be on top of a lot of cases these days. Unfortunately a good many cases are simply never known to anyone. A friend of mine said one time he thought that there was a lot more of the abuse going on right now in North Dakota. I disagreed. It has always been there, the case is simply that it was under reported and swept under the rug throughout time. I bet him at the time that every family knows a family victim or knows someone abused or knows a perpetrator. He did not take me up on the bet as he knew it was true in his own family. It was a hard thing for him to admit.

Thank God for Alfalfa Girl. In one recovery group I told my story. There was an exercise to help each other take steps toward recovery. In this one a paper plate was fashioned with a piece of yarn. We hung them around our necks with the plate on our backs. Group members were each given a bright marker and could write encouraging words on the paper plate for us. I still have mine on my bedroom wall. One friendly guy in our group wrote "You are special, Alfalfa girl." It stuck and others called me that too. I liked how it felt hopeful and certainly made me feel better about myself in some small way since then.

Jenny settled back into her training with the usual bump in production. This disruption was shorter than usual. Her instructor helped her get through the inability to focus. Ms. Connie met with her frequently. Dr. Bennington saw her from time to time also. Our team approach worked well.

I was Jenny's mentor in the mentor-mentee program which is how I first met her and other students. I looked forward to my monthly meeting with them. I was assigned three students: Jenny, Darla, and

Darren. I always provided a treat for them. The trio bounced into my room and each staked a claim on a chair.

Fifteen-year-old Darren still displayed some pre-pubescent confusion. As he walked into the room he smacked Darla on the back, harder than he intended it seemed. I shot a look at him that might have dropped a large, fierce animal.

"What do we say about putting our hands on other people?" I reminded him.

"Just teasing her," he retorted with a youthful, smug, self-satisfied half grin, half sneer on his face. He was letting me know I was out of step with him. I was sure that was true.

"In this office, that does not work. We respect each other. No hitting, no punching, ever!" I said emphatically with direct stern eye contact to make my point.

He pivoted off the subject. "Do we have treats today?"

"We do if we can respect each other." I answered.

Jenny studied my face again. Darla was leaning forward eagerly ready to talk as usual. It was hard for her. She was so much more mature than the other two. She was highly motivated and ready to please. She came from a religious family. She was a bright girl, her nursing training instructor told me on several occasions. Her parents were good, hard working people, commonly known as the working poor, which qualified her for our program. She had blond hair and deep blue eyes and rosy cheeks. She carried a little extra weight around the middle.

They were the working poor so often poorly understood by gate keeping politicians and economic deniers who unfortunately saw poor kids as burdens and the drain on public resources. They missed the potential so many kids possessed and their proposals would grind them out of the system if they could.

Benjamin and Joan Olson were good parents and supported Darla in her dream that she could be anything she wanted to be. Her father, a security guard at a local hotel, believed that with his whole heart. He saw so much of the other side of things, he wanted better for his daughter. The parents were always interested in her training.

Her mother worked at a local diner as a waitress. She earned a high school diploma but sought no other training. Her family received food stamps due to her father's illness and she was determined to work, education or not. Darla's mom always said there was no money for any more schooling for her after high school. Her parents thought she should work. They still fostered the once common notion that women would be cared for by a husband. In their minds, college was an unaffordable waste of time for their small family.

Elsewhere on center, the trio was an odd fit. They did not hang together socially except in my office. And even then, it was hard for them to bond as others might. My basket of candy bars whisked around the room quickly. As they munched I asked each student to let me know how things were going for them. Darla and Darren were into the first year of training. Jenny was the only one nearly ready to go on her unpaid work experience if we could get her past some of her other problems.

"I think we should get to go to the worksite even if we are not done with everything. We could learn so much and you stop us," Darren opined for the tenth time. He loved his little challenges to me. It was a game for him.

He chose the welding program. I handed him one of the welding brochures. He seemed mystified. This was the program you agreed to when you came here. Your training was geared to educate you so you are skilled and ready to go on a jobsite. That way you can more easily gain from the experience part of it. He shuffled his feet a bit. He liked having the attention of all three of us at one time, but he really did not quite know what to do with it. He did not like being presented with reality either. So he pushed it.

"When can I go? When can I go?" he angled.

I offered a compromise. "Let's start looking at what kind of work setting you want to work in." Sometimes that provided kids with extra incentive. If he saw the end game, maybe it would help him focus. "Now tell me how you are doing in your program," I encouraged.

Darren ticked off some skills that he accomplished since our last monthly visit. He did not bring up a problem he had in the dorm. So I raised the issue.

"How did things go in the dorm for you?"

He rolled out his sheepish look for my benefit but I was not buying.

"I got a write up for leaving my clothes on the floor. But it was not my fault. At home my Mom always picked up my clothes and I just forget to do it."

I smiled at him and shook my head at him in not buying it fashion. "Your Mother doesn't live here. We have talked about responsibility, Darren. Imagine what the dorms look like if all the students leave their clothes on the floor!"

He ducked the issue by childishly stuffing the last half of his Snickers bar in his mouth. Sugary chocolate drool oozed out both sides of his mouth and down his chin.

I resisted the inclination to comment on manners. He wanted child like attention. Depriving him of it would be much more effective. The girls reacted by fixing frowns on their faces and he knew they would.

EEEUUWW. The girls audibly expressed their discontent with his bad manners. He did not care. He basked in the extra attention and icky feeling it gave them. I expected him to open his mouth and expose the chewed up treat, but he did not today.

It was Jenny's turn now, but she motioned to skip her and move on to Darla. I nodded.

Darla was gleeful about joining the conversation.

She was an eager sixteen year old blonde girl who was focused and motivated. She had a round pleasant face and could express herself very well. She exuded a lot of energy around herself. Her communication was largely upbeat and positive in most instances where I observed her. She was a smart girl when it came to academics, but she didn't always come off very friendly with some kids on center. I overheard students say she was "stuck up," which was not the case in my observation of her. I saw her as wanting to be liked and popular and it was that part that created the problems for her, it seemed to me. She just seemed to try too hard. She was her usual chipper self today.

"Our class got to go to go to the hospital on a field trip yesterday. We visited pediatrics. I love that. I think I would love to work with little kids," she said.

"I am glad you are learning that about yourself. You can take your time to decide. There are many aspects of nursing. My sister works with older people in a nursing home. She loves doing that," I offered.

"No, I don't want to work with old people. They smell. My grandpa pees himself all the time. My mom got him these diaper things, but he always smells," she jutted her chin out in her emphatic declaration.

Jenny pursed her lips and let out a deep sigh. To her it must have seemed that having a smelly grandpa wouldn't be the worst thing. It was hard to know what she was thinking. I did note that she reacted to Darla's statements with interest.

"Jenny, how are things going for you in your training?"

"I made a cake this week, but the middle sank. It tasted good. We cut it and ate it in class. I like the middle gooey like that anyway. But it was not how it was supposed to turn out." She declared. She paused uncomfortably. She studied my face again. I did not understand what she was searching for when she did that.

Darren sounded the "time up" alarm. He practically had one foot out the door already.

"Time to go!" he laughed. They slid their chairs back and headed out the door.

Once it closed I picked up the phone, but a moment later, Jenny poked her head in the door.

"Can I talk to you?

"Sure." I said, half expecting it.

"My Grandma wants to come to center to talk with me. She said she would not bring him with her this time."

"How do you feel about that?"

"I am kinda scared, but if he doesn't come...well..." her voice trailed off.

"Have you talked to Ms. Connie about this?"

"Yes. She said she would be with me if I want."

"Can I help you with anything?" I asked.

"When can I go out and work?" she asked as eagerly as possible for her. Her request took me by surprise, but I saw it as a positive thing.

"You have a couple of skills yet to do, but let's talk about where you would like to work. We can go look at some of our worksites or do a day shadow before you pick a place. Food service has lots of choices for you. We have a lot of partners, everything from grocery stores, restaurants, coffee houses, cafeterias of many kinds and bakeries," I said.

"I still have my meats to do and then the full meal. It is happening so fast. I don't know if I am ready," she said.

It takes a long time to trust yourself and she wasn't anywhere near it in my view. I knew the pressures kids felt with their first work experience and I knew this would not be the best time for it. We would have to see how she progressed in her program. A lot would also depend on how she would do emotionally. She faced so many challenges yet.

She brightened. I knew that internal place well. She needed and wanted to move away from feeling trapped in her own skin to a place where she could make her own decisions. The insecurity, past failures, negative messaging from others and fear could be paralyzing for kids like Jenny. We tried to model ways for her to overcome those fears. We all wanted her to find that natural independence all children deserve to find in themselves.

It seemed as though she tried to thread her way through her life to find some emotionally safe places for herself. She tossed me a brief wave and disappeared out the door.

I was out of the loop on the Grandma info. I picked up the phone. "Connie, Jenny was just in my office for our mentor session.

"I meant to call you," she said. "What is happening is that there is a move to bring charges against Alex Turner. But it is complicated because child protective services dropped everything when Jenny moved to center. They figured she was out of harm's way here. My guess is that the Grandmother is posturing to get Jenny to deny that the molestation happened. I'm afraid Grandma wants to set up the meeting to intimidate Jenny. I think Turner is actually driving that train. I am waiting for a call and more details. At bare minimum Jenny does not need to be put through this again. I have had some success with her. She has come a long way, but she needs more time. Her confidence level is better but not there yet."

"Does she have to see Grandma right now?"

"No. I have advised against it. Social Services will make the call, but Grandma is furious. I am working with our own mental health team and we will keep you informed," she said.

Grandma appeared to be a woman who was uncomfortable in her own skin. Some time ago she asked for my cell number and I gave it to her. The other day I got a series of bullying texts from her. I have documented all of it and taken it to security. From our training I knew not to respond and I issued her a cease and desist order, but she just kept texting away. Sad to watch ignorant people just hang themselves out to dry.

"Does she have your cell number?"

I felt a jolt go up my spine.

"Yes she does," I answered.

"Block her! Block her now!" Connie advised.

I wasn't sure how to do it so we called Bob from Security and he helped me get it done. I used technology but only had a minimum of competency or comfort level with it.

"Also, put her into spam if she is on your computer and block her on your Facebook if you have one. Since you haven't heard from her, you likely won't I hope. She is a piece of work. It appears she has a lot of unresolved issues," Connie said.

I followed the protocols and let everyone around me know. I have her blocked on my cell phone and computer now. Security wants me to get a restraining order, but my thought is that she is too timid to pull anything. I really doubt she would try anything face to face. She is far too dishonest and manipulative for that to happen. She is one of those users and takers.

It felt like a long day. I spoke with the local hospital, a restaurant and a pancake house to run preliminary discussions for placing Jenny on a worksite. With that ground work laid, I would visit with Jenny about doing some shadowing. I grabbed my jacket off the hook and headed home.

The ten minute drive to my small story and a half craftsman house was just the transition I needed. I was still thinking about Jenny though.

Jenny joined the legions of women whose lives were shattered by rape or molestation and feared reprisal if they told anyone. Combine that with the debilitating shame and worthlessness that followed, the damage may be long and deep.

It was surprising that any of us survived it. I was told early on that one way to get even was to not just survive, but thrive. I hung on to that thought for dear life in my weak moments. That did not mean there will not be setbacks. There will be without doubt. But they do not crush you like they would without the notion of thriving. For me, that meant my degrees as a place to start.

Supper was simple tonight. Cottage cheese, a slice of rye toast, and a bowl of raspberries with some camembert cheese suited me perfectly. It was my go-to type of menu when fatigue stopped me from cooking a meal.

I couldn't shake the depression I felt setting in. Normally I could self care with music, quiet and rest. But it did not seem to be working this time.

My counselor of many years gave me a dolphin pendant. She instructed me to hold the dolphin and transfer the feelings to it. I pulled it from under my blouse. I never went anywhere without it. I held it. I chose the dolphin symbol from others because of its playfulness and how strong it always seemed. Those were qualities that buried themselves deep with my pain for so many years. I spent many more trying to find them. There were times I could too easily find the ugly little girl with braids and the hand me down plaid dress.

She was always with me. I slowly learned to treat her kindly and lovingly. She was the one, who at age nine, experienced her cousin's abusive action when he pulled out his fully erect penis, brazenly saying, "Hey, have you ever seen one of these before?" She was terrified and she nodded her head yes. Her stomach felt sick. No words would come. Having helped diaper several baby brothers, she had seen small ones many times.

"Whose was it? " He wanted to know. She felt too ugly and dirty to answer him. It felt like someone throwing mud on her.

He was in his early thirties and a rakishly handsome man. He was a player and a bully. She was alone with him that day although in a family of ten, she could not remember why no one else was around. She heard family stories of him beating his wife and children. She kept her eyes open, but allowed herself to see nothing.

He stroked himself and invited her over to put her mouth on it. She decisively shook her head no and sprinted from the room into the bedroom to hide under her bed. He did not follow this time. She could not tell anyone about it. She knew her parents would never believe her.

He was a veteran and had served in the army. He married an Asian woman. She was back in California right now with his two children. He was visiting his mother who lived on a farm outside of town. No more came of it that day. A day later he left. But that little girl in the plaid dress always felt dirty about it. Always! And she never ever told anyone about it. I learned later in life that he sexually molested his own two little girls as well. I did not find out until I was nearly thirty.

In my mind there was virtue in the dolphin. I had none for so long. I held it in my hand until it warmed. It felt comforting to wear this pendant.

Once, a dear, elderly neighbor who we always called Grandma gave me a vintage gold cross necklace. My friends wore them. But having been told more than once that I was nothing but a dirty little girl and Jesus would want nothing to do with me, I could not wear it. As children, my brother engaged me in some experimental "you show me yours and I'll show you mine" children sex. Mother caught us. After the beatings and for weeks afterward we were not allowed to go to Sunday school. That was when the "dirty little girl" speeches started and lasted for months. I did not put the necklace on. I never could. I tucked it into a piece of red tissue paper and lodged it in a drawer in the back of one of the only two dresser drawers that were mine. My little sister dug it out months later and broke it. It was no loss to me. She was little and cute and received no punishment for putting her hands on it.

I grasped the dolphin more firmly in my hand to let the metal warm. I imagined her splashing in and out of the ocean. She was clean. I liked that she was so clean and pure. I felt a tear run down my cheek and drip on to my chin. The little girl with braids never did feel clean or pure her whole lifetime.

I grabbed a Zquil dose and headed to bed. My bedroom was up a level on the half story. I surrounded myself with pillows and words of encouragement framed on my bedroom wall. Some days I read them to support my kids at the training center. Some days I read them for myself.

Connie made a lavender wreath for me. It hung on my wall next to the bed. Its natural scent reminded me of the alfalfa field. It felt as luxurious to me as my soft lavender sheets and comforter.

I kept a picture of the little girl in pig tails and the plaid dress on my bed stand by my bed. I picked it up and kissed her goodnight. I told her I was sorry for what happened to her with those awful men.

Jenny and I scheduled a day trip to the hospital cafeteria. We met the Manager, Deborah Olson, a youthful thirty something woman in an attractive red suit. She stood out strikingly amid the sea of grey cafeteria uniforms around us. She invited us in to her office. Her NDSU Management degree was perched on a bookcase behind her.

She looked at Jenny gently and told her about her shadow job. Her assignment was to take the food carts to the hospital floors to deliver the food to patients. Jenny leaned in and listened intently. I pulled my chair back to allow the conversation to flow between them. As Deborah outlined the responsibilities of the job, Jenny brightened.

My experience told me that in her mind she could actually see herself performing the duties and that was a huge step for her. I also knew from experience that first impressions could be deceiving. We set up a one day shadow for Jenny. She would go into the setting as an unpaid worker, but would be asked to perform the required duties while she was there. She could add the experience to her resume. It seemed like a perfect fit as there were many things about cooking that she did not like and accomplished with great difficulty in her trade. Confidence in herself eluded her often in her training. But she did not quit. I did not want to set her up to fail on this experience.

"What do you think, Jenny?"

With rare brightness in her eyes and a smile on her face, Jenny looked intensely at Deborah. She grabbed the moment for herself and did it with surprising gusto. "I want to try this," she said more eagerly than I had ever heard from her.

Yes! I wanted to yell out loud. Jenny found a piece of herself today.

"Ms. Emily, can I do this?" she asked.

"I will talk with your culinary instructor and tell you yet today," I responded.

Back at work, I strolled over to meet with Ms. Connie for her assessment. "Our meeting at the hospital went well today. The cafeteria Manager will start Jenny with a one day shadow. Tell me she is ready to do that," I encouraged.

"I think she is for a short term. Then let's see how it goes," Ms. Connie responded.

"She still has to plan and serve her dinner before then. She cannot go out until she has done that. That is happening on Friday," I said.

Ms. Connie nodded. "I know. She invited me," she said.

"Me too."

It's no small thing, this dinner. Students are required to properly prepare and serve four people a three course meal. It was a practical test for her. "She told me she will be serving a pork roast, mashed potatoes, peas and strawberry shortcake for dessert." I said.

I left Connie's office and headed to the culinary arts room. The instructor, Mr. Jones, met me at the door. "Come in. I want to show you the things Jenny chose for her table setting for Friday," he said. "Jenny chose a red tablecloth with blue and red plaid linens and a small floral centerpiece with little angels on it. She liked the angels. She said she was happy to have angels with her during her dinner."

I smiled. I knew she loved angels. Angels in several forms and colors graced her small dorm room.

Friday night, I wore basic black pants and a light sweater. Dressy but not overdressed. I wanted to send a clear signal to Jenny that I took this dinner seriously.

Jenny greeted the four of us and graciously asked us to take our places at her well-appointed table. It was attractive and inviting.

"Your table is lovely," I commented as the other three staff members nodded in agreement.

She smiled broadly. Moments bathing in this many positives were rare for Jenny.

The tantalizing aroma of her pork roast and its accompaniments drifted from the large vocational, instruction kitchen and filled the small office. It converted easily to a dining room this evening. It felt like fine dining.

Jenny disappeared from the table and emerged with a tray of salads. She served each of us. With every step around our table she studied us. The colorful salads graced each place setting now. "I have three kinds of dressing," she said, disappearing and returning with the dressings.

Confidence can be an elusive thing but it is usually easy to spot if present. I could read it all over Jenny this evening. This was truly her earned moment. I prayed it would all go well for her. She slid a tray of garlic bread on our table. "There is bread too. I made it myself," she said.

The four staff asked her all kinds of questions about her favorite foods and preparations.

She seemed to relax more and more. She admitted that cutting the meat was not her favorite thing. "It has to rest first. I didn't know you could cut it wrong, but the first time I made a roast I did it wrong," she said. "Before I came here, I did not know anything about meat."

We noted her little jest at herself. She left and emerged with her beautiful platter of roast pork trimmed with carrot curls and kale strips. We commented on how good it all looked and smelled. She delivered her mashed potatoes and peas. We ate family style in these sessions. I could see her relaxing. Most of the hard part was done and she settled into serving us, keeping vigilant watch over our reactions.

The pork was tender and well seasoned. Someone asked her about it.

"I thought about having applesauce with it, but I changed my mind," she offered. "I like onion and thyme seasoning the best. That is what I used tonight."

By now she was almost beaming. Success can be a flimsy thing when you haven't had a lot of it. You can try to bend it to your own needs and anticipate outcomes. Good preparation helps mitigate all of that and can propel one forward as it seemed to be doing with Jenny this productive evening. But the bending of it also means it can come back to slap you down if that preparation is not good or long enough.

This evening, Jenny bent success her way. It was damn well time for her to get the chance. She worked hard on her project and learned what she needed to accomplish for this stage. No one handed her success on a silver platter as happens with some people.

Staff complimented her for the creamy mashed potatoes and the peas with pearl onions. She dutifully refilled coffee and water and never missed a beat.

We had eaten well at the hands of this nervous little girl. Her lessons were well learned. It was about time for her. She did not have the capacity to understand she had just streaked ahead for her day shadow.

She brought the strawberry shortcake with whipped cream. She refilled our coffee and for good measure I decided to announce her next step. I wanted to provide her a moment she could relish. "Jenny, could you come here please?" I said. She moved closer to my chair.

"This was an excellent meal and I want you to know you will start your job shadow at the hospital next week. Instead of just one day, let's get a feel for how you like it and we will see if you can do a week. It is your choice. If it goes ok for you we can talk about more time with Miss Olson." I said.

The other staff applauded. I wanted her to experience a well-deserved proud moment. She seemed nearly overwhelmed by it. A genuine tear slipped down her cheek. This time it was a tear of joy!

When you haven't experienced much success, it is hard to know how to handle it. Jenny stared blankly for a minute. A few more tears streamed down her face. Happy tears, tears born of the success she had never experienced before. She wiped her eyes in a half embarrassed but grateful swipe with one hand.

Staff members were quick to put her at ease. We took turns encouraging her.

Connie took the lead. "Jenny, we have all been there. To you it might feel like all of us are very successful women. While it is true we all have our own special accomplishments, you need to know that we all had our bumps and our rough times too. Here is a thought that helped me in the past: bumps knock you down, but living life gets you up again," she said with a smile aimed right at Jenny.

I chimed in to the discussion. "This meal and your success in your training are huge successes. You own them. You worked hard when there were many challenges for you. The future will be the same. Work hard and you will find the future success that you deserve. No one can stop you now except you," I stated and patted her on the back.

Miss Barbara leaned over to give Jenny a big congratulatory hug. Everyone collected their things. It was time to go.

Jenny had to stay behind to clean up her dishes, so we all pitched in to help her so it would not take so long. With the last pan wiped, I gave her a little hug and started my way across campus to my car.

December in North Dakota could produce a variety of weather environments. When I was a child we saw winters with minus forty degrees and six or more feet of snow much of the time. Climate change greatly altered that constant for us now. On this day, there was very little snow on the ground. There was just enough to cover the brown grass. That was my favorite. Things always felt new and clean to me again with that first snowfall. This year temperatures remained mild until just lately when they dipped to near zero. A week before that some rain mixed with snow iced the sidewalks. I walked gingerly. It would be cold drive home this evening. I turned up my Christmas music loaded into the CD player of my Sebring convertible. The Chicago symphony poured strains of "Silent Night" into my ears and courted its calmness into my evening.

That ended abruptly when the car in front of me slid sideways on the icy street and flipped around almost facing me barely missing my car by inches. That vehicle completely blocked the westbound lane. I saw it coming and pulled over to the side of the street. I inched forward and rolled down my window.

"Do you need help?" I asked.

A youthful twenty-something driver emerged from the car along with a stinking swirl of cigarette smoke. He spouted a litany of swear words I had only ever heard my brothers use. "I am going to be late for my class now. I better move my car," he exclaimed angrily.

He was right. The car was sitting crossways in the street and would not be seen very well by an oncoming vehicle.

"I am going to put my flashers on until you get on your way," I said and rolled my window down a bit more. At least an oncoming car would see that something was wrong. He righted his vehicle and aimed it east toward Minot State University, my alma mater. I could still see my breath in the air as I drew it in deeply trying to rid myself of the fatigue I gradually started to feel. While he maneuvered his beat up old car around carefully, I thought of Jenny and her pork roast and it made me smile.

I had not heard anything about her pedophile and his pending court issues. I vowed to catch up on Monday. With her impending shadow, I did not want complications for her to have to deal with.

I always put my Christmas decorations up on the day after Thanksgiving. Until this year! This year I was late and I vowed to get my tree up over the weekend.

Tonight it would be a slice of turkey, chamomile tea, Pumpkin bread and a pleasant look through the ornaments with stolen pleasure. I treasured the only ones remaining from my childhood most. They were white icicles and as I child I loved them. They glowed in the dark, which we kids found magical back then.

With eight kids in our family there wasn't a lot of money for extravagant decorations. Neither of my parents had much of a Christmas in their lives growing up. Without much money they managed to put Christmas together for us to create a lifetime of great memories. The Alden Catalogue and credit at the grocery and hardware stores made that happen for them I learned much later in life.

Mother remembers getting a large candy cane for Christmas once. Dad remembered not getting anything for many years. The years they could afford it for the children, his mother made chicken broth and dumplings for Christmas. She lined clean socks up along the window of their home and slipped an orange and some peanuts into it. She put some red ribbons pilfered off an old dress on the table around the plate of oatmeal cookies. That was it—that was Christmas for him. There were 18 children in his family. My Dad's father raised goats and other small animals for food.

My mother was a genius in the kitchen. It was clear she and my Dad wanted their children to enjoy holidays they never could. We delighted as she dug out the tin snowmen, gingerbread men, star and candy cane shaped metal cookie cutters. The red metal box that contained them was sacred. Mother brought it down from its year round perch only once a year. It felt like a grand occasion. We all took turns picking our favorites. She rolled out the sugar and molasses cookie dough on the heavily varnished eight foot sheet of plywood table. It also doubled as the dining room table.

We were allowed to carefully cut the shapes. We stirred the powdered sugar frosting and dribbled the McCormick green, red and yellow colors from the little brown bottles into each dish. In the corner, the radio played Christmas Carols. With several pans in the oven already, the whole house filled with rich, molasses cookie aromas.

I was oldest and the only one allowed to help with the hot cookie pans. I liked feeling the responsibility. I stuck my tongue out at my younger brother who clamored to get one of the pans. I held it up and out of his reach. I stuck my tongue out at him again for good measure. Being the oldest rarely had its advantages but this one was delicious.

Outside the forty below zero winter cold and harsh winds raged as it piled sweeping, deep drifts across the streets. Snow storms happened often enough to feel commonplace and as children we barely noticed them while we were tucked warmly inside our less than modest home.

We did not own a car in those days. My father put on his six buckler boots and heavy grey parka. He strode forcefully through the knee deep snow banks to the store just down the block. He brought back some cinnamon candies for the gingerbread men buttons. We focused on the sugar cookies until he returned. We laughed as he shook the snow clinging to his parka.

The four little kids played around under the table and poked their heads up from time to time to get some of the left over dough that could no longer be formed after so much flour had been incorporated. Mom baked the scraps that were fair game for snacking as we worked. We dunked our misshaped treasures in the bowls of frosting for an even better but rare treat. That kind of latitude was unheard of throughout the rest of our lives. A six foot tree towered over us in the corner. Fifties cone shaped lights spread cheerful blues and greens and reds. The colors reflected off the silver tinsel glinting the colors around the room. A delicately painted, cardboard angel sat on the tree top. I loved her. She seemed so happy with her gentle smile and her spun fiber white hair and wings. I wondered if there were really angels. We had dozens of sugar cut out angels on the large table waiting for icing. No one in my home ever talked about angels. Only as an adult did I realize my family made nearly 40 dozen cut out cookies each year with that precious angel looking over our work. I never thought about it until now.

Monday morning I headed to work early. I wanted to meet with Jenny as she caught the training van to work. We already reviewed proper dress and other requirements for the worksite. I waited near the security office for her. She made her way down the hallway threading her way through students headed for class. She waved.

"I want to wish you good luck today," I said as she sped by me. She rushed through our conversation as though she did not want the extra attention in front of the other students. So I waved and headed down to the faculty lounge for a cup of coffee. I rarely ever went there. My office building was a half block away. When I walked into the room, I heard conversations already in progress. I stopped my entry with just a crack in the door. I did not want to interrupt or get caught up in the discussion.

Miss Malia Luigia was on fire about politics of the day. "My son is in Afghanistan on his second tour there after two in Iraq. What do I tell him? Huh, what do I say to him? You are out there risking your life for a second class country? Some fricking banana republic? Hell no! My Jorge is out there fighting for all of us!" she said hotly. No one argued with her. The room grew quiet after she stopped her passionate statements.

I smiled at everyone and quietly closed the narrow opening in the door. Although I agreed thoroughly with her, I knew this exchange was not going to end until the period was over or a long time after that.

Miss Luigia was the only Hispanic instructor employed with us on center. She spoke fluent Spanish and helped a great deal with our Spanish speaking students. She was extremely good with the kids in our program. I respected her a lot. So did everyone else.

She was the daughter of immigrants who first settled in California to do the backbreaking picking in the fields there. Later they moved to the Fargo area where they also worked in farm fields. She grew up in Fargo and her family was fortunate enough to be mentored by a local Lutheran church there. She and her brother graduated from Fargo High School and they both attended North Dakota State University where she attained her teaching degree and her brother earned a degree in Physical Education.

Fearful that she would lose her son, she tried to talk him out of his last tour, but she often said that her son's dedication and willingness to serve along with the other young men and women was just proof to all of us that America still is and always was great. I respected her patriotism, sacrifice and dedication, as did everyone else.

I checked my cell. I gave Jenny's supervisor my cell number in case she encountered any problems. I was not expecting any as her confidence level continued to spike lately.

I headed for the counselor's office and peeked in through the open door. Connie waved a cup of Starbucks at me. "Do you want some? I have another cup and no known diseases. I can pour you some." She did and I sank into the chair by her desk. Again, the lavender in her office caressed my soul. It always reminded me of my precious alfalfa field. The coffee welcomed me. Starbucks is a favorite haunt and I unloaded a lot of my good money for their strong coffees. I vowed to get one of their special unity mugs soon.

"What is happening with Jenny's Grandma and companion?" I asked.

"He ran. He packed up and left Jenny's Grandma and fled the state or so the story she tells goes."

"Will they go after him?" I asked.

"I doubt it. I don't think he was ever charged with anything yet. Grandma is devastated by her Prince Charming's split. She called security to see if he came here. We are on alert here just in case. We alerted the PD. They have a strong working partnership with our security people. I left you a message on your office phone."

"I haven't been to my office yet. I went to see Jenny off this morning so I did not go there first. Do we have to be worried about alerting her worksite?" I asked.

"Let's talk to Bob in security." She picked up the phone and asked about the extra alert. I could only hear one side of the conversation.

"Yes, I think that is a good idea," Connie said into the phone. "I will ask Ms. Emily to do that right away." She hung up and turned to me. "Call your contact at the hospital and let her know what is going on! That will create a safety net in case he didn't really leave the area. Our advantage here is that he does not know she is at work. If he came this way he would be looking here and center is on alert. Do we need to tell Jenny?" she wondered.

"I honestly don't want to disturb her work experience. Let's put every precaution in place and let her enjoy her work today. Get Bob back on the phone. Let's make some plans. I know how these predators work. They are very cunning manipulators," I said. She nodded knowing the truth too.

Bob's deep voice crackled a bit over the ancient speakerphone. "What about her work pick up? She is off at four today," he said.

"Bob, I will pick Jenny up from her work experience today. I do not want to take any chances as she moves from work to center. Are you ok with that?" I finished.

"It sounds like a great idea. Confirm with us when you have her safely in your car," he said. I nodded in agreement.

"In fact, I may go to the hospital and touch bases with my friend Jerry who is a security person there now," I said.

I called Deborah Olson and told her what had happened and cautioned her to keep her eyes open, but not to say anything to Jenny yet. She agreed. I called my friend Jerry at hospital security.

Jerry had military style security training and had worked hardcore cases in his past during his marine days. As he aged, he sought work in other, less demanding types of security. He had actually worked for a time on our training center, so he was familiar with both realities. I explained about Jenny's perpetrator grandpa figure.

"Jenny's Grandma says she thinks he headed for Texas, but we are not sure. Law enforcement is working on it now. But we want to cast a net of caution in case he doubles back this way," I informed him. I felt rushed in trying to get him enough information as quickly as I thought he needed it.

"What does he look like?" Jerry asked.

"He is an attractive man just under six feet or so, grey hair and beard, walks with a bit of a limp on the left side from a construction injury. He likes to wear military fatigues and a tee shirt. Every time I have seen him he is wearing that kind of clothing," I replied.

Chapter Two

THE ASSAULT

There was dead silence for a moment.

"Jerry, Jerry?"

"Holy shit, Emily, I think I saw this guy here this morning during my second floor rounds. Meet me on the third floor room 200. I am going to check something!" he said. Click and he was gone.

The hospital elevator seemed to get to the third floor like sliding molasses. Finally it came and I jumped in. My heart was racing. Jerry opened the door to room 200. He busily reviewed some video on his monitor. "There, that's the guy I saw. Is that him?" he asked. I let out a howl and nearly fainted. 'Yeah, that's him! How the hell did he know she is here?' I felt my voice rise.

"No time! Where is she working?" he asked hastily.

"Cafeteria," I said quickly.

"You call Olson and I will alert my guys! I am on my way!" He raced out of the room.

I called the cafeteria. No answer. I called Deborah's Cell.

Deborah picked up. She seemed out of breath trying to talk. I didn't even get my words out. She must have noticed my cell number.

"There is a problem!" She barely seemed to be able to squeak out the words. Deborah sounded extremely upset. "Are you here? Come down here! NOW! Jenny was attacked!"

I nearly dropped my cell. I caught it, shoved it in my pocket and headed for the elevator. Slow. Slow, slow. Everything felt like slow motion. I ran to the cafeteria.

Deborah was clearly shaken. "I got your message and went out to check on Jenny. She and one of our other aides were just taking a tray to second floor. Just as they came out of the door, a man grabbed her. He slapped her and put his hand over her mouth. He told the other girl to get the hell out of there or he would get her too. So Mary took off and came back here to tell us what was going on!" she stopped a moment to take a breath, and then continued. "Damn bastard, then he pushed her up against the wall and pushed his hand into her panties. He raped her with his hands right there in the corridor. She dropped one of the pans and peas and carrots spilled all over the floor. So far that is all I could get out of her." Deborah finished with an emotional sigh.

"Where is she? In your office? Alone? Please tell me she is not alone!" I had so many questions.

"No, one of the cooks is with her," Deborah said. We raced to the office.

Jenny was sitting on a chair in the corner, sobbing out of control. She was hysterical. "I am going to die! I am going to die! I am going to die!" she said over and over.

It was in Jenny's best interest for us all to remain as calm as we could.

We moved out of earshot of Jenny as Deborah caught me up. "Jerry called the emergency code that means medical and security are on their way," she said.

I pulled over a chair and seated myself beside Jenny who was still sobbing into her rolled up cafeteria apron.

Deborah had no sooner spoke than Jerry rapped on the door and announced himself. Deborah moved out of the way and stepped outside the room. I stayed with Jenny who had fallen silent by now with a faraway look in her eyes.

Jerry took a call on his radio. He stepped outside the door to take the whole call. I moved closer to Jenny. She moved away from me.

Silence had served us well a few other times. I decided to let her take the lead. To me it was her signal that she needed time right now. I respected that. My heart broke for her.

At that moment, a nurse specializing in sexual assault arrived. By this time, Jenny was sitting in her chair sucking on her thumb wrapped with a wisp of hair. She was rocking back and forth in that little fetal position again. The nurse spoke to her quietly. She motioned for me to stay in the room. Jerry promised all of us he would stand outside the door. "Jenny, I am Sonya. I am going to take care of you right now. I am going to put you into a wheel chair. If that is ok? Just shake your head yes." Jenny did.

"Let's go down the back elevator where we can find you a special room so you can lie down. Shake your head yes if you would like to lie down right now," Sonya said softly.

Jenny shook her head yes, but then looked up at me with panic on her face and pleading eyes.

"Do you need a hug?" I asked.

She shook her head no. I was prepared for that answer.

"Do you want me to go with you?" I asked.

At that point she reached for me and nodded. Sonya reached for the wheelchair in the corner and gently put Jenny in it. She carefully tucked a warm blanket around her.

"Do you want some hot chocolate before we leave the cafeteria?" she asked. Jenny shook her head no.

"I have some mints, would you like a mint?" I offered.

She nodded and I pulled a couple out of my purse for her.

Sonya took control of the wheelchair. Outside the door, Jerry joined us and announced he was going to walk down with us. We went down a back elevator to a quiet, pleasant little room.

Jerry motioned for me to wait a moment. Sonya wheeled Jenny into the room.

Jerry had good news. "We have him! PD was here right away and a couple of my staff and an officer cuffed him and they are holding him in a secure room right now. The PD is on the way with a squad car to transport him to jail. But I am taking no chances. I am going to stay right here!" Jerry said. He still wore a grave look on his face.

I reached to shake his hand and he hugged me back. I was so comforted for his friendship and all he had done in this situation. I did not fault him for the pedophile getting around the system. It is what I have come to expect of predators and pedophiles. That is how they gain their power many times. They game the system. I knocked on the door lightly, announced myself and Sonya indicated I should enter the room.

Jenny was shaking yet, but she had stopped crying. There were no tears left. Sonya just finished taking her vitals. Now she carefully guided Jenny to the gurney and covered her with a warm blanket. Jenny folded herself into her fetal position again. Sonya asked if she could put a warm rag over Jenny's eyes. Jenny nodded.

"Does that feel ok?" she asked

Jenny nodded again. No words yet. Jenny moaned.

"I want you to rest for a couple of minutes, Jenny, I will let you know everything that is going to happen," Sonya said.

Jenny seemed to settle in at that point. Sonya made a call for a kit.

I stepped outside the door to call Connie. Jerry still stood watch outside the door.

"Calling Connie," I whispered to Jerry. She answered her cell. "That crazy bastard got her in the hospital," I said gritting my teeth with anger. "Security has him now and they will transport him to the Police Department," I said.

Connie filled me in on the campus end of the drama. "Emily, we know how he found Jenny. He walked on to center through the back driveway as the kids were on their way to classes. He just happened to pick one of the girls from Jenny's dorm to ask where to find her," Connie said.

The students did not understand what he was up to because he introduced himself as her Grandpa. So one of the students told him she was at the hospital working.

The students reported how it went down.

"Little bitch!" The grandpa screamed at the kids. He took off running back to his car parked on the street. Then the students reported the incident to security here. Bob called the hospital immediately but did not get in touch with the right people at first. It took a couple of calls. "This was all unfolding just too fast and some events at the same time it sounds like," Connie said.

I felt faint but reached inside for some extra strength. I filled Jerry in on the center information. "I am going back in. Emergency personnel is with her now," I heard myself say in a whisper.

"How is she doing?" Connie asked.

"She is very broken, very broken. I am afraid for her. I don't know any other way to describe it. She is no longer the confident little girl who left here this morning. He did a number on her," I half yelled into the phone.

I choked back my own tears. One foot in front of the other! I told myself. I was shaking now. Someone came by with a carafe of coffee. I asked if I could get some. The young man went brought me a large covered cup. I sipped a few times and tried to compose myself and knocked gently. When I entered the room, Jenny had changed positions but was still curled up facing Sonya. Sonya leaned over close to Jenny and asked her if she could tell what happened to her. She also explained we could wait if she needed more time.

Jenny never opened her eyes. She murmured something indistinguishable and shook her head yes. She took a deep breath again.

I perched myself at the end of the bed on a chair and reached over to lightly stroke her foot. She pulled it away. No touching could be tolerated right now, not even good touches. I understood that. I feared for all the levels of violation she must be feeling right now. Women who know this kind of inhuman damage understand its mind numbing, searing pain. We also know what feeling brittle is like.

In the silence that ensued, my brain brought back a memory I had tried to forget many times. I was babysitting at a cousin's house for their children. My bed was made on the couch. As I slept I awakened to a hand moving up and down my body from my smallish, fried egg breasts to my genitals. I remember being half asleep and drowsily being pulled from slumber bit by bit. I remember the hand being very large. A finger broke through my inner folds and it shoved deep into my cavity. I was awake now, and tried to let out a scream. The seventeen year old slapped his hand over my mouth. I could not breathe. I tried to push him away. He moved from his crouching position and sat on my torso with a hand on my mouth and a finger repeatedly prodding my vagina. I was strong enough to push against him and knock him off me. He stood up, pointed to his penis and said, "This is waiting for you next time." I was young enough not to know completely what he meant. "If you tell anyone I will beat the hell out of you," he said and arrogantly strutted out of the room. I never told anyone.

Sonya reached for what I assumed must be a medical kit. "Jenny, when you are ready, can you tell me what happened?" she asked in a quiet, reassuring tone of voice.

No words. Silence. A big sigh. Then an unexpected explosion of emotion.

"I am going to die! I am going to die for sure now. I am going to die!" She mumbled at first and then her voice slid into rage mode as she seemed to chew the words angrily inside her own mouth. She shrank back into her reclined position as though giving up into a small puddle of a little girl.

Jenny sucked her thumb, hair wrapped around it, and seemed to fall into a fitful slumber of escape. Sonya answered a page and told the caller she would be in room 120 as long as it took. An hour passed and Jenny slumbered most of that time. She stirred a bit sometimes mumbling in her sleep.

Sonya bent closer to Jenny. "Can you tell me what happened?" she asked quietly and kindly. Jenny shot an answer that hit me like a bullet to the head. She was fully voiced now.

"You know what happened! You all know what happened! All of you knew it would happen again! No one listened to me! No one listened to me!" she accused in as much voice as she could muster. And that was it. It was all that could come out of her. Her rage was

53

as full-throated as it could be for now. She spoke for every victim everywhere ever. Too many blue skirts! Too many blue trousers!

Sonya backed off a bit. I turned my head so Jenny would not see me cry. I was glad she could not read my mind. Their voices are never heard! Never heard! We are never heard!

Jerry had things under control in room 200. A team of officers arrived almost immediately as did three members of Jerry's hospital security team. Jenny's perpetrator, Alex Turner, was cuffed and secured and walked down to a waiting squad car. He was transported to a much deserved jail cell. Jerry said they were in the process of collecting evidence from cameras back at the center and hospital cameras.

I tried to hope there might be justice this time. The injustice cowers in the millions of Jenny's and Alfalfa girls who live through the assaults. There are no protectors for "the locker room talk," no protectors for the pussy grabs or the sneaky breast pinches or sliding hands. If, indeed, it is some kind of arrogant game, we were not asked if we want to play. And it is not God damned funny! It is sexual assault. I don't care what sitting congressmen say. I don't care what incompetent pastor types spew over the airwaves. It is sexual assault. One pastor from another state opined that he thought incest was voluntary. I shot him a tersely worded six-page letter to set him straight on his clue less position, knowing he would never acknowledge me.

Jenny slowly found her voice. And when she did, it oozed out of her slowly and painfully.

"He called me names…" a long pause. "Again. Slut… Pig. He said…" she haltingly stated, "It was my fault. He grabbed me. He put his hands down there." Long pause. "It hurt. He touched me…all over and stuck his tongue in my mouth. " She wrinkled up her face. "He kept rubbing his pants in front…It happened so fast." Long pause… "I am not sure if I remember everything… It happened so fast. He chased off the other girl." Her voice trailed off to a whisper. "I tried to hang on to the pan of peas and carrots. They fell all over the floor. He told her to get out or she would be next. The girl ran away. I asked her to help me but she still ran away. " Tears clouded her eyes now. "Everyone goes away," she trailed off weakly and she quietly sobbed into her own shoulder. "Everyone goes away!"

Her slow succession of words emerged like cracked glass. Slowly, the story floated outside of her—all of it. Sonya had a recorder handy so all she had to do was push the button. There was no time to ask permission ahead of time when Jenny started to talk.

"This is a recorder, Emily. I recorded what you said. Is that ok with you?" Sonya asked gently. "If you don't want me to keep it, I will delete it right now," she added.

Jenny closed her eyes to process the question. Then she nodded her head to give consent.

"Do you remember anything else?"

Her shoulders drooped. She licked her mouth as though her lips were stuck together. Sonya offered her water through a straw. She sipped and bit down on her own lip as she told us "He said if I told," she paused painfully, "he would kill me." She struggled again and pulled at her own hair. "He says that," she paused as tears splashed down her cheeks, "every time."

"Jenny, you do not have to worry about him anymore. He is in custody," I offered. It did not comfort her. She was agitated about the information.

"Jail? He will kill me! He will kill me! He will! He will get out and he will kill me!" she whimpered and pulled the sheet over her head.

I proceeded cautiously. "No, he is locked up now. Right this minute he is behind bars," I tried to reassure her.

She pulled the sheet off, raised her head a bit then dropped it back on her pillow with a thump, closed her eyes and rocked her body back and forth curling once more into the fetal position.

Sonya motioned me to join her by the door. She shared her professional opinion with me. "This would be devastating enough for an adult, but she is still a child in every meaningful way. I think she needs more time. We need to examine her yet and I do not think she is ready for that right now. I don't even want to bring it up. She is too fragile. I think we should see about keeping her here for observation for however long it takes for her. I honestly think we need to give her the healing time she deserves." she advised.

I nodded and agreed with her. I was comforted that this whole mess landed in the hands of competent professionals. While I had plenty of experience to bring to the table, the professionals had all the cards in my view. I respected that.

"She is so vulnerable. I fear for how fragile she seems. We all want what's best for her. She has had so little validation of her feelings with the repeated trauma over time. I agree with you," I said. "I will take care of everything back on center. I promise."

"Let's talk to her first," Sonya said. I nodded.

We returned to Jenny's bed. Her eyes were open now and she was staring blankly at the ceiling. The light was still gone out of her eyes as she stared upward. Sonya spoke.

"Jenny, we would like to keep you here at the hospital overnight to make sure everything is all right. How do you feel about that?"

"He is in jail, right?"

We both nodded.

We saw her body relax. She looked at me."Will you be here?" she asked

"I will stay as long as you need me. But, I do have to go back to center and fill out your paperwork and let them know. I will be here when you wake up in the morning. Maybe we can have muffins together. The raisin cinnamon ones you like," I said.

She shrugged and resigned herself more than agreed. There was no expression on her face and it scared me to death. There was just that hollow little girl with her soul and spirit brutally stolen from her, again!

There are inner places we all find when we need them. Some are comforting, some are painful, and some offer us a brief respite.

None of those spaces are the same from person to person. Each person finds it or does not find it. Those inner spaces are crucial for many kinds of survival. They are crucial for simple peace of mind for some people. Some inner places are traps. Some are confining. Some foster creativity or relief or leaps into another reality. I thought Jenny was looking for that inner place. I prayed she would find it. And then the reality of the situation grabbed me back from my thoughts as I blew her a gentle kiss. It was as close as I dared be to her right now. Her body would likely not tolerate any touching at all right now.

Locker room talk my ass! I thought angrily.

"I will get the exam and protection moving for when she is ready," Sonya said.

I checked my pockets for my keys and headed out the door. It felt like weeks had swirled by us in this one day. I was very tired as I pulled my car up to the training center. I dialed Connie's number. "Can you meet me at my office?"

"Sure," she said and was there before my Keurig could pour out the second cup of French Roast coffee. She rapped lightly and let herself in.

"I tried to get some information," she said.

"I know but everything happened so fast. The bottom line is that he made his way into the hospital. He found her, threatened her and her co-worker who fled to get help. Then he brutally, sexually assaulted her again. She was fragile before, but I do not know how she survives this," I said as tears started rolling down my face. I could not hold back the sobs. I felt my shoulders shaking uncontrollably. "I told her we would protect her. I told her that. I was stupid! I am one more adult who lied to her. I should not have promised anything." I said. I could barely form words out of my own mouth.

More sobs. A dam broke inside me and the tears would not stop coming. I felt embarrassed and tried to recover my emotions. I could not. It felt like going over the edge of a cliff and trying to hang on to a handful of air. My whole body shook from the grief. I could not stop it. I tried. I could not stop it.

Connie took the coffee cup now spilling its contents on the floor. She set it aside and hugged me. As women, we sought to find an emotional safe place together. "We will get through this, Emily, we will. We are survivors, both of us. I want you to sit down now. Here are some tissues. Take a sip of coffee."

"Jenny," I started to say.

"Not now, Emily. I am more worried about you right now than Jenny."

"I am so God-damned sick and tired of the fucking perpetrators getting away with this shit." I slid out of professionalism at that point, practically yelling. I picked up a book and slammed it back down on my desk. I felt myself slide downward toward an inner abyss that I experienced in the past, but I did not care. I want them all to pay. I want them to pay the way we pay. And I am at my wits ends with these powerful perpetrators, especially those in the millionaire and billionaire club. The blue trousers win again and their little dogs, the Blue Skirts too. So damn many blue skirts. It is hard to decide who claims the highest prize for soiling the national conversation. It is nothing more than a mindless tailspin of denial, diversion and deliberate normalization of criminal behavior that rewards public apathy toward sexual assault. I can't stand it anymore. I can't. There are too many Jenny's and too many Alfalfa girls.

Connie listened to my rant and moved her chair closer to me, but she kept reading my face and I could see the concern in her green eyes. I felt like I was breaking into pieces and could not pull them together. I could not stop the tears. Connie handed me another tissue. I blew my nose.

"Should we call Dr. Bennington for you?" she asked.

Bennington is the center psychologist. His professional wisdom is available for students, but he also recognized that staff might need counseling too when unbridled duress appears from dealing with student issues.

"Just give me some time first," I said. When my head felt like it stopped spinning I wanted to talk to Connie. "What do we do now?" I asked not caring if I received an answer or not. I focused on information a bit to try to find my bearings again. I thought Connie should be updated on the developments. I drew myself up and started to talk. "Security still has a lot to do. The hospital and police are reviewing the recordings of the incident. They have him on video coming into the hospital and may have the whole assault recorded from the hallway cameras where it happened," I told Connie between sobs. How I want there to be cameras that caught this! This time we may have proof. You know the times he violated her before there was no proof and her little voice against him and with her blue skirt grandma's royal cover up. There was no proof. What's new about that?

"What about Jenny now?" Connie asked.

I was grateful to have Connie right now. "They are keeping her for observation until morning. I will go up and be there for breakfast with her. Someone has got to be there for her. She has no one," I said.

"Did anyone notify her grandma? Connie asked.

"Oh my God! I did not even think of it. She's a blue skirt but she should know. Jenny is her legal guardian." I said.

"Blue skirt?"

"A set of two poems I wrote in my early twenties. I will show it to you sometime." In my mind and especially with the fatigue I felt, I thought everyone knew about the blue skirts and the blue trousers.

"Emily, you do understand that if all of this is recorded, grandma's denial or concealment will get blown wide open. She could be prosecuted as well when that happens. I doubt grandma understands any of those repercussions. She was just pleasin' her man." Connie said cynically.

"You are right. Jenny first! Could you handle that part for us now? I asked. I felt like I needed some space and to withdraw for a time to clear my head and deal with my own feelings. I felt myself spiral downward emotionally. I felt weaker and weaker. I felt myself wanting to ditch some things that felt overwhelming to me.

"Maybe you call Sonya at the hospital and see what the next step is," I half pleaded.

"My guess is that their protocol forced her to contact Grandma yesterday, because she is Jenny's legal guardian and because Jenny is a minor," she commented.

"I think that is probably the case. I have Sonya's cell in my phone." I jotted down the number for her. "I am going home. I have not eaten and my head is splitting." I told Connie.

She gave me an extra hug and I headed out the door. "I hate to see you go in this shape. This is serious, Emily. I really think you should talk with Dr. Bennington for a few minutes," she said.

I shook my head no. I could not deal with it right now. Some floodgate felt threatening to me just one shade outside my conscious awareness. I did not know what it was. I just wanted to be alone. I yearned for an alfalfa field. But home would be just fine now.

"Let me know when you get home. I will touch bases with you later," she offered kindly.

I hated jumping into a cold car for the drive across town. But somehow the cold helped me this time. The crisp winter like air felt surprisingly good on my face. Beyond that I felt a sinking feeling more foreign to me than anything I had ever suffered for a long time. It felt like an unstoppable spiral downward. Down and down! I looked for some sort of normalcy to pull myself back. My thoughts stopped on the snow.

North Dakota was experiencing a very mild early winter so far. It had only snowed once and barely covered the brown vegetation everywhere. I hadn't even pulled my snow boots out of storage yet.

It was dark enough for my solar Christmas lights to have illuminated already. It made me feel a bit cheerier as they twinkled and greeted me. I always put them up on Thanksgiving or next day.

I was too exhausted to cook. Tonight I chose bananas and cream and rye toast for supper. I added a vitamin for good measure. But vitamins were not going to do it now. I could tell. I felt emotions swirl.

I opted for some Boston Pops Christmas music. I was famished and the food helped mellow me a bit. I sent Connie a text to let her know I was resting at home. I shut my eyes and imagined black. It was an old trick to help myself center again. I needed to sit down.

I loved my recliner and snuggled into it. I wanted to find Alfalfa Girl this evening for a bit. I wanted to feel safe. I should have felt comforted once that the pedophile was caught, but I had no confidence he would pay. I was unable to separate those two things yet.

I dozed off and on and found myself back home in my small town. I was standing beside a ratty little egg shaped trailer house with garbage and beer bottles strewn and broken all around it. It was an early September school day and I stopped by to pick up my newly found friend Elizabeth. I never knew her last name. Sometimes we walked the four blocks to school together. I could smell the bacon and eggs cooking as I stood outside looking at the frosted, round window in the door. I heard some scrambling about inside. I knocked again. The trailer appeared to be about 18 feet long. It was the cook car for a family of custom combiners. The four-member family lived in the trailer too. Elizabeth and her toddler brother tagged along with parents who operated their one combine custom harvest operation from it. Hired men were fed from that trailer. I heard more scrambling inside. Finally the door creaked slowly open. I might as well have been looking at the dark side of the moon. What I saw did not register on my inexperienced brain on any level.

The table was pulled out to the middle of the room blocking the door. Elizabeth's mother labored at the tiny little stove making breakfast. Elizabeth's dad sat across the table from two workers. Elizabeth was tucked in between the workers on the end bench which now served as seating for the other side of the table. They were with tightly quartered folks having breakfast. Elizabeth was still in her pajamas. Her pajama top was open to the waist. The worker on her right side moved his hands over her smallish breasts in front of everyone in the trailer. And now in front of me! The unshaven, unkempt man shot me a crooked, toothless smile. I froze. That kind of smile usually meant trouble. Elizabeth's Dad barked at me. "Elizabeth will not be going to school today. She needs to help her mother here at home. Now git!" he said.

His bronze, sun tanned face wrinkled into disapproval at me. He conveyed visibly that he was annoyed that I was there. I was afraid again. Very afraid!

I spun around on my heels and hot footed it out of there as fast as my skinny legs would carry me until I was hidden from view by anyone in the odd little trailer. It felt bad. It felt very bad. I did not know what to do with those feelings. Oddly they felt like some I experienced before. Just bad! All the way to the core of my body bad.

As I matured, I formulated enough information to know that blue trousers and blue skirts sometimes set a very low bar for their young children to grow up in. Certainly Elizabeth's life experience fit that description. I figured that out over time.

Elizabeth and I continued to be friends during the short time she was in our town. We never spoke of the incident ever. When she left town a few weeks later, I never saw her again. But I have wondered about her many times. I cannot imagine what her fate might have been in a family like that.

I finished my bananas and toast and thought about my other friend, Dixie. Her parents used to put her Mother's drunken brother in bed with her. That is where he was assigned to sleep on his visits.

Dixie asked if he could sleep somewhere else and her mom scolded angrily. "Where do you want him to sleep, on the floor?"

Her mom did not know the irony of her sentence. That is where Dixie really slept. Uncle Andy would not keep his hands off Dixie during those sleepovers and Dixie took the heavy comforter from the end of the bed and curled up with it under the bed out of reach. Drunken Uncle Andy barely ever noticed.

Dixie cried herself to sleep those nights. The blue skirts and the blue trousers remained clueless about their part in Dixie's abuse. The family never spoke of it ever. Don't tell, don't tell don't tell. It is the subtle, harmful mantra we all understand too well.

I awoke several hours later when the final strains of "Silent Night" filled the room. I headed upstairs to shower. Normally I took long bubble baths, but opted for the short shower instead. I just wanted to scrub the filth I felt off my body. I scrubbed a little for Jenny too.

I rose early and headed to the hospital to see Jenny. I was no sooner in the front door of the hospital when Grandma popped around the corner. I would have spoken to her, but she glared at me, stuck her chin out and pulled her elbows up to barrel right past me. I was not surprised.

"Lord, this cannot be good," I thought.

I checked for the room number at the same moment Connie texted me to say she was on the way. Third floor room 313! I waited in the lobby for her. She arrived shortly.

"You probably haven't heard. Sonya contacted Dr. Bennington. He thought Jenny should be kept under full time surveillance for awhile. Remember how she always says she is going to die?" I nodded.

"They do think she is suicidal after this recent assault, so she is in the mental health ward under observation. Sonya called me last night. I wanted you to sleep last night, so that is why I did not call you. You had a pretty rough day yesterday."

I nodded in agreement. "Jenny's was worse," I said.

"I saw Grandma here a moment ago and she snubbed me."

"I don't know all the particulars, but I don't think they let her in to see Jenny. She was screaming something about that lying little bitch and so she pretty much eliminated herself from helpful recovery, I think. Sonya told me to text her when we arrive."

She texted and Sonya told us to meet her in the lobby next to mental health unit.

Her news was mixed. Throughout her admittance, Jenny repeated the "I am going to die!" exclamations to Sonya and other staff. That is what generated the protective measures. The nurse lightly sedated Jenny to settle her down and they did not let Grandma in to see her. Grandma spent the night in the nearby waiting room outside the ward. She may have hoped to manipulate her way in.

Connie motioned me to sit down next to her. "You know, Emily, this situation has mushroomed beyond what we have the capacity to deal with at work. Jenny cannot go back to center. We do not have the resources to help her there. I doubt they would release her back to Grandma at this point. None of that has been decided yet. But the reality is that we are essentially done with this case now," Connie said.

She spoke reality to me, but my heart would not wrap around it. I fought back tears.

"This case? This case? Are you kidding me this case? There is a little girl lying in a bed in there who has been hurt badly. Very

63

badly!" I found my center enough not to scream the words, but I surely wanted to except I respected and revered Connie enough to know that she did not intend her words to be harmful. My heart grew heavier as I recognized that Connie was right.

"Do we just walk away? How do we do that?" I asked.

"Let's wait and see what Sonya has to say," Connie said.

At that moment Sonya walked into the room. She was dressed in her pale blue uniform with her dark hair pulled into a roll at the base of her neck. She did not wear makeup. She did not need any. Her dark brown eyes and ivory skin made her very attractive. She walked toward us with the impressive gait of a professional woman in command of herself. Her warm humanity exposed itself all over her face as she smiled and greeted us.

"Jenny had a rough early evening. When we see women at this stage it is not uncommon for them to reflect the damage and trauma of the assault. There was blood and tearing evidence that he penetrated her with his hand and she was quite hysterical until we could get some meds into her. Dr. Kraft, one of our psychiatrists was on duty and he saw her. He also knows Dr. Bennington from your training center. The two of them consulted last evening and since Jenny is already familiar with Bennington, they decided he should take the lead. He came in last night, but she was sleeping and he observed her for a while and left. He was in for rounds this morning and talked with Jenny. She told him she was going to die. Bennington wants to see her later today. He wants to talk to her when she is more awake. So we will follow the standard protocols for her or anyone in this situation. From this point on only Dr. Bennington can give you information on a need to know basis. He agrees she cannot go back to center."

"Can we see her? I asked.

"Bennington has to make that call," she answered.

"Can we at least leave her a note so she knows we were here?" I asked." I promised her raisin bran muffins." It was an odd thing for me to remember, so I called down to the cafeteria to have one put on her tray. Sonya agreed to get Dr. Bennington's permission for us. He could grant permission for the note by phone.

We thanked Sonya for her help and headed reluctantly out the door. We stopped at the gift shop and bought some cheerful cards and dropped them off at Sonya's office. I picked one with pink roses so she would feel her Mother close to her I hoped.

"I am coming to your office when we get back to center. You look dreadful and right now I am worried about you. Do you have any leave time coming?" Connie asked.

"I was saving it for Christmas but I do have about three weeks," I managed the response.

"Good. I will run by Starbucks and get us some coffee and see you in a few minutes in your office," Connie said.

I walked into my office and it seemed like months not just days since I was there last. I was in tears again. It did not feel like my office. I felt like I was sleepwalking through someone else's life. I did not even know what to do in this office. I did not even know what day it was.

Connie arrived within moments. "Do you still have a counselor?"

I nodded. "But it's been a long time since I have needed to see her."

"Call her!" Connie half suggested, half ordered.

"OK, I will do it later." I said warily.

She gently placed her hands on either side of my face and forced me to look into her eyes. "No you won't. You call her now and see if she can see you today. As your friend and as a mental health professional, I want you to see her today if she has an opening," she said with a grave look on her face.

I felt compelled to call at once. Dr. Judy Wisc was already on my contact list and something very visceral and relieving flooded over me when she picked up. I was sobbing by now and asked her if she had an appointment.

"I will make one. Come over right now."

Connie welcomed the news and volunteered to give me a ride. But like Jenny wiping her eyes on her sleeve to assert her independence,

I wanted to drive. I had to. Right now it was a gift of strength I could give to myself. At least I could drive my own darn car!

Connie left to clear up all of the morning events with administration. She cancelled my mentee meeting and my afternoon appointments. She also updated "need to know" administration and instructors with limited information about Jenny's status. Sonya agreed to let the hospital cafeteria manager know that Jenny would not be back any time soon if ever.

Outside, it was snowing lightly and the streets were very slippery. I took my time. I drove in North Dakota winter weather since I was seventeen years old. I knew better than to over drive the conditions. But I was crying now and that did not help with visibility. I could not stop crying.

On one hand I looked forward to my visit with Dr. Wisc who I called Judy most of the time. We were in our sixth year of counseling together as patient and counselor. I started working with her at the time of my divorce. My ex husband had found his way to the bottom of a bottle which did not help with the heavy meds he was on for his schizophrenia. We divorced after one of his heavy drinking episodes.

Chapter Three

ALFALFA GIRL

Dr. Wisc's small office was comforting. She loved nature and it reflected that with its many paintings of trees. She had plants and flowers and some dioramas of trees and often used tree analogies.

We had worked together previously to help me get past childhood abuses. She played a soft Pachelbel when I walked in. She knew it would comfort me.

She gave me a few moments to compose myself. Tears were still running. It came from a well of grief so deep I could not identify it or even find it just now. She gave me all the time I needed. I sniffed into some tissues she handed me. I straightened up in my chair indicating to her that I could talk now.

"Tell me what is happening to your tree today?" Judy asked.

I struggled for an answer and the one that came out was painfully honest without me even recognizing it. "I don't know."

"Is your tree strong today?"

"No!"

"Is it bending in the wind?"

I thought about that for a moment. "I think not just bending." I sniffed a bit. "I think it is bent over and close to breaking!"

"What happened?" Her question was simple.

My answer was long and complex as I recounted the whole story about Jenny and her grandmother and the boyfriend abuser.

I sobbed my way through Jenny's story and somehow by just telling it, I felt better. I emotionally grappled to find control of my emotions and it was a horrid feeling.

I finally stopped crying and wiped my red, teary eyes.

"I see more than one tree in this forest. I see a whole forest of trees," she said.

The adage you can't see the forest for the trees popped into my head, so I said it out loud. "I can't see the forest for the trees," it was half answer half question.

"Or the tree for the forest," Judy said. "So, I know all about Jenny now, but you are the one whose heart is wounded today. What is it about Jenny that hurts so much?" she asked.

Several answers popped into my mind, but one of them clung to the tree branch stronger than the others. "The injustice of it all," I answered as images of women victims I had known passed through my brain like a cruel movie reel.

"Is it Jenny's injustice?" She asked.

"Yes," I said almost authentically. Then I thought a bit more, looking for all of my feelings in the merry go round of my mind just now. "No," I said cautiously, but did not know why.

"If the injustice is not for Jenny, who is it for?" she asked.

"Me," I said, feeling selfish about the answer. My brain felt fuzzy. I had another answer on the tip of my tongue. I searched around in my head and found an answer and it felt like a shaky aha moment. "I feel the injustice of it all…. for Jenny and all the girls and women. So many lives ruined."

"Do you think you can carry that injustice for all of them? She paused a moment. "Is it up to you to do that?" she asked.

She had such gentleness about her even when she asked hard and pressing questions. Judy handed me a tissue. Tears fell somewhat harder at that point.

"Don't we ever freaking get over this? Is it ever over?" I half mumbled.

"Think about the trees, Emily. If you walk through a forest, many trees have scars on them. They repair themselves over time and they are still there. In most cases the scars are visible, but sometimes they are not. You are a tent camper. Have you noticed the trees with scars at all when you are camping?"

I paused and said. "All the time!"

Dr. Wisc settled back into her chair and looked thoughtfully at me. Her hair was drawn into a pug on the back of her neck. Her glasses hung on a gold chain around her neck. She had a plain but very welcoming face. It was a trusting face, wise with all of its years of counseling experience. There was very little she had not encountered before in her practice. Still she made me feel unique in my situation. Just looking at her face comforted me. That did not mean she couldn't ask the hard questions. She could and often did. I liked that about her too. She sat a moment or two longer before she spoke.

"Look at what you have just told me Emily. Every step of the way with Jenny you told me you felt pain for her. Look how hard all of you worked to prevent the situation that happened!" she said softly and paused again. "Now I want you to do something for me. You are a gardener too. I want you to close your eyes and think about that new apple tree you planted in your yard last spring. I want you to think about that tree as its nutrients and soil and sunshine give it what it needs to grow and repeat again to grow some more," she said.

I did the visualization. It helped to a point. I was far too distracted emotionally to point myself in the right direction. "But that is all new. The tree gets to start from scratch. We do not. We just keep carrying the scars and then something comes along and opens them up," I said thinking I was flexing my intellectual side.

"That's the part we need to work more on. Can we bind up that fragile damaged tree and give it a chance to grow again?"

"I don't know how," I said feeling at a loss for the moment.

"Yes you do. You have been doing it for a lifetime or you would not have made it this far. You have a whole world of people, family, friends who love you. You also have a handful of undergraduate degrees, a Masters, almost a doctorate and a successful 30 year career." She said and leaned closer to me. "You moved on. One step at a time! One step at a time!" The repetition of her statements was deliberate and soft. "Many girls and women do not get that far," she said with her green eyes engaging me the whole time. Did you ever give up on yourself?"

"Once, I was suicidal," I responded weakly but honestly.

"I know you were, but you are here aren't you? Close your eyes. What is happening to your tree now?"

I closed my eyes but there was that damn forest again. Not my own tree in the backyard. Visualizing took so long I thought I should just say something. Anything. Silence pervaded. Under my eyelids, I searched for the tree. Then I saw it behind the other trees in the forest. One of its limbs was bent and nearly broken. I told Judy about it.

"What do you want to do?" she asked.

I closed my eyes. "I want to fix the branch."

"Imagine you are doing that. Watch yourself go over and do just that," she said quietly and softly.

I imagined some soft material to straighten and bind up the limp branch. It was heavy at first, but I pulled it up and bound it to the trunk for support. It felt so heavy! Too heavy! Way too heavy!

When I opened my eyes, Judy offered me a hot cup of chamomile tea. I drew a deep breath. I felt better, but I did not know why.

"Tell me what you saw," she encouraged me to speak.

I repeated the scene to her as I had seen it in my mind.

"Tell me who the person was that did the binding of the tree limb," she said.

I closed my eyes again to double-check what I was about to say. I drew a breath. My own surprise was obvious in my answer. "It was Alfalfa girl. She did it. Alfalfa girl did it. She did it for me." A tear wandered down my cheek.

"Emily, you always saw her as the wounded one. Her heart was wounded. But there she is. Who is that Alfalfa girl really?" Judy asked.

The tears rolled again. I felt my arms hug myself and rock backward and forward. "She is strong. She bound up the tree. I thought it would be me," I said, looking at her through my tears.

She grasped my hand gently with a warm smile on her face. "Emily, it is you. It was always you. That little girl with braids and the plaid hand me down dress is how you made it all this way," she said.

Alfalfa girl, alfalfa girl, alfalfa girl. The words just kept flowing like a blessed prayer-whisper out of my mouth.

That night I fell asleep with my picture of alfalfa girl close to my heart. I loved that little girl. But I had so few good memories of her. She was always so full of pain. In the morning I found the notebook on my bed stand. It was the one Judy gave me to take with me after our talk yesterday. The brown cloth cover bore alfalfa plants skillfully painted on it by my dear, artistic counselor and friend. Instructions were written on the inside cover.

"Emily, the wonderful parts of Alfalfa girl are still with you. When you find them, write each one down. Your trauma prevents you from seeing all the wonderful things you need to feel again about Alfalfa girl. You need to find every part of her. It will help you in your journey," Judy had written to me.

I held the journal close to my heart. I wanted to start writing in it immediately.

I looked at the clock and it was nearly 6 a.m. Time to get ready for work! I was on auto again. I forgot that my supervisor granted me a one week leave of absence to help recover from the whole challenge with Jenny. It felt like a sinful luxury to crawl back into bed and get the rest I needed.

Judy talked me into taking some time to process the things that had happened. I resisted at first, but decided that she had only my best interest at heart so I agreed. And in my heart of hearts I absolutely knew I needed to take care of myself. I didn't fully recognize yet what had just happened to me.

Connie took care of the paperwork at work and we postponed meetings and appointments on my calendar for the week. She proved so many times that friendship was precious.

Mostly, I slept, but I used a bit of time to finish up wrapping my gifts and getting a few Christmas cards signed. I used to send a hundred Christmas cards and these days I sent out a dozen or so. I posted a greeting on Facebook to all of my computer friends. Wrapping presents was a form of therapy for me. I loved making them individual works of art. I collected all sorts of materials in a bin for that purpose.

I also went looking for Alfalfa girl as Judy suggested. I really did not know how to do that. I called her and asked her about it. She advised me to look at childhood and think about life back then. What was ordinary? What was not ordinary? What were some things you really wanted to do back then? What didn't you do?

I poured hot water for some spice tea and grabbed a bagel. I sat down in my plum colored living room. It was a color that had to grow on most people, but it was luxurious and inspirational to me. Outside the cylinder glass windows with the lead glass insets, the snow was gently falling. I lived in a part of town called Eastwood Park. It was a generous grouping of historic homes from Tudors to a few salt blocks and some craftsman homes like mine. There was a Queen Anne Victorian just down the street and a plantation style home next to it. I loved walking through that neighborhood any time of year. It was a quiet neighborhood with middle-aged folks, professional people and retirees. Not many children lived on my block. The historic and vintage nature of the neighborhood would not appeal to some people.

I settled into my recliner and gave some thought to Alfalfa girl and what she was really like.

I thought of her without her plaid dress, but loosely fit hand me down slacks, makeshift suspenders and oversized tee shirt. As I peeked in on her in my mind, I noticed she was very busy making mud pies. Her shoes and stockings were covered with mud, which Mom and Dad never liked much. She passed them out for the little kids to pretend eating. They pretended a lot when they played. The littlest child, Little Cindy, took a real bite. She ran for some water to fix it before we both got in trouble. Alfalfa girl showed the little kids how to make "scoop em and drop em cookies." Then she showed them how to make roll em and squash em cookies.

I dug out my journal. I had not thought of mud pies in forever. I started writing. I wondered how Alfalfa girl knew how o make mud pies. I do not remember anyone every having taught her. I wanted to define that for myself. I did not know how. I called Judy and had to leave a message. It was awhile before she got back to me, but she instinctively knew what I was about to ask her. "Are you journaling?"

"Yes, but I do not know how to translate the story."

"Don't. Just let the story talk to you. Don't judge it, don't interpret it. Just experience it."

That was a new one on me. I had been in academia so long that just simply experiencing it was foreign to me. I closed my eyes and brought back the scene. I watched alfalfa girl play with the four younger siblings. They ranged in age from 18 months to 5 years old. Alfalfa girl was in charge of them. It was her job to keep them safe and entertained. How did she know that was her job? No one ever told her. She just knew somehow. And she did it well every time. She did not want the little ones to get into trouble and receive the horrible beatings that would result.

They did not have fancy toys. Most of the activities were made up along the way. Alfalfa girl sent the two older ones to look for seeds or rocks or something to decorate the mud cookies. Now they had to go in the oven. She had to come up with an oven. She pulled up an old peach crate nearby and put it on two rocks. The dirt cookies rested on a sheet of cardboard the size of a cookie pan. She showed the little ones just how to do it. Cookies would air dry there.

Alfalfa girl was smiling. She did not seem to mind her charges or her play. She looked as though she was enjoying it. She noticed several of the little kids had mud on their clothes by now.

That stopped me right there. I could not think past that moment. It felt dark and I wanted to stop writing. I put the final notes into the journal. There was more, but intuitively I knew to stop writing there.

I ran my fingers over the delicately painted alfalfa plants on the cover and smiled. Judy was just so darn competent on every level. I admired her greatly. I was surprised to see how quickly the morning flew by. I was also surprised at how much more relaxed I felt. Maybe I should check in on Jenny. No, Connie was going to do that and would call me if anything urgent came up. I gathered up some clothes and headed for the washing machine. More than a load waited for me this morning.

There was a knock at the door. I looked out the window. It was a deliveryman from the Flower Nook. I opened the door to a polite young man who handed me a beautiful bouquet of roses. There was no card on it. I asked the boy who sent it. He did not know. He said I could call the office and see who paid for it if I wanted to know. My tummy rumbled, so I decided to put it off until after lunch.

I opted for a can of tomato soup with crackers to soak it all up. We ate that a lot as kids and we loved it. Most of the time mom served it with grilled cheese sandwiches. I did not have any cheese so an apple would have to do when I got around to it.

My writing was turning to scribbles anyway and I stopped for the moment. I was so used to a filled schedule, that free time was disarming for me. Being this rested was also foreign to me.

I grabbed my cell phone as I nibbled the last of my apple. I looked up the number of the floral shop.

I explained the roses without the card. "Could you please look it up and find out who bought them? I would like to know who to thank." I said.

"This was a credit card purchase made online. The name on the credit card is Alex Turner. Does that help?"

I swallowed hard. It was Jenny's perp. I felt faint. My address! How did he know my address? I needed more information and what the hell did it mean that he sent me red roses? Me. What the hell did that mean? I couldn't think. The evil of the man turned my stomach over and over. I headed to the bathroom to throw up my lunch. I felt dizzy for a while and saw those stars you see behind your eyes sometimes. I headed for my recliner again. The episode niggled at me. Was I wrong to be alarmed that a pedophile sent me flowers? My brain turned to fuzz and I leaned back in my chair. I saw pictures in my mind of him raging at center and felt disgust at his attack on Jenny at the hospital. I played it over and over again. I decided to call Judy.

She was clear in her response. "I don't want you to do anything right now. I will make some calls. We need to know if Turner is still in jail and we need to let the police know about the flowers. We should also let security at center know and alert hospital security. I am very suspicious of his motives right now. I can't help wonder if Grandma is involved in this. Let me make some calls. I don't normally do these things, but Connie will help and you are in no shape," she said.

"I know you want me to rest, but I can't rest right now. I want to make these calls. It would help me to do this for myself," I said.

"I could see Judy smile through the phone call. I think you should too, but I did not know if you were ready to do this. Keep me in the loop." Judy's insight was staggering.

Judy was right to question Jenny's Grandma's involvement. Although she was not the predator she was a class one enabler for him...a true blue skirt! She excused him, failed to hold him accountable or responsible. She allowed a double life of secrets and behind the scene phone calls, texts and emails that allowed for a grand conspiracy against Jenny to take place nearly daily. Jenny, in her own innocence had not figured all of that out yet. Unfortunately the horrible disappointment would hit her in the face someday down the road. I started making the phone calls. Jerry at the hospital seemed like my first best step. It would be a friendly ear. He picked up right away.

"This is Emily. Do you have time to talk?"

He did and I explained the situation to him. He jumped right into it. "First things first! This smells bad to me. Let me check with PD and see if he is still in jail. He should be but you never know. Can you find out when the order was taken?"

I let him go to get the information and get back to me when he could.

The phone call alone was dizzying for me. I wanted answers. I wanted them now. But I took a moment to collect myself. I reached for the bowl of anise mints and popped one in my mouth. I decided to wait before I called center. Jerry would handle the rest for me, so no use in alarming people for no reason.

I mulled it over and over in my mind. What did the flowers mean? What was the message? I reviewed in my mind what I know about manipulators. They like to keep you off your game. They relish your discomfort and prop up their egos at your expense. We could see this happening all over national conversations right now. The climate was not good for anyone.

Stop that, Emily. Stop that and focus, I told myself.

My cell rang. It was Jerry. "I have some bad news for you. Something happened, it's a long story but Mr. Turner is out of jail. He got out last night. I told the PD what happened with you and they are sending an officer over there to keep an eye on things until we find out what the hell is going on. We have some plainclothes officers in the lobby and at the nurses' station at the hospital. Grandma tried to get up to see Jenny today, but the psychiatrist is still not recommending a visit from her. She is madder than hell right now. I saw her stomp out of here, elbows flaying in every direction. She thinks she is helping her boyfriend, but she is a train wreck waiting to happen from what I have observed," Jerry said.

I agreed. A brainless pawn run amuck and I could not even think about all of that right now.

A few moments later a young woman knocked at my door. I saw her through my oval glass door window. Her squad car was parked in front of my house. She was a black woman with lovely dreadlocks and thick-rimmed glasses. She had a notebook in her hand.

"Emily Sorenson?" She asked.

I nodded.

"My name is Officer Sylvia Grinell. May I come in for a moment?"

I motioned her inside.

"I would like to see the flowers you received."

I brought the vase to her and she noted that there was no card on it. "That's the way it came," I said.

She took a photo of the vase."I am planning to be on duty here and look after things until some of the details of this case are sorted out," she said.

I offered her some tea, but she declined.

"Can I destroy these now?" I asked.

"I would just hang on to them. It may be they want it brought in later or something. It may be evidence, so no I advise you to hang on to them," she said. She saw the dismay on my face and added, "Just put it somewhere out of sight for now," she said warmly. "They want me to exchange my car for an unmarked one, so an officer will be by to pick mine up in a few minutes." She no sooner had the words out of her mouth than we saw the exchange happen out my window. I felt some relief for my safety then. I stuffed the vase of roses into a bottom cupboard in the kitchen. There were so many unknowns right now. I tried to fight the depressing feelings that were floating in my mind.

The officer came back in and just at that moment she received a call and turned away to take it. I moved over a bit to give her some space.

"That was the Chief of Police downtown. He called to tell me that Mr. Turner is back in custody. The first place he went was to the hospital. He met up with his girlfriend there. Hospital security saw them in the lobby and contacted the police. I am to remain here until he is behind bars again. Grandma left the hospital and we don't know where she is or what her role is yet. I will stay with you," she said emphatically.

Jerry had never called me back and now I understood why.

"He just doesn't give up, "I said letting out a huge sigh.

"When we encounter the serial predator, we see that all the time," she said.

"Serial predator?" I said before I realized it slipped out. "You mean Jenny is not the only one?"

"I cannot give you any details," she said, "but there is list of predators online and you may want to check it out." She told me where to look and I jotted the information down.

The phone rang and it was Jerry. "Is there an officer with you?" he asked.

'Yes, she is right here," I said.

"Good. Turner and Grandma were here again. We stopped them in the lobby and he went back to jail. Grandma is royally pissed off at you. She cussed up a storm down there. She blames you for the accusations against her boyfriend. You know how the scumbags always have someone else to blame for their troubles. I think that Jenny has been so grateful for your leadership and your help to her that when she shared that information with Grandma, the old bat couldn't handle Jenny's admiration and respect for you. When the two officers led him off to jail, he yelled back to her, 'You keep after her.'" Jerry continued. "We don't know if he meant Jenny or you. Until that all gets resolved, PD will keep someone at your house."

I felt comforted by that and yet not so in a strange way. I did not welcome the intrusion into my life. "What was with the flowers?" I asked Jerry.

"My personal opinion is that they wanted you to know that they could get to you. They get their power from making people afraid and then try to call it respect. Go figure. It's hard to say with some of these nut bags. I dealt with a nurse this morning that got a bullying text from another co-worker. She insulted her and even threatened her in a series of texts. The nurse called me and I told her to give a cease and desist warning but the damn fool texted four more times after that. She was fired. We don't put up with that level of stupidity here," Jerry said. He turned his conversation to me. "How are you doing?" he asked.

"As best as I can. I realize that Connie's advice to take time off was the right thing to do. Although I have to say today has not been so restful for me."

"I called center to keep them in the loop. The staff there always appreciates updates. Just as a precaution they are going to have some officers patrol over there too. Nobody knows where Grandma is now or what she will do." Jerry said.

"God damned blue skirts," I said.

"Blue skirts? What's a blue skirt?" Jerry asked.

"Long story! Sometime I will share it with you," I said.

"OK, I need to make rounds again. Keep your chin up. The police chief and I are good friends, I told him to take good care of you. He said you worked together a lot in the past when you placed students in the office at PD. He has your back, Emily," he said and hung up.

They were good people. It was comforting to know these two guys had my back. I felt so much better. I leaned back in my recliner. Officer Grinell returned to her car. She was talking on her phone. I wasn't sure if she was coming back in or not. I left the door open a crack so she could come in if she wanted.

I felt at loose ends and did not know what I would do next. My head and stomach hurt from all the tension.

I decided to just sit for a bit. The low winter sun poured through my front window and warmed me. The beveled glass inserts sent a series of refracted rainbow light droplets across the room. I must have dozed as it startled me when Officer Grinell gently rapped on my front door.

"I just want you to know that I will be leaving now. Jenny's Grandma went to the training center. I have been called down there. My understanding is that the department will still patrol by here today. But if you see or hear anything that concerns you just call 911. I gave them your name and address."

I thanked her. I felt sad that she was leaving. I felt so safe with her here. Those of us who spent so many years of our lives not feeling safe around people appreciated a welcome sanctuary the few times when we did.

My ex husband used to try to keep me emotionally off balance by stomping around and raising his voice. He knew those signals would send chills up my spine and he liked the control. I put my Christmas CD in. Boston Pops again. They were my favorite. *Strains of Angels we have heard on high* filled the room and I settled in for a little nap. An hour or so later I awakened with a sore neck from having plopped into the chair at an odd angle, falling asleep with my head tilted sideways. The CD was still playing on a continuous loop. *Let it snow, let it snow, let it snow* filled my head as I walked out to the kitchen.

My stomach told me it was time to eat. I didn't feel like it so I looked around the spacious kitchen to see what needed to be done. I decided nothing NEEDED to be done.

Bake some cookies! When I grew up my parents did not have much. Yet our house always boasted the aromas of fresh baking and homemade meals. Nothing would be fancy as I had not pre-shopped for this impromptu kitchen fest of mine. I dug out my Mother's old cookbook and fingered my way through it. I settled on the Molasses cookies. I knew I had all of the ingredients in the cupboard. I had one of my Mother's old cookie sheets and I pulled it out. I was sure hundreds of thousands of cookies had graced this cookie sheet in its lifetime.

It wasn't long before I imagined my Mom splitting off a chunk of dough for me to roll. We rarely spent much time alone together. With ten family members in a household there was negligible solitude to cherish as I could do now.

Life was uncomplicated. She wore a white bandana with a curious red spot on it around her head and one of dad's old tee shirts. I was an adult before I figured out that bandana was a Japanese flag that he snagged during the war. He never spoke about the war, ever. She and my father had one child after another until there were eight of us. I never knew how she managed everything emotionally or physically. Everything was hard. No running water, only a ringer washing machine, no indoor plumbing or bathrooms until I was in high school, she had few conveniences. And yet she was a chef in her own right.

Life was very hard for them with little money and no luxuries. But standing beside her next to the corner cupboard with my chunk of molasses cookie dough, I felt rich. I felt important and for a short time even wanted. Alfalfa girl rarely felt wanted in her lifetime.

Mom knew about timing. The littlest ones were napping and this was the get it done while you can time. She rolled the dough first and I cut out the gingerbread men and some camels. We had a scratchy old record player with Christmas favorites playing in the background on this day. It was almost never taken out when the little ones were up. It was simple then.

My mother and I tangled often and harshly throughout our lifetime. But at this moment I saw the little girl with the braids and plaid dress smiling. She relished the attention she so seldom received more by default than intention. Eight siblings tend to squeeze out the one on one time. After the oven she was allowed to put the red cinnamon candies on for buttons and the white icing for eyes and mouth. I did not know Alfalfa girl felt deprived about attention. I did not remember her smiling much. But she was the oldest of the eight-pack of kids and had many responsibilities beyond her years.

Alfalfa girl spent hours herding the two older boys out of trouble. She could not stand to watch the beatings they got. But cookie making with mom was different. It felt special even if it was not by most measures.

We kept plenty of end pieces for the little ones. Mom's cookie sheets bore the testimony of thousands of gingerbread men over the years. She said the sheets were the best because they were "seasoned" over time. We had so few moments like this just Mom and I together. I saw this little girl for the first time in many, many ways. I had given myself permission to remember her. I liked her for the very first time. It helped ease the painful memories of an overburdened mom too. She must have felt burdens she would not have been able to express to anyone back then.

Soon molasses and ginger aromas filled up my own kitchen and four dozen cookies graced my kitchen counter. I surrounded myself with shabby chic white and beige decor. It was so perfect for the vintage home. The crackled glass lighting splashed lovely ambiance all around the room. I had molasses on my arm and powdered sugar frosting on my face much the way Alfalfa girl did all those years ago. I was really getting into these cookies. It was good for my heart.

Connie and Dr. Wisc both wanted me to relax and not busy myself with anything, but I really was having a hard time doing that. The precious solitude beckoned me to free myself from pressure and "human doing" stuff. No work they said. Dr. Wisc wanted me to reconnect with the little girl with braids and a plaid dress. I took out the last pan of cookies and gently placed them on the cooling rack. I raced to my journal to remember the happy little girl while I could. I struggled with not commenting on her or assessing her importance or describing what it all meant. It felt hard to do that.

I raced to get it all into the journal while I could. Cookie baking was not work today. It was therapy. Now it was time to enjoy. I pulled out a small crystal Christmas tree plate and took four molasses cookies. It was supper for sure. At age 50 I could eat cookies for supper if I wanted. I enjoyed my foray into decadence and lingered over every delicious bite. I did not take time to frost them. I just dipped them into a small bowl of frosting, licking my fingers as I went along.

I desperately wanted an update on Jenny, but I knew if I did that to myself, I might get dragged back into her situation and it was becoming more and more obvious to me that I needed this brief hiatus. My crying jags were not so frequent anymore. The pain in the pit of my stomach was not as bad either.

I was tempted to turn the television on for the news, but I could not bear the awful conversations going on in our nation's capitol, I resisted with my recent copy of *Elle Décor*. I thumbed through the pages of interior design ideas. I wanted to make a change in my stairway to the second floor. I wasn't sure what I wanted except to be true to my vintage craftsman style home.

I headed for a bubble bath. I plopped on the floor for a few exercises first and then headed to the lovely claw foot tub.

The only reason I could afford the beautiful tub was because it had been damaged and Menards put it on clearance. I did not mind the damage and was able to paint some faint vintage flowers over the scuffs allowing the gouges to add depth and texture to the delicate wild flowers. I redesigned my bathroom in vintage fashion including brushed bronze faucets and hardware. It was pure luxury for me. Just pure luxury! I reached for my Eucalyptus and Spearmint bath oil, ran the water and snuggled down for a long soak in the tub. Alfalfa girl reminded me that the bath oil smelled oddly close to the fragrance of the alfalfa field. Not the same but refreshingly similar as only Mother Nature can do. Alfalfa girl chose the bath oil. I smiled. I like Alfalfa girl even more. I closed my eyes and enjoyed a long soak. Alfalfa girl came back again. She reminded me of the luxury of leaning back and closing my eyelids. That was a rare thing for either of us.

Alfalfa girl was raised by strict parents with a lot of rules. It was pretty much a no nonsense existence for her parents and family. As the oldest she helped get the family meals. She actually enjoyed some of it.

Once she geared up to surprise her mother by baking a cake. She did not know what confection sugar was and made the cake with it instead of granulated. The recipe was ruined and her mother did not appreciate the wasted ingredients in such hard economic times. The scolding was brutal and she tried to make up for it by cleaning out the cupboard. Actual forgiveness for the sin was unknown. She never knew if it worked or not. Forgiveness on any level for Alfalfa girl was totally unknown. I saw that for the first time. *What happens if you can never feel forgiven for anything?* I paused only slightly on the thought and moved quickly to my journal to write it down. Alfalfa girl hated peeling potatoes most. She never seemed to do it right. Mom could peel them razor thin. Every scrap of potato was needed for such a large family.

I grasped the oval shaped bar of soap and finished my soak with a good foot scrub with a brush. I stepped out of the tub, blew out the candle nearby and dried myself. I grabbed the robe off the vintage hook and headed to bed. I hugged the picture of Alfalfa girl. I knew more about her tonight than ever before. I turned on my sonic noise machine and let the sounds of the ocean rock me to sleep.

When I awakened in the morning I was stunned to look at the clock. It was nearly 9 a.m. I never slept that late even on weekends. My body clock normally awakened me at 5:30 am. My habit to rise early to prepare leisurely for my days engrained itself into my body clock. I avoided rushing and morning chaos, which I shed early in my adulthood. I included a short exercise routine, a short walk around the neighborhood and some downtime with music to collect my thoughts before scooting off to work each day. It had become a ritual over the years.

But this week was different. It was time to treat myself and the notion of another day of finding Alfalfa girl appealed to me. My journal filled with notes. I admitted to myself that when Judy suggested the process I was more than skeptical. I decide to treat myself to yogurt, raisins and walnuts with a molasses cookie for breakfast. I opened the last packet of chamomile tea. *Now what do I do with myself?* I wondered. I am not accustomed to so much free time.

I realized that my Christmas tree still rested in its box along with the ornaments. Good project for the morning. I always found pleasure putting up the tree. I needed to be selfish this week and ignore my usual habit as a news wonk. I was out of touch with all of that and needed to be. I could catch up later when I felt better. Still, Jenny crossed my mind. I wondered what had become of her. I felt guilty about not following up even though I was not supposed to get involved in it any more. I felt uneasiness. It bothered me like a dull toothache. I paced. I picked up my phone and put it down again. This is not restful. I cannot just sit here. I picked up the phone and dialed Connie's number. We chatted for a bit and she resisted telling me anything about Jenny.

Finally, she gave in. "I will stop by after work tonight," she said.

I felt good about that. I knew her motive was to talk to me face to face and see for herself how I was doing. I turned my attention to my Christmas tree. I put on my Lori Line CD for tree trimming music. It was an artificial tree, but one with great detail of sprouting needles and pine cones and tender green needles on the tips. I stopped buying real trees several years ago when an expensive pine dropped all its needles in three days.

I unloaded all of the icicles from my childhood tree. My tree had a Victorian flair to it. Many friends and family had given me glass Victorian ornaments and I savored every one.

At the bottom of the box I found the four nature ornaments that my brother gave to me just before he died. All of his presents were under his bed and we found them after his death. I treasured them. I unwrapped some bronze ornaments from my friend, Jena, who died from cancer two years earlier.

I strung the small, white lights and the pearls, careful to make each loop uniform. I added the large plum balls and found the best balance for them. I added the tiny glass angels and frosted ornaments last. The tree felt complete now. I wrapped and put all of my gifts under the tree. It felt good to me. I always took extra time with this part to savor it and make the creative feeling last.

I pulled together a plate of cheese and crackers to offer Connie. I put on a pot of mint tea.

Connie rapped on the door." Hellooo" she called from outside.

"Your yard looks so festive," she said.

"I went to solar this year and it is so much easier. I have some camembert and crackers. I made molasses cookies yesterday. Here, have some," I offered and waved her to sit down in the other recliner.

"I can't stay long," she said as she balanced a piece of cheddar on a cracker. "Jenny is doing as well as she can. They are keeping her in the hospital as long as they can. One of the things they learned in her therapy is that molestation was the least of her problems. She had a vaginal infection and she had been raped at least once if not more. They think it may have started some time ago."

Tears ran down my face. I felt a sob welling up. Connie teared up too.

"I need a hug," I said.

She hugged me for a bit and then I needed to sit down.

"Dr. Bennington from center and Dr. Kraft, the hospital staff psychiatrist, have been working with Jenny." Slowly Connie revealed the real nightmare of Jenny's life. "There were all kinds of signs. Alex exhibited overt sexuality with Jenny in overly affectionate moves and hands on her. Lots of people saw it. There are even pictures of her on his lap, unnatural clinches, hands near her breasts, a movie of her as a teen bouncing up and down between his legs and other terrible pictures that most sane people recognize as unnatural and certainly not innocent we now know. They were sick photos to say the least. The doctors are convinced that her grandmother knew about the pedophilia all along, but she did nothing about it so he wouldn't leave her. Many things Jenny said confirmed that grandma knew. It does not sound like she participated, but she definitely knew about it. Jenny will not be able to go back to that home. Something will be done legally, the way it sounds. The big change is that there is evidence now. And clear-cut evidence from those videos at the hospital and at the center! They are keeping Jenny for recovery. Grandma is still a loose cannon. She came to center that day and made such a scene that they arrested her for disorderly conduct. But she was out again soon after. I do not know what the situation is now, but nobody is taking any chances right now."

"Blue skirts. They are all the same!" I said.

"You really do have to tell me about these blue skirts sometime."

"I will tell you now. When I was a young woman I attempted to write a poem about my molestations. Words failed me time after time and somehow the notion of hanging the pain on abstract words and ideas came to me. There are Blue Skirts and Blue Trousers. The Blue Trousers are all of the sexual predators who molest, rape and defile girls and women. The poem includes all the lawyers, politicians and powerful men who deny or protect perpetrators.

"Blue skirts are all of the women who knowingly or through denial or cover up or enabling or spurious, religious fervor assist crimes to go on undetected or unpunished. They help maintain the vacuum of indifference, denial and protectionism that allow the crimes to continue in so many lives and communities. They contribute in so many immeasurable ways to the pain victims go through. I feel as much venom at them as I do the men. Blue Skirts and Blue Trousers are a set of two poems I wrote way back then for my own healing. It helped me a lot then and only now am I revisiting that time."

Connie looked surprised and said, "I'd like to read them sometime." I nodded.

"I will see that you get some copies when I find them. I have them packed away right now."

Connie stood to leave but paused. "Are you resting? I recognized your PTSD after that first whole day of the whole Jenny situation. Please do take care of yourself. You are the only one who can," she said and hugged me on her way out. "Do you need anything?"

I shook my head. I felt comforted after her visit. I have not always had someone to nurture this part of my painful life experience. I allowed myself to selfishly wallow in it.

I went to the kitchen and selected a pear from the refrigerator. There was some cheese and crackers left and that finished off my supper for the evening.

I looked out the front window. The snow was falling in huge fluffy flakes. It fell gently to the ground. Now this was true Christmas snow. I hated ice and wind and snow blowing sideways, but this snow is relaxing and beautiful. I turned on the television to catch the Concordia choir on Prairie Public. The rich choral voices soothed me. I opted for a glass of wine and relaxed to the music. It stopped snowing, but the evergreens across the street bore a regal, white mantle of snow. With my tree lit up beside me and nature gracing me with its beauty I sat back to enjoy the rest of the concert.

With two days down and only three plus the weekend to go, I felt my sanctuary time slowly melting away. I grabbed the journal and paged through the quickly written notes. I wanted to visit Alfalfa girl again.

She was there on the pages just as I had written her. But she was not fully revealed yet. I could sense that. But I did not know what the blind spot was. Once in one of my recovery groups, I had been taught to "trust the process" and that seemed like a good idea now. I held the journal close and fingered the alfalfa painting once again. Nothing came to me. Maybe it should not yet. The choir finished the last of the Halleluiah song. I went to bed.

Day three at home dawned with a furious blizzard. No news for me lately. I could not tolerate the bigotry right now. A life threatening blizzard was on its way. It slammed into North Dakota and shut down interstates 94 and 29. It shut down city traffic with drifts several feet deep everywhere. Nothing was moving in Minot or in the state. City crews focused on emergency routes as they should. People do not understand the immense burden the crew faces I opined in my mind. It was not uncommon for us to be shut in for days growing up. In fact, it felt like special holidays. So I was not intimidated by it now. Inside was the best place to be. I thought of all of the years I commuted to my jobs and drove out in the battle of humans vs. snow, wind and ice. Being home in my lovely house felt so precious to me it practically dropped me to my knees in gratitude.

Cream of wheat and raisins would get me off to a good start. I checked my supplies to see how long I could maintain supplies during the blizzard. I knew how to stock up for winter. I could be shut in for a long time. I was comforted by the blizzard for so many reasons. No one would be coming over and I certainly couldn't go anywhere. I relished my solitude.

I turned up the heat a bit. The east wind impacted my house the most. I dug out a boned ham to make a pot of bean soup. Soup bubbling away on the stove was a surefire way to make home really feel like home. My mother used to like to make bread, something I tried but never could do right.

Alfalfa girl grew hungrier as she got older. She did not know why. She had begun to gain some weight. Her body was changing and she did not get good information from anyone about any of that. More than once she sought the comfort of food to make herself feel better. The body changes were more than weight. She redistributed her weight all over her body. She did not wrestle with the boys the way she used to nearly daily. She slowly emerged with a young woman's body much earlier than any of her friends. The immature boys in her class poked fun at the bumps on her chest and she fought her Mother when wearing a bra came up the first time. She was not ready for this change and did not understand anything about it. Mother did not help with useful information.

Alfalfa girl was about eleven years old when her cousins came to visit the family. Mom and Dad made a big thing out of the visit.

They were all the way over from Montana and the family did not see them often. The family of ten owned barely enough beds to accommodate their own members. But that did not matter. This company felt like an adventure to Alfalfa girl. Six little makeshift beds in the form of blanket bedrolls grew bumps across the living room floor. The youngest seemed to think of it as a party and they noisily and anxiously called dibs into their new sleeping spots. Their beds went to the grownups.

There were two of us who were older. Jake was just a few years older than me and we both joined the grown-ups in the dining room.

Cousin Mark brought a six pack of warm beer in from the car. Mom and Dad and Mark and his wife Shirley each had a bottle of Pabst Blue Ribbon beer in hand. Jake and I did not. We just sat quietly and listened to the gown ups catch up. "Well, look at that girl of yours. She sure has grown up a lot now hasn't she," Mark joked. There was something about him! She dismissed it almost as soon as she thought it. She did feel a burning urge to get out of there.

She asked Jake if he wanted to go across the street to the park. He agreed and they were off to look for glass pop bottles. For every one they found, they could return it to a store or cafe and get two cents. She was saving that money in a pink plastic piggy bank in the corner cabinet. It would be a new dress someday when enough money collected there. She looked forward to buying the new dress. It would be a welcome and unique experience from her hand me downs. Alfalfa girl did not mind all of her cousin's hand me downs. There were always adjustments to make but she did not mind that. Next year she could join 4H and learn how to sew some herself she hoped.

Jake and Alfalfa girl split up and he covered the North side of the park and she covered the south side. They gradually worked their way back to the center of the park and the bandstand. It was in bad need of repair, but many summer concerts had been given in it by high school bands during its prime. Jake found three bottles and she found one. He quickly offered her one of his to make it an even two. Jake was a lanky, clumsy looking kid with dark brown hair. He had an awkward way about him, but she liked him. She had not seen him since we were about six years old. She almost trusted him, not something easily done for her. Then they played on the tire swings and chased each other around the yard in a grand game of tag. They flitted freely and carelessly through the summer breeze. The family raised rabbits in a cage in their yard and he was fascinated by them.

"Can we go back and look at the rabbits?" Jake wanted to know.

She perked up. Alfalfa girl talked to them sometimes. They listened to her sadness sometimes. They did not judge her. They just looked back into her eyes. Once when her mother throttled the hell out of one of her brothers, Alfalfa girl hid behind the rabbit cage and cried about it to the rabbit. The rabbit did not cry, but it folded its ears forward. It did not like the screaming brother either. She could not fold her ears forward, but she put her hands over them to silence the screaming brother and his beating.

She nodded and they headed back. She tucked her pop bottles into a safe place in the shed. He put his in the 1953 black Dodge, their family car.

The rabbit cages stood off by themselves. Alfalfa girl always wondered why the poop looked like raisins. They sat by the rabbits and just watched them. Her next younger brother, Ronnie, goaded the little brother into eating it. He did and there was hell to pay from mom and her belt. She did not take a liking to her children eating rabbit poop!

They looked back at us moving their noses up and down and up and down as though they were trying to sniff something. Their eyes rarely blinked.

"They look sad don't they?" Jake said.

"I don't know," she responded halfheartedly. She did know. They sat for a very long time and just watched the rabbits' noses peacefully sniffing up and down, up and down.

Jake broke the long silence. "They don't like the cage. They want to be free. We all want to be free," he said very matter of fact.

Alfalfa girl looked at how small the cage was and remembered the time she let the rabbits loose and crawled into the cage herself. One of her brothers flipped the lock and she could not get out. She had to pee and peed through her clothes on the wire pen floor. The rabbits lit out through the rugged snow fences toward the ditches. Alfalfa girl got one of the beatings of her life in the off case she wanted to make some kind of habit out of crawling into the rabbit cages in the future.

Emily drew back from the window and the raging blizzard outside. She moved to the journal and wrote.

Free. We all want to be free. Jake. Rabbits in a pen. Alfalfa girl in a pen. Want to be free. Blizzard. Cannot go out. Want to be free. Unlike before the words were scattered and incoherent. She wrote anyway.

Jake gave me a bottle. Didn't have to; he just wanted us to be equal. It would be the sole time in her life that she felt equal to anyone for any reason. *Equal* was scribbled down the rest of the page and off it. It was the most puzzling of all of the journal entries. And yet one of the best!

I looked it over and over. I toyed with trying to figure it out. Don't try. It just is. Don't try to figure it out. She wrote more. Cousin Mark. Cousin Mark. Cousin Mark.

Emily started to cry. She did not know why. She pulled the picture of the rabbits and Jake quickly back into her head to feel the experience again. Nothing would come.

Alfalfa girl showed up. She beckoned Emily, no, wait; it was Jake. She summoned Jake to the alfalfa field. She had never done that before. No one else ever knew about the alfalfa field. She showed Jake how to make his own bed down into the alfalfa. He laughed and rolled around flattening down the alfalfa just a few feet away. It was not the sacred experience she always had. He saw it as more of a game. She didn't like that. It felt irreverent to her somehow, but she did not blame him. He could not know what this precious place meant to her. It was her own fault for having invited him.

"See, if you lay down in it, no one can see you," she told him.

"Why do you do this? Jake asked.

"To be free and safe," Alfalfa girl answered.

"Oh, like the rabbits?"

"I don't know," she said. And she did not know. Neither did Emily.

I pulled away from the journal with tears in my eyes. I saw Alfalfa girl again. I loved Alfalfa girl. I did not remember ever feeling anything about her. I did not know why but the tears ran just now. I looked at the journal page. The words TO BE FREE were spelled out in large, darkened letters. I read up the page a little. The letters around the words, NO ONE CAN SEE YOU were fainter and only partially legible as though the pen suddenly ran low on ink. It was not the case. I read and reread the words, Tears splashed down my face and dripped onto the page, partially blurring the no one can see you. Alfalfa girl knew what it felt like to feel invisible. She knew what it was like to need to disappear so no one could see you. She knew. Alfalfa girl knew. She knew. She knew it in every part of her body.

The cousins from Montana never stayed very long, but when they were there Alfalfa girl avoided Cousin Mark whenever she could. When it comes to those kinds of men, once they violate you, you just know. You know all of them. It's in the swagger, the arrogance. It's in their wanton, careless, personal invasion and its damage to body and soul that are gone in just moments sometimes. The selfishness of their acts on innocence rides smugly on their faces. Once you know it, you know it. You can feel it. They don't seem to know they wear it like an entitlement. They smile it like an entitlement. They mock with entitlement. They just do. And it is a sad and devastating recognition to women and girls who spot it.

He seemed to know that she was in the outdoor toilet alone. More than once he found his way into her space. This time it was the creaky, drafty, weathered old toilet.

This time he knew that if you pushed on the rickety old toilet door and lifted slightly, the block on a nail that served as a crappy door hitch would come loose and you could go in. This time was no different. With Jake lingering nearby at the rabbit cage, Cousin Mark gave in to the short time. He only touched her lightly inside her panties this time.

"No hair yet." He smiled all evil all over his face. "I like it that way. Not spoiled by anybody yet." He sneered and peeked out the crack in the door for his chance to get out. Then he slithered out as quickly as he had slithered in.

It was a smooth getaway for him. But not for her. She thought about running to the alfalfa field. No use with all the extra people around. It would be like crawling into the rabbit cage again. There would be no escape anymore today or tomorrow she told herself.

She headed to the kitchen to see if there was anything to eat. Maybe stuffing food down would make the sadness go away.

The cousins from Montana only stayed one night. Cousin Mark owned a broken down little garage and he had to get back to it for work. He once worked in Minot for the big Chrysler Corporation. But he was monoxide poisoned once and from that time on his decision making was poor and eventually he and his wife pulled up stakes and went to Montana to live. The family thought it was the poisoning incident, but no one knew for sure.

Jake and all the kids bellied up to the family table for bowls of ham and bean soup. It was cheap enough food to fill hungry bellies, but nevertheless a favorite for everyone. There was corn bread and brown Karo syrup too. Alfalfa girl liked hers last as a kind of dessert. There was a gallon jar of milk on the table with the familiar aluminum scoop in it. Milk came from a dairy farm up north of town. Milk in store cartons cost too much for such a large family.

After supper the grownups headed to the living room. They all sat around smoking Camels or Lucky Strikes. Alfalfa girl and Jake headed outside to get away from the smoke. They did not like the clouds of smoke in the air or the smell of it. They could not figure out why the grownups did. They found a ratty jump rope and tried to jump together, but they both fell down.

"Hey let's see if we can run over to the café and turn in our pop bottles," Jake said.

Quick permission was granted from the adults still visiting inside. The two were off.

The lady at the café was a very large woman with dark brown skin. Many thought she was an Indian. Her red plaid dress did not flatter her rotund body anymore than the hair net over her short, black curly hair. She was a rough speaking woman and Alfalfa girl thought it would be better if Jake asked for the pop bottle exchange this time.

Marell, the café lady, was busy wiping up the malted milk machine. She was annoyed by the kids or so it seemed.

"Can we sell these pop bottles to ya?" He asked cordially enough.

But she was in true form and barked back at him with a scowl. "You think I'm made out of money? Who wants to know?" She popped the questions in rude shotgun fire style. She always did that. The Pepsi Cola and Nesbitt companies paid her for the returned bottles but she trotted out her deception every time. We all knew it but Jake did not.

She didn't see Alfalfa girl behind the tall counter. As she came around the end of it, Marell laughed and pointed her chipped, red painted fingernail finger at Alfalfa girl. "Oh, You! I should have known it was you. Get over here." She pointed at Alfalfa girl.

Despite all the roughness, Alfalfa girl liked her and in a genuinely unknown way she felt sorry for her. She did not know why. Marell threw her head back and pitched a guttural laugh that might be heard far down the street. That was her "I am just kidding laugh" Alfalfa girl knew that laugh well.

Alfalfa girl's mother hated Marell. She was her father's sister. Her buxom size did not seem to matter. She played the field despite her marriage to an older farmer near town. He barely spoke English and she seemed to be able to manipulate him in any way she wanted. He had money until she spent most of it on trinkets and foolish things in Mom's opinion and she told it around more than once. All kinds of stories of Marell were told all around. Women of the town whispered that Marell never missed an opportunity to flirt with the first man who came along. She flirted shamelessly with other women's husbands. Some said even young boys now and again, but most folks thought that was a lie. Her mother always called Marell a painted, shameless hussy.

Marell acted out all of the worthlessness she felt right out in front for everyone to see. No one knew the horrors that took place on her in an empty chicken coop when she was just a child. She remained the painted woman until she died of cancer. She was buried wearing the bright red lipstick which only contributed to the whispered gossip in the small town. Despite the gruffness and the hard human exterior, Alfalfa girl liked her.

Once she invited Alfalfa girl to their farm. They took minced ham sandwiches and a bottle of root beer down to a big rock to sit on and gaze over the small, blue pond nearby. They found snails on the rock and Marell let Alfalfa girl hold some of them in her hand. She listened as Marell talked about the snails.

"You know, the snail is stupid. People can just step on them if they want and they cannot get away. They can't run away or anything. When people do things…" her voice trailed off. She drew herself up and said, "I feel sorry for them." She gently laid a snail into Alfalfa girl's hand.

Her eyes grew deeply sad. A lifetime of hurt slid down Marell's cheek in one solitary tear that July afternoon and no one would ever know about it. Marrell hoisted her considerable frame off the large rock and waddled off toward the house. She was done talking and perhaps done feeling for now. You can't feel either. It's not allowed. Alfalfa girl knew all about that part.

She never told. Neither did Alfalfa girl. Like so many women before them, whatever Marrell's story was, it died with her some years later. Alfalfa girl knew there was one, but it remained so private for the woman it could not be shared. She never told. Neither did Alfalfa girl.

Marell did not always use her forgiving laugh signal. You just didn't always know if she was kidding or not, and Alfalfa girl figured out you just had to be careful around her. Turning in the pop bottles was no exception.

"How many?" Marell barked.

"Two each." she said almost apologetically.

The plump owner doled out the four cents to each of them as though it were hundreds of dollars and said, "Don't come here again tomorrow. They better not have any chips in them. I am not made of money you know."

Alfalfa girl motioned to Jack to scoot out of there as quickly as they could and they did. Alfalfa girl pocketed her pennies quickly and they bounded down the street toward the back yard.

I had fallen asleep in my chair. This time there was no comforting Christmas music playing. The wind howled outside and the sun had moved completely over the house to the west side of her yard. The living room had darkened and I turned on the beige, fringed, cloth reading lamp near my chair.

A bit of dust floated down and reminded me that the room was due for a thorough cleaning. I fingered the alfalfa plants on the journal over and over. I pulled up my laptop stored between my chair and the end table. It was always there ready to go. I had not used it in days, which was unusual for me. There were 131 emails and 21 Facebook messages. I did not want to get into Facebook very far as I was also finding it overwhelming recently. There was an informative posting from the National Weather Service. It predicted the storm would last for a couple more days. I shrugged.

Having grown up in North Dakota and experienced many brutal winters, this was not a big deal to me. I liked winter. But at an older age now, I was glad for the opportunity not to have to go out or struggle with my red Sebring on icy roads. It felt like a rare gift to me to stay at home.

The weather report was a signal to dig out my long, green hooded goose down coat and heavy boots. I would likely need them. I stuck a note of reminder on the refrigerator.

It was time to get some supper. The ham and bean soup cooled and was just right for eating. I scooped a bowl. I packaged the rest up in single serving snap lid plastic containers and dug an ice cream bar out of the freezer for dessert. It is a simple dessert for someone living alone. I always chose the yogurt ones to help stave off my fight with cholesterol. The chocolate covering was an indulgence I chose.

My cell rang. It was Connie. "I thought I should update you on Jenny," she said.

I must have breathed deeply enough for it to register audibly.

"Oh, it's good news. I would not call you with anything but good news right now."

I relaxed. I knew she would not.

"Social Services have worked with the legal community to officially removed Jenny's grandmother as her legal guardian. There was a lot of evidence against her. She knew about the molestations and the rape all along and did nothing to protect Jenny. She put her own interests above Jenny's. My own opinion is that she was not capable of discerning the situation very well," Connie said.

"Where is her grandmother now?"

"No one knows. She has dropped out of sight."

"She knows where I live. Should I be worried?" I asked.

"Don't worry about that right now. I will check with our guys in security and see what we should do. I think she is more bluster than anything, but when people are that unhinged you don't know what they will do. Take the necessary precautions, locked doors all of that. She mentioned you in her rant on center. Jenny is very fond of you and she talked about you a lot. Grandma was intimidated by that and probably a bit jealous too, so you are definitely her target. Security said that one of the things she ranted about was "putting you in your place and that would get your respect." It's a twisted way of thinking about respect. Make sure you have doors locked," she said again.

"Yup, I have been doing that all along. I have 911 on quick dial. They were on alert several days ago," I said. I needed more information about Jenny. "How is Jenny doing with all of this?

"I don't know all of the details, but from my previous sessions with her I know she never really bonded with her grandmother. So, we think she won't be feeling that much of a loss. But starting over in another family, especially if it is a foster parent situation will be a lot for her. Hopefully she will find out how to trust. I doubt if she has recovered enough for that to happen right now. When you grow up like that being constantly violated it changes your world forever, as you well know. I never did share that research with you. Oh well, another time. Training was probably the best thing that ever happened to Jenny in her life. Now all of that has been taken away from her too. I don't know the details, Emily. I will talk with Dr. Bennington again and see if there is anything we can do for her. Social services picked up her belongings from center last week, so she has all of her things. She was asking about her drawings. The doctor said she was overjoyed to get those back. It was about all she has that was meaningful to her the way it sounds," Connie finished.

"Can you find out if we can see her? There is so much happening... so many changes...I am hoping she will not feel abandoned. I would really like to talk to her," I half pleaded.

"You are in no shape right now. You keep working on you and I will see what I can find out. Any luck with the journaling process?"

"Yup. Alfalfa girl is all over those pages. I have an appointment with Dr. Wisc tomorrow so I will see what she has to say about it. Thanks for the update and keep me posted," I finished the discussion and clicked off my cell.

Foster care. I mulled it over in my mind. I had seen the best of the best and the worst of the worst with some of the kids in our program. I wondered about creating a bridge of people she trusted as she moved into the unknown stage of her life. I felt disloyal putting the whole situation aside, but I had to do it.

My stomach growled at me so I headed to the kitchen. I flicked on the light and when I did I thought I saw something move past the kitchen window. I walked over and wiped the moisture from the glass. It was only clumping snow flying by. That must have been what I saw. No one would be out in this weather.

"Lord, stop that," I scolded myself. I took an orange to the living room with a cup of hot tea and just let my mind wander.

It is 1959, with too many Hardy boys and Nancy Drew mysteries under my belt. My friends and I got in a lot of trouble from that. We were always exploring old buildings in town. We looked for secret passages and hidden treasure and all of that. One summer day we geared up to explore an old house south of town. The three of us, Georgia, Joanne and I all rode together. We did not know what to expect. We dropped our bikes. I suggested we might want to hide them, so Georgia and I did. Joanne joked about how she did not think that was necessary. She did not. We tucked ours behind the lilac bushes in the yard.

We opened the creaky door. It was not locked. It barely hung together and was part way open anyway. The glass was broken out of the door and most of the windows. The once beautiful old house now weathered as its paint scaled off its siding. A shutter hung loose. The chimney crumbled long ago and spread its red bricks all over the yard. It was the perfect setting for a spooky Halloween story.

We encountered stairs directly in front of us. With each step our shoes crunched all the broken glass beneath our feet. We arrived in what must have been a small bedroom at one time. The steel bed frame was all that remained. There was a closet. We looked into it. The door sported a black curtain with huge red roses all over it. It was faded now and the material was paper-thin in spots. We pushed the curtain open all the way. Dust billowed from it. We choked it back.

Suddenly we heard a vehicle drive up outside and stop. We went to the window to look. It was a farmer. He must have seen us when we rode up to the house.

We did not talk. We motioned to each other to head for the tiny closet. I had to pee but ignored the urge. There was an old cooking pot on the floor. I turned it upside down and sat on it. Georgia and Joanne stood. We heard the farmer coming up the stairs. One step at a time; it seemed he would never get to the top. Crunch, crunch, crunch! Closer and closer!

We pulled the shaggy curtain over the doorway and tried not to breathe. We sat frozen in our spots. The farmer crunched up and down in front of the curtain. Crunch, crunch, crunch on the glass. Back and forth!

Back and forth in front of the thin gauze of material that separated us. Crunch! Crunch! Back and forth! Finally, we heard him leave the room and crunch down the stairway. I really had to pee, but I realized I had been holding my breath. I let it out in a loud burst. My friends did too. We did not talk. We waited for the sound of the beat up old Chevrolet pick up to start. Only then did we dare venture to the window to look. We saw him back around to leave. There in the pickup box, Joanne's bike stuck up in the air like a prize monument or something.

"I told you, I told you," I said.

She looked forlorn. "What do we do now?"

None of us knew, but the sun was well past the house to the west and I darn well knew that I did not dare miss supper.

"We need to get back to town," I urged.

Three girls and two bikes. Now what? We all seemed to question it at first. I scooted behind the lilac bush to pee. There is one thing about water trickling downward. It does not care where it goes. It landed on my pants, socks and shoes.

"I can't walk back. I will never make it with my side," Joanne said.

I knew she had trouble with her appendix. I decided to be the one to walk. "You two just ride to the end of the road and into town. I studied the terrain a brief moment and I made a strategic suggestion and drew it in the dirt with a stick.

"I will cut across the field and you two ride back on the roads. My dirt drawing formed an uneven triangle. I should be able to meet you when you get to that point," I reasoned.

It was a great plan, but my total ignorance of plowed fields did me in. Every step I took, I sank into the soft, plowed dirt. Every step forward felt like two back. I was making no time at all. I saw the girls riding along and I felt doomed that they would arrive at the meeting spot well ahead of me. I kept plodding away. I studied the sun. I knew it was way past six o clock, suppertime, and I knew I was in deep trouble. You could not be late for a meal without consequences and serious ones at that. I tried not to think about it. My whole body ached as the plowed field kept trying to suck me down into it. After what seemed like hours, I came up to the ditch along the three mile stretch that led out of town. The girls started to laugh. Not just a giggle but a damn belly laugh...both of them.

"Look at you," Joanne laughed.

I had not noticed the dirt that swirled around me with each step. I was covered from head to toe with only my white eyes visible. I licked my lips. They both bent over laughing. The jig was up. No story I could make up would account for the dusty figure I presented this moment. They laughed some more.

"Look, we still have to get to town and I am in 'deep crap,'" I said.

Joanne gave me her bike to ride. She and Georgia took turns walking and riding back to town. We stopped at Joanne's house first to tell her parents about the bike. Her mom and dad laughed about it and the way we looked. We did not know who the farmer was, but Joanne's dad did know who it was by the location of the land. So he vowed to go to see the farmer, Ronald Orville, to get the bike back.

That was when innocent exploring took on a life of its own.

Joanne's dad, George, did not fare well in his discussions with Mr. Orville.

"I will not give back that bike." he insisted in the first meeting. There is a lot of damage to that house. Broken windows and door busted up. I will sell the bike to take care of the damages those girls caused."

The old Hume place as it was known was a beer drinking retreat for dozens of high school boys over the years. The damage occurred over way too many booze parties for decades. Orville knew full well that the girls did not vandalize the house in the few minutes before his arrival that day. Mr. Orville saw his chance to make good on a few dollars and he was not going to give up. He refused to return the bike.

Joanne's mother and dad were horrified and decided to get satisfaction in their own way. They bought Joanne a new bike and then put a small ad in the local weekly paper. It read, "Joanne Rowel and Ronald Orville both have new bikes. We hope they both enjoy riding them."

I smiled as I remembered the sweet, subtle justice of the whole affair.

It did not deter us from keeping up our Nancy Drew explorations. But we just never took our bikes again.

I looked over at my journal. I was puzzled that this memory came to me the way it did. Alfalfa girl did not help me with it at all. I did not know what to make of it. I pulled out the journal and wrote the whole incident in it just the way I remembered it.

As for my punishment, I went without supper, of course, and my mother grounded me for three whole weeks. I put the memory into the journal noting that Alfalfa girl never showed up in the memory. It puzzled me.

I confirmed my appointment with Judy for the next day. She said she had been wondering how I was doing, but knew that I would call her if I needed anything.

"I think there is a big snow drift behind my garage and I do not know if the city will get it plowed out by tomorrow." I said when I called her.

"Let's do this," she said. "My streets are open. Should we just meet at your house?"

I agreed. I caught up with some well overdue dusting in my home. The mantle on the historic fireplace really needed a wipe down. I poured a glass of wine and headed for my bathtub and some comforting Eucalyptus and Spearmint time.

The next morning bright sunshine greeted me as it reflected brightly off the newly fallen snow. The front yard Christmas decorations were completely covered by a three-foot snow bank. I noticed that the plows had already moved through the neighborhood carving a single open trench like pathway. At least Judy would be able to get here. *Not true,* I said to myself as I looked outdoors again. The ten-foot path to my door and the steps were covered in snow. It took me about three hours to clear them one shovel full at a time. I ate a bagel and peanut butter mid morning. I looked through the journal. I wanted to experience Alfalfa girl another time before Judy arrived. The words on the page seemed as though they had been written years ago and not in the past week. Alfalfa girl had more to show me, I sensed, but I did not know what yet. I would ask Judy.

She did one of those drum roll knocks. *da da de da da* pause *da da* knocks. We sat down at the small dining room table together.

"Tell me about Alfalfa girl," she said. The straightforwardness did not surprise me, but I was not ready for it. I drew a breath. I fingered the drawing on the front of the journal in hopes it would focus my thoughts. The pause was uncomfortable for me. I am so used to knowing my thoughts and expressing them readily.

I did not know this time. I really did not know.

Judy suggested we read the entries together. I agreed. I thought it would be useful. I opened my skinny little journal to the first page.

"Read it to me," Judy said.

I started reading to her about the mud pies and making them. Judy listened intently. She provided no discernible response.

I read the parts about making the mud pies and baking them.

"Is this the first memory you have of mud pies?" she asked.

"I don't know. I don't think so because she just knows how to do it," I said. It seemed like a very thin answer to me.

"Not you...her. What do you see about her?"

"I don't know the answer to that one. She is happy. She is happier than I ever remember being any time in my life," I said.

"What else," Judy said.

"She seems to like playing with the little ones. She is not angry or anything. She seems comfortable in her role there." I said.

"Is she creative? Judy asked.

It had not occurred to me. "Yes, she sure is. She is sending them off to get things to decorate the mud pies and mud cookies. She even made an oven to bake them," I said.

"Do the little ones like her?"

That seemed like a loaded question to me. "I don't know if they do or not. But they listen to her and they are laughing and enjoying the mud pies."

"Write those observations down in your journal now right beside your other notes," she suggested.

I wrote them down on the edge of the page. The words *likeable, responsible, sharing, creative, afraid of doing something wrong,* took their places in the margins. I crossed out *creative* and put *inventive.*

"What did you just do?

"I changed one of the responses. I changed creative to inventive," I told her.

She questioned my response. "Why can't there be both?"

I shook my head. I did not know.

"You eliminated one of the possibilities that Alfalfa girl gave you. I want you to put them both there."

I agreed and put *creative* back on the list.

"Tell me about being afraid," Judy said.

"I was afraid all the time," I said.

"Afraid about what?" she asked.

"Just afraid."

"No, you said you wrote *afraid of doing something wrong.* What happens if you do something wrong?"

"You get your ass beaten off," I said.

"Emily, we all do things wrong. We humans are not perfect. No one is. We will all make mistakes and most people do not get beaten up for it," she said. "What does Alfalfa girl do in your scene? Did she make mistakes?"

A tear ran down my cheek. "Yes she did. The kids got mud all over their clothes and so did she."

"What did Alfalfa girl do even though she is showing you she made a mistake?"

"She did it anyway," I said.

"What word would you put on your page seeing her now?"

It took me awhile to find a word to fit my thoughts. "Courage," I said almost apologetically.

"Yes, she had courage. She gave that to you."

My heart welled up inside my chest and tears spilled down my face.

"Just let them come, Emily, let them come. You are really meeting Alfalfa girl for the first time in your life. How are you feeling about her?" she asked.

I had to think about it for a moment before I could answer. "I don't know." I stammered through the words. "Love mostly I guess and some sympathy for her, I guess."

"No you are not guessing, you are feeling and what you are feeling is real. Don't get in the way of it." Judy said.

"I am sorry she had to go through so much," I said.

"And what about you, Emily? How did you survive?"

I felt like I could not answer any more questions. "I need to stop now," I said.

Judy agreed. "I have a client coming in to my office in about a half hour or so. He said if he could not get out of his yard he would call me and he has not," she said, checking her cell phone. "Are you off next week?" she asked me.

"Just for Christmas Eve and Day. I need to get back and do some catching up from this week."

"Look, if you need to take the whole week next week, I will recommend it for you. But I want you to decide. What are you doing for Christmas?" she asked.

"I planned to go to my family, but if I don't feel any stronger by then I will probably just stay home. I would like to see Jenny, but I do not know if they will let me or not. Connie is trying to find that out for me. And what are you doing?" I added.

"My son and his family are coming and we will do church and then the traditional turkey dinner. There are my two grandchildren and we will open presents when they get into town," she said.

"I bought Jenny a gift and I really want to take it to her." I said.

"They should know if she is up to that or not. Call and find out," she advised.

"I have the weekend now, so I will leave you a message on what I decide to do," I told her.

She sipped down the last drop of her tea, put on her black leather coat and checkered scarf and headed out to her car. I watched as she walked down the still slippery sidewalk. She always knew. She always knew. With her thirty years of experience she always knew. I had such profound confidence in her. We had not discussed Jenny at all and I felt it was by design on her part.

I tapped Connie's number. She picked up right away. "Do you think the doctor will let me up to see Jenny?" I asked.

"I think it could be arranged. Dr. Bennington has been working with her and I understand it has gone well recently. Do you have the number?"

I did and connected with him. "Dr. Bennington, this is Emily Sorenson. Do you think I could visit with Jenny tomorrow? I have a Christmas gift for her."

"Yes, I think it would be good for her. We are working with a good family for her now. She is scared and fearful, but that is to be expected. Tomorrow is Saturday. I will make arrangements with the staff there. She is still quite fragile, but I am hoping your visit will be helpful for her," he added.

"Can I take some treats up to her?" I asked.

"I think they will allow it, but they would certainly check them over. I will give the clearance for you from this end," he said.

I thanked him and hung up the phone. My mood soared. I wanted to make it special for her. I pulled her gift out of the dining room cabinet. Wrapping gifts was a passion for me. I aimed toward beautiful and special. No stick on bows for this woman. I bought special handmade wrapping papers. I pulled out a print with a lot of red in it for the holidays

I removed the angel locket from its silk pouch. Jenny loved angels and this one was genuine gold. I hoped she could use it much as I have done with my dolphin all these years. The card also had angels on it. I wrote a special note in the card, wrapped the delicate paper around the box and secured the card to it. I fashioned the beautiful gold ribbon into an attractive bow. I pulled a strand of greenery off a nearby decoration and tucked it into the ribbon for a little something special. The vision of putting the seeds on the mud pies came to me just then and it made me smile. Alfalfa girl was front and center in wrapping this special gift. I was so excited.

The next morning I jumped out of bed, grabbed some toast and a cup of instant coffee. I looked out back of my house to see if the plows had gone through. They had not. I felt disappointed, but nothing was going to stop me. I put on my jeans and a dressy sweater and called a cab.

The dispatcher said it would be an hour. A lot more people were taking cabs since the storm. I did not care. The cost would be under twenty dollars. I felt practically giddy!

The cab arrived. I was surprised at the amount of snow dumped into Minot. I had not been out to see it for myself and I really had not paid much attention to the news.

I was accustomed to the normal protocols for getting into the mental health ward. Once it had been my home for six weeks. I did not have many visitors, but saw the routine many times.

I waited in the visitor area. They would bring Jenny to me. A staff person would be present to supervise the gift to make sure that there was no contraband.

"Miss Emily," I heard my name called from a distance. I turned around and she ran straight at me. I put out my arms and she hugged me and hugged me. I held my own without shedding a tear, but they were close and I spoke.

"I missed you," I said.

"So much has happened," she said.

I nodded. "You have never been far from my mind. I have kept in touch with people."

"I heard you were sick," she said.

"I am fine now. I just needed a little rest," I said.

"I have something for you too," she said.

I couldn't imagine how that could be as she did not get passes from the hospital. It didn't matter.

"This is the only real present I have. Thank you so much. A church group brought up some packages. I got a nice blanket and a little bible from them. One of the nurses gave me a box of candy, but she gave everyone one. This is a real present."

"Open it," I said.

She carefully and deliberately touched every part. She stuck the greenery in her hair and playfully modeled it for me.

"Looks nice," I said.

She smiled and refocused on her task. Soon the wrappings and ribbon were in her lap. She opened the box and looked at the angel. She wiped her eyes. "It's beautiful. I love it. I love angels. Can I put it on? Can I put it on?"

I motioned for the nurse and we asked her. She said she could put it on but that they would have to keep it in the nurses' station when I left. It was a 16-inch chain so precautions were necessary. I understood. She put the chain around her neck. She jumped up and proudly danced around showing it off. Then she aimed at me suddenly and hugged me.

"This is a special angel. When you have bad feelings, you hold her until she gets warm and just give her the bad feelings. I have a dolphin." I showed it to her.

She fingered the dolphin gently. "I like my angel better. I don't know anything about dolphins," she said.

"I have some Christmas cookies for you. I hope you like Molasses cookies." I opened my cloth bag and pulled out the tin. "They are gingerbread men. I used to make them with my mom when I was your age," I said.

"We never did that. She was gone before we could do that and she just couldn't bake anymore toward the end, "Jenny said blankly. "Miss Emily, do you know what happened to my house? I mean my grandma and everything?"

I shook my head yes. "I have been keeping up with things. How are you feeling about all of these changes?" I asked.

"It always changes. Everything always changes. It is nothing new to me. I am glad not to go back to center. I think it would have been bad for me. I am glad not to go back to that trailer house with grandma. There are too many bad memories there for me." She stopped suddenly, took a breath, and finished what seemed to be a practiced speech to me.

"But how do you feel?"

"I feel sad, Miss Emily. I feel sad. I feel alone all the time. I just feel alone," she said so quietly.

It sounded like a kind of grieving to me and I held her hand. I could find no words. I just looked at her, gently pulled the curl back off her forehead. It was a safe place and time for her to grieve. I tried to find words of comfort but nothing would come to me. We sat there looking at each other. I think our souls touched, but I do not know how.

She broke the silence. "There is a family they think will work for me. I got to meet the family. It is a minister and his wife and their daughter. They were all very nice, but you know living with other people is hard. I don't know how it will work out for me. I won't have my job shadow anymore. I don't know how it will work out. I am sad about the job. I wanted to do my best and be on my own!" she spewed the words quickly.

She talked like she had given up on her dreams of independence. A lot had happened and it seemed that her future must feel cloudy to her. "You know, Jenny, there is a lot of opportunity out there. There are a lot of people who like to help others. I have worked with many students who changed paths for a lot of different reasons. Just because one path closes up doesn't mean there aren't others. I resisted the "one door closes another opens" cliché although it sat right in my throat waiting to come out.

"I know a lot of people in many different kinds of training. You can do many different things. I have one more thing for you," I said. This gift was in a gift bag. I handed it to her.

"I thought we were done with presents. Oh, I forgot," she said putting the bag aside for a moment. "This is for you." It was an envelope with a card in it.

I opened the envelope and read the card. "To Miss Emily. You are the best one to me. I will never forget you." There was an unfolded piece of drawing paper in it. I turned it over and it was a hand drawn rose, slightly colored pink with a lightly colored green stem. It was just like her drawing. The heartfelt sharing of her Mother's rose symbol with me nearly brought me to my knees.

"Are you sure, Jenny? Are you sure," I asked her.

"I drew this one for you special. There are only two people who get this rose from me," she said and threw her arms around me in a big hug.

I hugged the drawing close to my body. "I will always keep it close to my heart," I said.

I fought back the tears. I did not want to break down in front of her. She seemed quite strong. I needed to be the same. "Ok. This is the last gift for you," I said.

She reached into the bag, removed the tissue paper around it and gasped. "It's a camera!" she said. "A camera! I always wanted a camera but grandma said I was too young and he said girls were too stupid for cameras."

"You have a lot of good memories to come in your life and you can record every one of them as you want. You are free to do that," I said.

"I will have them keep the camera in the office for me," she said.

I took the camera back for a moment. "Here I want the most important picture to be the best one." I pointed the camera at her and told her to smile. *Click.* It was a great picture.

She took the camera and motioned for the nurse to come over. "Take a picture of us," she half shouted in glee. The nurse posed us a couple of ways. I put my arm around Jenny. "Now, take it," she told the nurse. *Click.* The Miss Emily and Jenny photo was recorded forever.

We finished our brief little visit with the gingerbread men. She had never eaten one before. "I like them," she said. I want to keep one though. Will it keep?" she asked.

I assured her it would. "If you let it lay out and dry, it can get as hard as a brick and last a long time. We used to put them on our Christmas tree when I was little and when we took them off after Christmas they were very hard and dry. But they can be brittle too. They won't take much banging around," I said.

Someone turned on Christmas music. *Little Drummer Boy* was playing and I responded to it. "I love that song. My class did it when I was in grade school for the Christmas program," I said.

"I never went to a Christmas program at school. It was after my mom died. Dad said they were a waste of time. We had to make the costumes at home and he was pretty mad about it. He was supposed to make me an elf suit, but he didn't and grandma didn't want to either. He told the school I could not be in it," she said with a harsh reality tone in her voice.

My heart broke. I felt disgust for her family and sorry I brought it up.

"That was who they were, Jenny. Now it's time to find out who you are. If you like Christmas music, you can always go to a church somewhere and they will let you enjoy it. Or you can listen to it on a CD. You don't have to be in it, but you can always listen to the music and enjoy what you like. You can learn to play an instrument and play some for yourself. There is nothing stopping you from doing whatever you want now. Let me tell you a story.

"Several years ago, I was very sick. I had surgery on my back. It took several months to recover and it was during Christmas. I always bought a fresh tree at Christmas, but could not that year. I had no way to get it up the three flights of stairs to my apartment. I bought some elegant, glass trees of different sizes and put them all around my apartment. It worked out just fine for me. I missed the real tree, but I just let my creativity fly and it was delightful. Just because things change or are different doesn't mean you can't fill your heart up any way you want." I told her.

Jenny smiled at me. "I never thought about filling my own heart up. I will put this angel on my tree too. It will remind me of you," she said.

I hugged her tightly.

The announcement that visiting hours were over came all too fast. I wasn't ready to go.

"I love you," Jenny said and it hit me like a brick. I was not expecting that.

"I love you too, honey. I will be in touch with you again, as soon as I can," I said. As I walked out the door, I wondered if all of that was appropriate by some standards. Some may judge that I was too invested in Jenny. I decided it was their problem. I did love this little girl. It was just that simple or just that complicated, depending on how you looked at it.

I walked out the door. I would call the cab when I reached the lobby. I stopped in the lobby to make my call when Dr. Bennington strode up to me. "Hi, Emily. How did your visit with Jenny go?"

"She certainly is more at peace with herself than she once was. I hope that with this new family she has a chance at some sort of normal life. She does not know what normal is. She does seem to think her learning chances are over, so I visited a bit with her about that," I said.

"She will need a lot of time, Emily. She has a lot of adjustments to make. I know you know that." He smiled and turned toward the elevator. "On my way up there now! She does not get many visitors so I want to see how she fares after your visit," he said as the elevator door closed behind him. He headed out of the lobby. My cab arrived and I headed home.

The weekend seemed no different to me than the rest of the week. If you aren't resting up from a workweek and a schedule all the days seemed the same to me.

I arrived home just at dark. There was a note thumb tacked on my door. "You think you are so smart. You have so many words. You will pay. You are my business until this is settled." No signature but the incoherence was a dead give a way. Oh, Lord, Grandma. I looked around me. No one in sight. I took the hawk flashlight out of my purse. I refused to carry a gun, but bad things happen to good people, so I bought an ultra powerful military style flashlight. It could blind someone temporarily especially if the flasher is turned on. I pulled it out of my purse and turned it on the wide lens. It produced near daylight at once. I quickly illuminated the bushes, the side of the house and down the street. I saw nothing.

I unlocked the door. I flashed the light around the hall and living room. Nothing! I sat down on my couch and dialed 911. The dispatcher said an officer was close to the neighborhood and on the way.

I barely had time to pull my wits together when the officer knocked on my door. "Emily Sorenson?" he asked.

I nodded.

"Sergeant Billevus," he said. "The dispatcher said you have a threatening note?"

"I do," I said and pulled it out.

He read it and put it into a plastic pouch for safe-keeping. "Do you want to fill me on what is going on here?"

I nodded but thought we could save time. "Officer Sylvia is fully aware of this situation. Can we call her?"

"She is off tonight, so I will get the information."

I filled him in the best I could. I was out of the loop on anything concrete about crazy grandma. "The last I heard she had kind of disappeared. So I don't know. She has verbally threatened me a couple of times with lots of witnesses. Officer Sylvia has all of the information about the roses incident," I said.

"I am going to call for surveillance. We take these things seriously. People end up dead in some of these cases," he said.

"Are you going to leave now?" I asked

"Not until back up arrives," he said. "Do I have your permission to do a walk-through of the premises? I want to make sure no one is in the home since you just arrived too," he said.

I could hear discussion on the radio on his shoulder. "That's me," he said. "Situation secure for now, but definitely a threatening note on her door. 411 10th St. North. I will stay for now. Officer on the way," he reported.

I felt weak. "Do you want some coffee?"

"If you have some, but don't make fresh," he said.

"I need fresh," I said.

I put the Kuerig on and realized I needed to make some calls. "I have to let a few people know about this," I stated. He nodded just as the other squad car drove up.

I tapped numbers out for Judy, then Connie, then Jerry. I explained the situation to all of them as a safety net for Jenny, center and myself.

Judy advised me to take the next week off. "This is too much, Emily," she said.

I was too heartsick to cry or scream or resist her suggestion. I do not know how this young girl ever survived these two crazy people. The Keurig stopped brewing. Sergeant Villehus filled out a report and took the coffee I offered him.

"The home is secure. No intruders," he reported into his radio and turned to me. "There is an unmarked car out in front of your house. We will not leave until the situation is resolved," he said.

"Do I need to do anything?"

"No, we will take care of this. Officers are headed to her home right now. We had her address from the roses incident." He shook my hand and left.

I looked out the window and saw him talk with someone in the unmarked car. My head was spinning and I was glad to done with it all for the moment. I did not finish my coffee. It would not go down. I dumped it down the sink, which seemed a fitting thing. All things should be so easy to dispose of.

I settled into my chair. I pulled the card and rose drawing out of my blazer pocket. It was delicate like Jenny herself. It was such a delicate wisp of reality for her to hang on to. But immeasurable in her survival I thought.

I reached for a pen and my journal. I started writing.

The soul survives somehow. Its reality struts and fades as it needs to do. It clings like a scared suckling baby if it has to. It weeps and laughs. It warps and straightens with tears and joy. It seldom remains static. It stretches. It recoils. It faints in despair and glows in miracle moments and finds solitude in dusk and euphoria in sunrise. It eases its way along, riding over valleys and bumps if it must. It does not complain or brag. It never touches the meek or the strong in the same exact way. It is there. It is internal reality, it is steadfast and eternal. Soul protects if it must and withers quickly when driven mercilessly hard. I wrote and wrote and did not know what the writing was about. I thought Jenny must be in there somewhere, but I did not know how or where. But it was good for me. I felt better and my soul was at peace for having scribbled the words on paper.

I awakened the next morning realizing that I would not be able to travel home for Christmas this year. With the death of our parents, we no longer have a single gathering spot for family. It was a huge change in our lives. Christmas used to mean thirty people or more in the large living room with lots of kids and lots of noise. But over time and aging, our families splintered off to their own homes and their own immediate families. Sometimes I felt heartburn about it but as Jenny said things change and change.

After several years of open and clear winter driving conditions, Mother Nature swept through the state with ferocity. We experienced three severe winter storms back to back in one month.

I made my decision to stay at home and observe the day with a healthy dose of solitude. Not loneliness as my ex husband once suggested in one of his bipolar rants. I have rarely felt lonely. Over the years I came to know how to pamper myself. I toyed with the idea of inviting someone over to my house. I would have to see how I felt and how things developed before doing that. Rest is rest and I needed large doses of it. I recognized a lot of fatigue yet.

My cell rang and it was Jerry from hospital security. "Grandma was at the hospital today. She had a present for Jenny and tried her best to get up to Jenny's floor. We denied her access and did not let her leave the present either. No telling what was in that box. Security tried to get a fix on where she is living. The police department has been checking and there are no tracks in the snow in or out of her trailer home. We asked her for a phone and she gave it to us, but it is her cell and we already had that. It doesn't work most of the time. We tried to impress on her that we needed to know where she is living in case of an emergency. She saw through that since she no longer had custody.

"She quit her job at McDonalds and we don't know if she is getting money from the boyfriend or what. The police are looking into that. She was ranting and in that rant she mentioned getting out to Burlington, a small town west of Minot. The PD is looking into that.

"Her car would be easy to spot it is an older model orange Bronco. We have the license from her time in jail, so they are looking into that right now. She still brings up your name and how all of this is your fault, so we still want to have all precautions in place."

"Did she get to Jenny?"

"No. Those doors are locked and we are monitoring for her all the time. Security stopped her in the lower level lobby," he replied. "If you see that orange Bronco, call 911 immediately, okay?"

"I know. I will. They were able to pull the unmarked car from my place, I noticed. Thanks for the update," I said.

I smiled at what good friends we had become. It wasn't always that way. Jerry and I got off to a rough start when I first started working at the center. He worked there ten years before I came on board. I thought he was too hard on the kids. Over time, I learned his sporadic gruffness was just his way. I learned to have a great deal of respect for him over time. He was a veteran of military security in several wartime hot spots around the world. He knew his stuff. I learned a lot from him over the years. Behind that gruffness was a solid gold heart. I saw his soft side when my brother died. He called me into his office and expressed his sympathies and shared some stories of his own with me. His life had been no bed of roses either. I valued with confidence anything he told me.

I toyed and toyed with asking if Jenny could come over for Christmas. I have much and she has nothing. But I could not decide if I was strong enough. With only two days until Christmas, I decided to check my misgivings. I called Judy."Hi, I will be spending Christmas at home and have been wondering if I should see if Jenny could come over for dinner or something. What do you think?"

"You have a servant's heart," she said. "But I do not think it is a good idea for several reasons. You have made some good progress from your PTSD. I think you need all the extra time you can get. The other thing is that with grandma still a loose cannon out there someplace, it might even be dangerous for Jenny if she showed up. I think it is best for both of you not to do it. You might want to make a phone date with her and call her. You could send her a care package from the gift store downstairs and make sure they give it to her at Christmas. That way everything would be able to be checked out before she gets it. They are pretty fussy about what goes in and out of there, you know. They have to be."

I did remember that from my brief stay in the mental health ward many years ago. I thanked her knowing she was dead right. My friend on center once told me "You can't make life perfect for other people. Life isn't perfect and it's not your job."

There was an alert on my phone about a bad blizzard coming into the state on Christmas Eve. It would include sub zero temperatures, wind gusts up to 50 mph and blowing snow. Roads were expected to drift over and many would be impassable.

A while later the snowplows passed through the alley behind my house. My garage opened to the alley. I could probably get out if I shoveled for a couple of hours. The blades pushed banks up against my garage door. It was the single drawback of living in this historic neighborhood. Being snowbound was nothing new to me. I didn't mind it at all. In fact it cleared the schedule most of the time.

I decided the Christmas delivery idea was a good one. Jenny would never suspect as we had our little exchange together already. I called the hospital gift center. They were quite helpful and I knew exactly what I wanted. "I want her to get a very pretty Christmas basket. Please make it beautiful and festive. I want it to include an angel. I saw the perfect one in your window. It's the white brocade lace one with lavender ribbons. I also want a box of chocolates and some Christmas cookies if you have any. I want a bottle of body wash and a diary if you have one."

The lady was very accommodating and wondered what scent of body wash. They had cherry and a few other fruit flavors. I hate food bath products. She had something called fresh morning, which I thought would be the best. "We have some small tins of licorice that say reindeer poop on them. Some folks have been buying them to cheer people up," she said.

I loved it. "Oh, my yes, please include reindeer poop." I chuckled to myself. They also had gift cards and I thought that would be a darn empowering thing for her at some point. I included a gift card with the basket. She could buy something for herself. I asked about delivery and she assured me they had a special volunteer who always worked in the gift store on Christmas day to deliver all of the special requests from the shop. I rambled off my message to her.

Dearest, Jenny, I could not forget you on this important day. The weather is supposed to be very bad but please enjoy these gifts to help you make your day as special as you are. Love, Ms. Emily.

The wind whirled the blowing snow through my front yard. I put my newest Lori Line Christmas CD in the player and settled into my recliner for a nap.

Chapter Four

"GIRLIE"

Before long Alfalfa girl visited me. It was a cold winter day. She was building a snow fort in the backyard with her brothers. Her mittens were wet and they had been out long enough for her feet to start feeling cold through the rubber boots. Spot and Suzy, the two family dogs, began to bark wildly.

It was George Olson, the neighbor from down the street. He was more than a bit eccentric. He wore a flat, plaid golfing hat. He carried a cane but never used it. Dad always said he carried it just to hit the neighborhood dogs with. The dogs did not like to be hit with the cane and they did not like him. It became a vicious cycle over the years.

Alfalfa girl used to earn some money cleaning his house for him from time to time. The going rate was twenty-five cents an hour. She felt rich as she brought home a dollar now and then for her few hours of work.

"Hey, girlie," he called at her. He always called Alfalfa girl that name. "I need that floor washed again. Can you come over in about an hour and do it? I have my nephew visiting here and he doesn't like all the dirt on the floor." That was understandable because Mr. Olson did not have a kempt home. In fact he was a hoarder and very little of his home was accessible or functional. His idea of clean was to smear off the food and chew spots building up on the rotting linoleum.

Alfalfa girl didn't care about that. She had so few ways to earn money and it beat looking for pop bottles at two cents each, something she could not do in winter anyway. She checked with her mom and she granted permission.

After lunch she gathered her drying mittens off the heat register, put on some warm socks and headed down the block to Mr. Olson's house.

"Yeah," was the raspy, grunted reply to her knock at the door. "Oh, it's you, girlie, get in here. There's the pail and there is the mop. It shouldn't cost me more than fifty cents to get this done. And when that's done empty those dishes out of the sink," he commanded, pointing his crooked finger at the sink heaped with food crusted dishes. The room reeked of food that was days old by the look and smell of it.

She put her black and grey plaid coat on a chair. The chair was full of cat hair from his cat, Murphy. Murphy always wanted to get into her scrub water, but she did not see the big grey cat anywhere today. She was glad. It got in the way all the time and slowed her down a lot last time she cleaned.

She climbed up on the nearby stool and moved some of the dishes out of the way to slip the scrub bucket under the drippy faucet. There was no hot water in his home and all he ever had for soap was some powdered Tide laundry soap.

She knew she had to put the soap in a dish and make slurry out of it. She did that quickly. She cleaned off the dishes and ran water in the sink. Some of the slurry would go into the dishpan to help with the food on the plates.

She hoisted the pail out of the sink to the floor. There was no broom to sweep the dirt up first. She rolled up a dirty rug and sprinkled some water on it. She pulled it across the floor a few times and it took up most of the loose dirt and debris off the floor. She grabbed the mop leaning against the wall. It was filthy as usual. She also knew from other times that there was no getting it clean with the cold water. She carefully mixed the slurry into the cold water.

He did have Hilex on hand, so she poured a generous amount into the scrub pail. At least for a moment it smelled clean. She added some to the kitchen sink water too.

She set about wiping down the floor crusted with unknown spots and bumps of food and even some tobacco chew that missed the tin flour can substitute for a waste basket. She felt satisfied with what little progress was actually occurring on the floor. It was not at all like her mother's linoleum. Even though the linoleum at home was worn down to the brown underlayment, it was consistently clean with scrubbings several times a week or even daily as needed. She scrubbed them too.

This floor had never seen that kind of care. Alfalfa girl scrubbed the floor as hard as she could. She dunked the soiled mop back into the already brackish water. The Hilex was all that saved her from feeling like she was rolling in filth.

Alfalfa girl did not hear anyone enter the room as she focused heavily on getting the first half of the floor done. Her dad and mom always prided themselves in doing a good job and giving good work for good pay. She was bent over with her butt in the air to put some extra strength on a built up spot

"Well, that's what I like to see," a masculine voice said with a slight slur.

Alfalfa girl was about to stand up when a large male hand swiped down her back, over her butt and made circular movements along her cotton pants touching her genitals. Alfalfa girl tried to stand up, but the man's other hand held her down with strength much greater than hers. He continued the movements a few more times. She had never experienced this kind of assault before and did not know what to make of it. She was more scared than she had ever been. She had to pee on top of it. One half of the floor was as clean as she could get it. She tried to stand up again and this time he let her. It was her first look at him.

He was a rough cut thirty-something, unkempt man with greasy, red hair and a straggly red beard with food lodged in it. He smelled of beer and cigarettes. His crooked teeth were brown from smoking.

She did not like anything about him and she tried to move away from his strong grasp on her.

"What have you got up here?" he said and moved his hands over breasts that were little more than bubbles right now. "It won't be long and those little buds will be respectable tits. Yeah, pretty nice tits," he laughed cruelly. There was a Miller beer on the table and he reached for it. It was already open.

She thought that was her escape. All she wanted to do was run. But his arms were too long and he nabbed her by the collar nearly choking her. A life-defying, squeaky rush of air escaped from her mouth and throat. He sat down in a rickety chair and pulled her into his lap.

"Now, looky here what you did to me."

She did not know what he meant.

"I think you should have some of this," he sneered and reached for the zipper in his pants.

He was powerfully strong and held both her hands in his one hand. He laid her back down on the clean part of the floor, which was still very wet with the Hilex water. He unzipped his pants and Alfalfa girl looked away at the ceiling. An old kerosene lamp hung from it. She fixed her eyes on a spider web hanging loose from it.

He kneed her near the groin and put his weight on her to hold her down. Alfalfa girl wriggled desperately to get away, but it only made him more excited. He pulled down her pants part way and by now he exposed himself to her. She focused on the spider web swinging off the lantern.

He tried to enter her, but could not.

She instinctively tried to close her legs and pull her knees up to stop the assault.

"God damn little bitch. You are all dumb little bitches." He growled spitting on himself and on her as he railed angrily.

She felt the painful ferocity of him entering her only partly. It hurt and Alfalfa girl felt herself start to whimper.

He tried again and again. She did not know what happened, but all of a sudden, she felt wetness all over her groin and top of her legs.

Just then Mr. Olson popped through the door.

"Well looky here you dirty little girlie, what we got going on here?" he sneered so much evil she did not dare look up.

The young man jumped up and sputtered something Alfalfa girl could not hear along with a string of profanity. "Some bitchen girl," he sputtered incoherently.

"Get up girlie," Olson growled his contempt for her. "I see you been having fun here with my nephew instead of doing your work. I haint gonna pay you no money for not doing no work. What the hell is the matter with you?" he raged on. The unwarranted assault spiked through her soul.

Her head spun and she stifled back her cries. She honestly did not know what had just happened except that it felt bad in her heart just like the other times. She had the same convulsing pain in her stomach. She felt like she was going to throw up. She tried to get up, but the floor was still wet and now she realized the whole back side of her skin and clothing was wet with dirty Hilex water. She struggled to her feet. Mr. Olson grabbed her coat and threw it at her.

"Go on get the hell out of here, you worthless girlie and don't come back. No money for you little whore. Yer all whores!" he hurled the insult at her. She did not know what the word whore meant then.

He threw her coat out into a high snow bank. She was wet and reeking of Hilex. Her boots were wet with the Hilex water and she slipped and fell head first into the snow bank. She felt her lip split open and the warm blood drain out and drip in the snow. She instinctively licked it with her tongue. She could hear her heart pounding in her ears.

Don't tell. Don't tell. Don't tell. Jesus doesn't like dirty little kids!

She worked hard to imagine how she was going to explain this to her mother. No money, heartbroken and confused, her mind would not give her the answer. Her mind reeled as she trudged her way home slowly trying to make sense of it. She reeked like Hilex and dirt. Clean, dirty? They were the same this day for her and too many other days of her life as well.

Making sense out of senseless is very hard. She decided to lie. The truth would not work for this attack. It never mattered anyway. Never!

Mom was busy changing the baby's diaper when she arrived home. "What the hell happened to you?" she blared. Over the years Alfalfa girl and her siblings grew used to the woman who had too much to do with no resources. They cringed but found a child-like acceptance of the loud outbursts from their mother. Blaring had become her signature voice to kids, family and everyone else. Part anger, part disappointment, part bone breaking fatigue, it overshadowed her whole persona. This time was no different.

"I fell down. The floor was slippery and I fell down when I was scrubbing," She lied.

"How much did you get?" she asked.

"Only fifty cents." she lied.

Alfalfa girl pretended to finger fake coins in her pocket. She even pretended putting them in her piggy bank in the corner cupboard. They never checked it, so she knew the little white lie would work.

"I don't feel good," she said.

Now, the privilege of going to lie down and rest just because you weren't feeling well was not in her family worldview back in those days. You sucked it up and put one foot in front of the other. The little kids were gathered around the radio listening to Fibber McGee and Molly. That was good. She could tiptoe right past them to take care of herself without any little eyes.

She went into the children's' barracks style bedroom. Three sets of bunk beds lined the walls from one end to the other. It was rare for her to ever be there alone. She shed the nasty smelling clothing and put them in a pile on the floor. She could worry about them later.

She found dry clothes and a towel. She put the towel around herself. The house did not have running water so she had to take care of herself the best she could. She reached for a jar of Vaseline on the dresser. Mom used it for sore baby bottoms. Her finger scooped a glob out of the jar. She rubbed it around her palm to warm it up. She put some on the small cut on her lip. Then she put some on her bruised genitals. She was still pretty sore and she could see some of the outside redness. Her body felt sore inside too, but she did not want anymore touching there.

She put on clean panties and dressed herself in her favorite lavender pants and striped shirt. She hoped she would feel clean. The Hilex reeked from the pile on the floor. She did not feel clean. She would not feel clean for a very long time. She sat down on the lower bunk. She felt like crying, but no tears would come. She drew several breaths and stared at the painted wood floor. She just wanted to curl up and pull the blankets over her head.

The radio show must have ended because a swarm of little kids billowed around her.

They wanted to play. She did not. She could not just now. She worked hard to stay upright. Her stomach churned and her head pounded wildly.

She took out the huge box of tinker toys and gathered the little ones in the corner. She knew they could do that alone without her. They jumped into the toys with glee and busied themselves.

Alfalfa girl just needed some time, a little time to filter through the assault and find a way to deal with it. How she needed that alfalfa field!

She knew she should own up to the Hilex ruined clothes as soon as possible. But she rolled herself over into the bottom bunk. She tucked in a blanket along the top bunk. It made the bed into a kind of tent. It was darker in there. It was not the alfalfa field but it allowed her some sacred privacy for a bit. She laid her head down on the pillow and the space swirled around her. Her throat felt tight. She tried to push the afternoon memories out of her head. They kept stubbornly trying to push back like a newsreel spinning out of control.

She put her hand over her genitals and let the warmth of her hand radiate into her body for a moment. It was simple but comforting. She felt like screaming, but there were no screams. She felt like crying but there were no tears. She felt rejected and worthless. This kind of worthlessness was the kind that wanted to settle in, take root and live there a long time. It was an unusual twenty minutes or so that she was able to find much needed respite in her makeshift bunk tent. Alfalfa girl just wanted to feel something, something....*anything....* normal in the shattered core of her body. She wanted to feel. She did not. She did not feel very much for a very long time after that day.

The life giving solitude of the makeshift bed tent shattered fast when the little kids thought it was a game and came jumping into the brief haven. Tinker toy time was over. So was her short, precious respite.

I awakened from my nap with a burning desire for a warm bath. I remembered the rape vividly. I drew a nice warm bath and immersed myself in it for over an hour. I added hot water from time to time and relished every single bubble. This bath was for Alfalfa girl. I let her feel the warm luxurious water. I let her feel the cleanliness of it. I let her feel the luxury of the plush wash rag. I just let her feel and feel and feel. It comforted me to know I could give back to her now.

I felt some hunger pangs so carefully stepped out of the tub. I looked around the room and compared my vintage bathroom and lovely décor to that dismal day when only Vaseline could ease the pain of the child and her sexual assault. I bet myself that Alfalfa girl's conquest would be the great stuff of "locker room talk" by some people's measure in our nation today.

With every towel stroke up my legs and arms, I reaffirmed my own power and strength. Still I felt a sadness I could not shake and recorded the whole incident in my journal.

I read and reread the passages. I felt myself sinking into a horrible depression. It was an eerie inescapable blackness. The pieces of the incident kept playing in my mind. I decided to call Dr. Wisc. She had time to talk with me, but did not have any openings this late in the day. She asked me to read the journal entry to her. I did and not a single tear would come despite the savage ugliness I felt.

"Do you see the work that Alfalfa girl has done here?" she said.

I could not respond. A lump in my throat held the words back.

"There are so many layers here, Emily. It's not just the rape; it's the violation of your humanity here. This is a complex and layered occurrence. How many times did he insult your body alone? At least three times. Plus, this was a work situation. Child or not, you were working at the time. So you are assaulted on your job and you didn't get paid for your hard work. Plus you are thrown out of the door like a dirty old rag and the blame of it all was thrust upon you. Then you didn't even dare even tell anyone about it because they would not believe you. You actually had two assailants in this incident. Trust me the older fellow knew what was going on," she said and paused.

"What you also had happen in your little world is a veritable capsule of what happens to grown women in a corporate culture of sexual assault all the time. Trust me, the older man knew. But he scapegoated you to save his own ass. Alfalfa girl bore all of this indecency, this mongrel, inhuman, deviant behavior. She bore it for you," she said.

"So many women bear it today. The corporate moguls, business as usual types and politicians just go off to their mansions and never give a thought to the utter pain they ejaculate everywhere. I am not using the word lightly," she said.

Now the tears rolled. I sniffed and agreed but still could not find any words.

"Do you see what she did? She put one foot in front of the other and kept on going. She kept body and soul together for you under the most extreme mentally and physically damaging conditions imaginable. Some girls and women never survive these types of things, but Alfalfa girl's instincts were a salvation for you. She successfully defended you from worse harm during the rape. She protected you on her way home by putting one foot in front of the other despite her extreme degradation. She protected you from any further abuse when she got home and her mother had all those questions. Even then she found a way to keep her status in the family flowing by concealing the lost earnings and finding a way through her own personal pain and agony to still care for the children. She even found a makeshift alfalfa field in the bunk tent. She is smart and creative and inventive. Then, for goodness sakes, she cleaned herself up without even any hot water or privacy. Now, having said that, it is not the way it should happen. Victims should be able to come forward without reprisal, but we are not there yet even as a so called civilized society of ours. We know that if we listen carefully to the news today. Washington D.C. is awash in it. I just don't know how we get the word out to your blue trousers and blue skirts," she said.

"Alfalfa girl made you strong. She allowed you to survive one more time. She carried all of that pain and grief for you. You not only survived your trauma but you excelled in the face of it. It takes a very strong girl and woman to do that you know."

I finally found words, as inadequate as they were, I found my voice. "I know. It helps me to frame it like that in my mind. Otherwise, I do not know how I would have survived it, honestly, I don't," I had to admit.

"Keep journaling. Alfalfa girl has been doing a good job of filling you in on all of those parts you never understood about yourself. She is the soul of who you are. You would do well to continue to embrace her often," she said. At that point Dr. Wisc's other appointment arrived and we ended the conversation.

It was getting dark out now and I turned on the Christmas music and my tree. I switched on the gas fireplace for some extra warmth. I felt as though I needed some extra care this evening.

I took out a Cornish game hen for Christmas dinner. I cubed some bread for stuffing and added sage like my mother used to do. I smiled as I looked at the cup and a half pile of dressing.

It was tenderly amusing to me because dressing at the Sorenson home would be made by the double roaster full back in the day.

It would have been prepared for a turkey that Dad purchased from a farmer. It arrived with feathers and the head chopped off. The rest of preparing that bird was up to my parents. Only once did I have to pull pin feathers. I thought it was gross and disgusting. It was at a tender age that I understood how a live bird got to a dining room table wafting its mouth watering aromas. I smiled as I finished up my tasks. I was grateful not to have to pluck the bird. I have it so much better in life than my mother ever did. I doubt I ever truly appreciated how much.

I settled on a package of frozen beef stew for supper with some mint ice cream for dessert.

There was a knock at the door. It was the UPS deliveryman with a package.

I opened the door. The package was from my sisters. They sent two lovely wrapped gifts. I put them under the tree for Christmas. I was glad I had sent them gifts through an online store. With all that was happening, there was little shopping time for me this year.

Since I was near the front door, I decided to look out at my ornaments on the lawn to see how they were doing in all of the snow and wind lately.

Then I saw it. The orange Bronco was sitting down the block from my house. I dialed 911. The dispatcher said they would send an officer immediately. I locked the front door and turned off all the lights.

Then I headed toward the back door and crouched down beside it. There were no windows and it gave me a get-away if I needed it. I piled my coat beside me and took out my pepper spray. I refused to carry a gun. The small spray vial was my defense weapon of choice. In the old days I carried a can of cheap wasp spray, knowing how it burned if you got it into eyes.

It seemed like forever before I saw the flashing lights reflected off my living room mirror. I headed for the front door.

It was Sergeant Billevus. I was so happy for a familiar face. "Is she in here with you?" he asked

"No. I called as soon as I saw the vehicle," I said.

"Two of us are here. I dropped the other officer off at the car. He just called me and the vehicle is empty. She is not in it. The motor is cold, so she obviously has not been in it recently," he said.

At that moment the other officer arrived at my door.

"May we come in?"

"Of course," I said.

"We have some new developments about her. She moved in with a guy in a town west of here. We think she might still be taking orders from the boyfriend though. Parking her car here is more than just nuisance. Together with her many public threats toward you we are looking at this case with new eyes. It is stalking and now we will pick her up. Has she made any contact with you since our last discussion?"

"No, I would have reported it," I said.

"I will make the call in," he said and talked into his shoulder mouthpiece.

There was a brief discussion back and forth for a moment.

"We are going to impound the vehicle." he said.

I took a deep breath. He asked to look through the premises inside and outdoors. The other officer pulled a scarf around his neck and departed to look through the garage and back yard.

"We are going to put an unmarked car outside again. It is not unusual for this type of thing to go on for weeks like this, so we will take every precaution," he said and slipped out the door to join his partner in the search.

I turned on the television to my favorite news channel just in time to hear about the sentencing of a predator found guilty of sexual assault of a five-year-old child in Williston. It seemed to be everywhere these days. I switched it off. I rested in peace knowing at least it was none of my pedophiles. Mine were all deceased now. No one ever knew about their crimes against me. I chose not to reveal it.

I retrieved my stew from the microwave and headed to my recliner.

Now and again I would catch parts of a national conversation disparaging women. I stayed out of it. I had seen too much in my life and the hypocrisies were well known to me. But for the sake of my own survival, I ignored as much of it as I could. I did catch the part where some pastor said that rape and incest were a gift from God. What kind of God does that man pray to?

I thought about the rape episode with Alfalfa girl. I never allow the use of disparaging words like tits, cunt, pussy, or anything like it in my presence. I will not allow anyone to reduce me or any other woman to demeaning slang body parts. I shut my eyes and focused on letting go of all of it.

I tried to rescue a little bit of down time for myself after all of the day's events. I watched *The Christmas Story*, an old favorite of mine. I had originally seen it back when our small town still had a movie theater. There was no television back then, so we were lucky to have seen it. Tickets were twenty-five cents then and that was a lot of money. Popcorn was a dime if the lady showed up to make it.

I finished my stew and the delicious decadence of mint ice cream.

My cell rang and it was Sergeant Billevus. "I thought you would like to know we have Jenny's grandma in custody. She claims she was just driving by on your street and her car stopped there. The officers tested the car and it was in working order so we know she was lying. I just thought you might be able to sleep better if you knew she wasn't lurking around your home. The vehicle will be towed out of there in the next hour or so."

I thanked him. It was good to know. My whole body relaxed.

There was another knock at the door. It was late for the postal service, but it was my postman with another delivery. I signed for the package and some magazines as well.

I handed him a Christmas card with a Starbucks gift card in it. I was glad I had done all of that earlier in the month before all of this crazy stuff started to happen.

I opened the package and it was from Connie. Lord. I had not gotten anything for her. I would have to get something to her after Christmas because now she would be off work for Christmas.

I put it under the tree with the others and finished the rest of my movie. I decided to enjoy some quiet time in front of the warm fire in the vintage brick fireplace with its carved oak mantle. I had a single stocking hanging from it. Pine needles and pinecones adorned the top of it with some rustic candles.

My surroundings were important to me. It is something I started doing in my adulthood. I invested myself in a sort of personal nest building. I created an environment of comfort and safety. I always saw it as an ongoing part of my healing process.

Dr. Wisc helped me see once that that was a predictable outcome of all of the abuses of my life. No matter where I lived I found a way to create a "soft place to land" for myself.

That is a luxury Alfalfa girl never had a single moment of her life. She lived a life of utter chaos.

As an adult, I am unable to tolerate chaos and it makes me feel crazy in a moment. I run not walk away from it any time it surfaces in my life.

This whole affair with Jenny had the potential of chaos in the making. I knew I was walking on thin ice. I could not make the moral decision to walk away from her, however. Given how many people ignored or walked away from Alfalfa girl in her life. I simply could not be someone who could or would do that.

I received a box of chocolates from center for Christmas before I left work. The time to eat them arrived. I made some chamomile tea and chose a caramel, my favorite. I picked out one more. It looked like a mint. It was and I savored both. Then I headed up to bed. Visions of sugar plums did not dance in my head, but thankfully no bad dreams did either.

Christmas Eve morning I awoke very late. It was nearly ten a.m. by the time I awakened. The sun shone brightly in my east facing bedroom window. It was a lovely room. The year before I studied evenings and attained my redesign certification and used all of the skills I had to tailor the room into my private haven. I obtained the certification to help earn some extra income. However, most of the work I did was for people I knew and did not charge them. I redesigned this room with lovely lilac floral print wallpaper. You could get away with that in this vintage home.

I chose shabby chic furniture. I purchase some old style dressers and end tables and painted them to look very old, being very careful not to match anything. I wanted it to have a collected look about it. My bed was an old bed I salvaged and painted white. It had a simple metal adornment in the middle at the top of the headboard.

I did spend money on good mattresses and bedding for it. I designed the attached half bath in the same manner. All of the bathroom fixtures and lighting were brushed bronze. The house came with vintage doors and windows and woodwork, so little had to be done to them except to add off white paint. I slipped on my robe and headed downstairs.

I wondered how Jenny was doing on her Christmas Eve. I would give her a call later in the day. But first I needed to go out and warm my car. I had not driven it in days and I like to keep fluids circulating from time to time. I had to shovel first. I struggled in the deep snow the short walk to the garage. My shovel was just inside the door. The temperature was decent today at about 5 above zero. Without a brisk wind dropping the wind chill, it did not feel that cold. I wore my goose down coat and bundled my face up. I stopped counting the shovels of snow at about 60. Finally, there was room to back out. The car started on the first try. I could see the moisture in the air from my breath. My survival gear was stowed in the back seat, but would not need it for a quick drive down the grocery store.

The small grocery store was a great little privately owned market. Their specialty was freshly baked caramel rolls every day. I didn't need many things, but did pick a couple of the decadent, gooey rolls for a special Christmas breakfast treat.

The streets were plowed out, but a new layer of snow had fallen and there were intermittent drifts that created some visibility issues. I was glad to get back home to my garage. I put my groceries on a plastic sled from my garage and dragged them behind me to the back door. It worked so slick.

Alfalfa girl pulled a sled many times. Sometimes she went with her Dad. The family had a Radio Flyer wagon. He put skis on it in the winter. It held two large cream cans which he used to haul water. The family hauled all the water from the community well. The water was used for drinking and cooking and for the five gallon slop pail, the only indoor toilet our family had. In the winter they melted snow in a copper boiler on top of the stove for baths. There was no bathroom. A round tin tub was placed in front of the oil stove. Precious little privacy resulted from hanging a blanket around chairs lined up around the tub. The kids all took turns taking a bath in the same bathwater. Occasionally Mom would add a dipper of hot water to freshen up the water for the next child. It was rustic, but no one knew any better then, so we accepted this rudimentary bath time. It was all that was available. Alfalfa girl was oldest and always the last child to bathe. Dr. Wisc and I talked a number of times about the ritual bathing was for me now. And she noted how significantly it played into my life. At least I didn't have to haul water.

So this pulling a sled across the snow in the back yard was nothing new for me. I felt a bit spoiled in fact.

Just as I stepped in the door, my cell rang. It was my brother. He was a cook on a Navy ship in the Mediterranean the last I heard.

"Hi Emily, Merry Christmas to you." he greeted me.

"Merry Christmas," I was overjoyed to hear from him. Many times we did not know where he was serving.

"Where are you?"

"We have a brief stop in Greece and tomorrow we head out again."

I did not ask where he was going. He never told us. "What are your Christmas plans?" I asked.

"We are going to a little church down here with a friend and some locals, then out to dinner and then to some kind of celebration the town is having. It is very warm here and doesn't feel like Christmas. It never does without snow," he said.

"Well we have plenty for you. I think they said about fifty inches some places in the state. We have had one snow storm after another this year." We talked a bit more and then it was time for him to go. I loved the brief visits with him and the call was unusual and delightful for me. I opened the door and moved indoors to the kitchen as we talked.

It was good to be back inside and toasty warm now. The snow had even completely melted off my snow boots by the back door. I settled in to give Jenny her Christmas Eve phone call. But the circuits were busy and I could not complete it. Lots of people connecting with loved ones I suspected. I had prearranged the time. Now I worried she would think I didn't call. Damn it. Finally the call went through.

A nurse answered the phone. She sounded discouraged. "Emily, I am afraid Jenny cannot come to the phone just now. She met with her foster family this morning. We thought everything went well. Even Jenny told us it went well. They were so joyful to see her and brought presents and a small tree. They so want to welcome her to their family. Everything seemed to be going well and a few hours later she had a panic attack so significant we had to give her medication for it. She is sleeping now. We called the doctor and he is due in here in a few minutes. She simply seems to be a bit lost right now. I am sorry. She was so looking forward to your call. She mentioned it several times today and told her visitors about it more than once. She seems to trust you above anyone else," she said. I ended the call and sat down in my chair. My heart hurt so much for Jenny.

Alfalfa girl stood in front of me now despite the fact I was wide awake. It was hard to understand the confusing feelings I was having. I felt my soul touch hers. I sat down and closed my eyes to listen to the silence. She was reaching out to me. She was in the sacred alfalfa field. She was sobbing and busily laying down the plants to form her little cocoon. It was her safe haven. She could go there any time to find the peace she craved or grieve if she needed to. She inhaled the earthy fragrance of it and relaxed as its gentle aromas comforted her. This time she laid down in it and her face was salty with the tears of her lifetime of pain. I could not see her mouth move, but she spoke to me just the same. Her trust was gone. Completely gone! Not just a little bit, but a lot. Her latest predator was a long time family friend. He had worked his way into the family environment. The whole family thought of him as a dear friend. Over time, he befriended Alfalfa girl. Over time he built trust with her. Then in one shattering moment he manipulated himself on her after grooming her for months to trust him. He did not penetrate her, but massaged his penis against her until he ejaculated. Alfalfa girl knew in her child mind that this was wrong and ugly.

She got up and ran as fast as she could to the alfalfa field. She could scream out there. She could cry and get the ugly feelings to temporarily evacuate her body.

What she could not do in the alfalfa field was fix the damage to her life. That did not stop her from trying. She heard her mother call for her many times. She remained still like the rabbit in the cage. She remained invisible. No one found her. She hid right there in plain sight. She would do that for much of the rest of her life.

I let Alfalfa girl guide me to the present. I lowered herself shakily to my recliner. Alfalfa girl could no longer trust even a calling mother.

Jenny cannot trust either. She cannot trust that a loving minister and his family could bring safety to her life. Her body and soul could not allow it at this point it seemed. Her damage was profound and deep. The hospital for all of its whiteness and sterility must have seemed safer for her at that moment.

I remembered that time as an adult when I was hospitalized as suicidal. I was headed to a local tourist spot to drive my car off the cliff into the lake. The rest of the world felt hostile to me. I remembered Jenny's first utterings about her soul. "I am going to die. I am going to die. I am going to die."

I got up from my chair and made some toast. I was hungry and sick to my stomach all at once. I felt overwhelmed.

My cell buzzed. It was Connie. "There is a new development with grandma," Connie said.

"Please tell me she is not out now," I almost begged.

"No, there has been a new development. While she was in jail, Dr. Bryn Cleveland, a very astute social worker that I went to school with was called in to visit with grandma about grandma's options. Bryn's specialty in her doctoral program is child molestation and sexual assault. While they were visiting with grandma, Dr. Cleveland learned that the boyfriend also threatened grandma if she told. By making grandma an accomplice he would continue to have free access to Jenny. She was also manipulated by him. She has been in touch with him all this time and she continued to pull the strings for him. That is why she launched her attacks on you," Connie said.

"Now what?" I asked

"She is being transferred to a mental health unit in Fargo. It is a tangled mess for them to work with, but you are safe and Jenny is safe," Connie added.

"Not true. Jenny is physically safe but she had a major panic attack over going to the new foster home for Christmas. Everyone thought she was ready for it. She did too it seems, but she was not well enough yet to deal with all of the trust issues she has going on. That is what I think, "I said.

"I agree. When you are dealing with Psycho Sexual Trauma Disorders, the damage is serious and impacts many areas of life we have not recognized in the past. More is being learned all the time with ongoing research. In fact there is new evidence out that the assaults can actually change the brain. Each victim is different. I am dealing with a young man right now who was repeatedly raped by a priest in his church. He was thirteen years old with all sorts of speech difficulties. He has been bullied by other kids as a result of it. We don't often readily see how deep the wounds are. I have an embroidered picture on my wall at home that says, 'If you could see on the outside, how many people hurt on the inside you would be surprised who they are and how many they are.' I have a colleague who is working on his PHD in sexual trauma. He has been doing studies in prisons. His findings are exhaustive and enlightening. Many of those incarcerated come from these vicious sexual childhood traumas. But that is another subject for another day. I need to get going here, so just want to say Merry Christmas to you. I hope you can put this aside and relax now. You need to take care of you right now, " she said.

I knew she was right. I felt sick. It was Christmas Eve and I was sick at heart here. I went to my journal to write, but nothing would flow. I decided to leave it all alone for now. I gathered my Alfalfa girl picture and the rose drawing from Jenny. I decided two things. I sat them on the table near a treasured Christmas candle. I lit the candle in their honor. They are both safe. They are both in the best place they can be right now. I cannot help them by agonizing over them and making myself sick. It was a liberating decision.

I remembered the caramel rolls. Now was a good time for one. I missed having one for breakfast. I made a pot of green tea and sat down with the gooey luscious pastry. Not good for the cholesterol but good for the soul. I savored each bite. I refused to let the pain destroy me.

I found ways to transport myself from my troubling thoughts to my present. I looked at my Christmas tree. It had a definite Victorian look to it. Maybe I would opt for something a bit different next year.

The doorbell rang. It was the UPS man again. He had a delivery for me. I was not expecting anything so it felt uncomfortable.

"We are working overtime to get everyone's packages to them for Christmas. The storm back logged us for four days. Merry Christmas," he said.

"Wait one moment," I said as I dashed to the kitchen and saran wrapped one of the caramel rolls for him. If a guy has to work on Christmas Eve to bring people gifts, this was the least I could do.

"I didn't get lunch today. This will be wonderful." He saluted me playfully and disappeared into the heavy snowfall.

The package was an unexpected delivery from my car insurance salesman. It was date nut bread. I put it in the refrigerator for later snacking, maybe with cocoa that evening.

I pre-recorded the Concordia Choir concert on Prairie Public. Now seemed like a good time to watch it.

First I made oyster stew for supper and it would be a quick fix later in my evening. For now I simply let the voices bathe me in joy and comfort. I felt my body relaxing. I had not realized how tight my muscles became over the course of the day's events.

An acquaintance of mine once remarked about how much time I spent alone in my garden or with my rock collection, reading or listening to music. What she failed to recognize was that my choice for solitude was just that—a choice. Since my chaotic childhood, chaos became intolerable to me. That meant physical and mental. Unnecessary chaos generated by people was the worst for me.

A colleague of mine once asked my help to store some things of hers. She was moving some things from one storage unit to another.

She said and needed a temporary place to park her things. In her case temporary really meant free. I agreed without understanding that fact or the length she would go to manipulate the situation for her own benefit and agenda. But Charlene was a hoarder. I did not know that when I agreed to let her store some things in my garage.

Weeks passed and the mess she created was driving me nuts. Despite my many attempts to get her to deal with her own things nothing improved and she did not remove her belongings. She would come by from time to time and make it look like she was doing something about it, but she simply just shuffled things around. She only took a thing or two when it suited her to fool me about it. No access or function was restored to my garage area for weeks. There was no closure or respect for personal boundaries. I felt violated. When I talked to Dr. Wisc about it, we agreed I would give Charlene written notice and have the document notarized. If she did not remove her belongings, I would call the Salvation Army store to come and get them. That is what I eventually did. She never spoke to me again. I wondered why this experience popped into my head just now. I thought it might be because I so relished the orderly function of my own space. It really was a mental health issue with me, as was cleanliness.

My concert ended. I felt lifted and at peace. Alfalfa girl helped me learn how to do that over the years. She carried my soul when I couldn't carry it any more.

The wind picked up outside and I could see the fiercely, blowing snow would make it hard for anyone traveling this Christmas. Many people would adapt to it. I was content to be inside and warm. Other years carolers came by on Christmas Eve, but the weather would prevent that from happening this year.

My high school choir went around our small town caroling for a couple of years but eventually the woman who made it happen moved out of town and it all fell apart then. I never watched news at Christmas. I did not want the world intruding into my space. I realized that I forgot to grab my mail by my doorstep mailbox. I reached the letters and they were a bit damp from the snow in the air. There were some bills, a flyer from Menards for special eleven per cent savings and several Christmas cards.

I opened the first one from a woman I went to high school with. We re-connected after many years and she is dear to me yet. She has an intelligent mind and we often exchange emails. There was another card from my former pastor. He and his wife moved to Michigan and now we only communicate by Facebook sometimes.

One last card surprised me. It was from a man I dated six months ago. He was over involved with his children and I always felt in the way. We could not even go on a date or a drive anywhere without them calling. The intrusion was so difficult for me that I decided it was not worth it. I ended the involvement. The Christmas card had two movie tickets in it. We used to go to a lot of movies together and loved discussing them after. I was not going down that road again. I tore up the card and the tickets and threw them in my nearby wastebasket. I was proud of my strength in this matter. It felt empowering to have some healthy boundaries for a change.

I stirred the oysters into the half and half cream with some butter and a little salt and pepper. I loved the little round crackers. They were a special treat in our family when I was growing up. But with so many kids, we could only have a few with our soup. Now I could have all I wanted. I just chose not to.

I put the tea kettle on to make my hot chocolate. It was Instant these days.

My mother labored over a whole two gallon kettle of milk with Hershey's cocoa powder, a bit of butter, a pinch of salt and tiny bit of vanilla. It did not last long in our household. She also made gigantic caramel popcorn balls, not the white or colored syrup kind. That was about It for celebrating Christmas Eve at our home.

Our family did not go to church as many families did. Our big observances of that kind were the Sunday school and School Christmas programs. It was about all they could manage back then. Our small community also held a Santa day where bags of candy and apples were given out to the children. Adults received tickets for drawings for hams and turkeys. My mother never attended Santa day. I suspect she was home wrapping presents knowing we would all be gone all afternoon. My dad won a ham and a turkey a couple of times. I simply relished the fun of it all and getting out of school a couple hours early.

I finished my oyster stew and moved on to the hot chocolate. I indulged in a couple of my favorite candies. Since childhood, chocolate covered cherries were high on my favorites list. I savored them with the steaming cocoa in a delightful Santa cup, a gift from a dear friend last Christmas. I savored the quiet Christmas music and the chocolate melting on my tongue. I delighted in the fact that I learned over time to be comfortable with myself. An old phrase, "Where ever you go there you are," came back to me. I was content for now.

More snow in this Christmas storm battered the state. Blizzard conditions and thirty degrees below zero meant treacherous conditions for travelers. North Dakotans are resilient. Most people hunkered down and did what they needed to do. It would be a fool hearty person who would take on conditions like tonight unless they had to. My yard ornaments became buried deeper and deeper in the snow bank in my front yard. I would leave them there until the first big melt or spring whichever came first.

My living room darkened gradually. I turned on the fireplace and settled in for the older version of the Christmas Carol, one of my all time favorites. I saved some chocolate covered cherries for this. I held my journal in my hand and traced the alfalfa drawing over and over again.

Dr. Wisc suggested that when I was ready that I should write a letter to Alfalfa girl. I decided it would be my Christmas present to her. I wrote carefully and lovingly.

> *Dear Alfalfa girl.*
>
> *I want you to know you are safe with me now that I have really found you. I am sorry that I did not know you for so many years. I am sorry that I did not recognize all of the important hurt and pain you*

carried for me when I simply could not. Grownups failed us both so many times.

Grownups, both men and women created the hushed environments where we could not tell anyone that we were getting hurt again and again. They did not respect the innocence of our childhood. I cannot tell you why because I do not know why. You were always there for me every single time a man or boy decided to violate me. I would not be here today if it were not for you.

So thank you for being the brave one. Thank you for being the one with courage. Thank you for finding our alfalfa spot to escape rest and recover. I would not be here without it. My very spirit would have died from shame. I would have died from degradation. I would have died from dehumanization. So I have much to thank you for.

I promise you I will be the one to build a safe spot for you from now on. No one will be able to hurt us like that ever again. I promise I will stay connected with you always. You were a good little girl. You did absolutely nothing wrong. You did nothing to cause any of these bad things to happen to you. I always thought we did. I was wrong. Most of my life I was just plain wrong about that. I blamed us.

I am sorry the grown-ups made it impossible to speak our truth, to tell our pain, to even understand or forgive ourselves. I am so sorry for all of it.

I promise not to blame. I promise not to carry guilt. I promise not to allow rejection of us. I promise not to let anyone hurt us like that again ever. If they try I promise we will respond appropriately. I promise to continue to seek healing for us. And most of all, I promise to love you forever even though I did not know how to for so many terrible years. Love, Emily.

I flattened the rose drawing from Jenny between the pages. I placed the Alfalfa girl picture in between the next pages. I closed the book. I held it to my heart. I had never known such peace. It was the finest Christmas Eve ever.

The next morning the North Dakota blizzard brought everything to a stand-still. I felt sorry for people whose plans had to be greatly altered. But I was comforted in the notion that families would have successfully adapted to the storm. They knew how after living here for years.

Technology would also be helpful. A friend of mine emailed me to say she and her family was going to watch the same church service on television and then Skype afterwards.

I felt lucky to envelop myself at home safe and sound. I saw the journal on the stand by my recliner. I smiled and blew a kiss to Alfalfa girl. She felt so close to me now for the very first time in my life. It was a blessed gift of healing.

I wrapped myself in my blessed solitude. I reached for the caramel roll and popped it into the microwave. I threw on a few raisins and walnuts for an extra treat. I cut a pat of butter and put it on the steaming roll. My Kuerig finished a perfect cup of coffee. I headed into the living room. I turned the tree lights and the fireplace on. I felt like a little kid getting ready to open Santa's presents. I buttered one of the caramel rolls and brought it with a cup of coffee in to the living room. Maybe it was because I knew I was doing it for Alfalfa girl for the very first time. Away in the manger played as I moved the presents to my chair and opened my gifts from my sisters first. They thoughtfully gave me my favorite Eucalyptus and Spearmint bath oil and lotion. The gifts were beautifully wrapped with lavender netting and a ribbon. The attractive baskets would look lovely in my bathroom until I wanted to use them.

I munched on another morsel of the caramel roll. I opened the gift from Connie. She also knew my penchant for calm. It was a lovely sachet of the lavender she grew herself. I knew just the spot for it in my bedroom. Her lovely hand-made card read:

Dear Emily, Here something to help you in your journey, Love and blessings, Connie.

Her handwriting was beautiful and neat. It felt good to have such a good friend and colleague.

I settled back into my Queen Anne recliner to listen to more of the piano Christmas CD. I allowed myself to just relax. I needed to remind myself to do that in the past. It did not come naturally to me.

I reminded myself to get my Cornish game hen into the oven for Christmas dinner. It was the perfect solution for a one person special meal. I accompanied it with steamed potatoes and Greek yogurt topping, broccoli, rye dinner rolls and a store bought pumpkin pie with whipped cream. It was simple but luxurious in my mind.

I spooned my pre-made dressing into the small bird. I coated the breast with olive oil and put it in the oven. I placed a setting of my best china on my small dining room table. My Christmas napkins were a gift from my sister and I treasured them with every use. I opened a bottle of pinot noir and poured myself a half glass. *A reward for the cook,* I thought and smiled.

Dinner was ready in no time and I enjoyed the lovely food. I remembered all of my childhood Christmases growing up. Mom and Dad always went out of their way to make it a celebration for us, something they were rarely able to afford at other times. I still have my last doll from them in a small chest my dad actually made for me. It is one of my treasures and repainted for my bedroom now.

I finished my pumpkin pie and Cool Whip. My thoughts turned to Jenny and the phone call I promised to make to her.

I dialed the number. The nurse answered.

"How is she doing?" I asked.

"Much better. They postponed the actual residency with the family until we know she is more stable. I will get her."

"Miss Emily, I miss you. Can you come and see me? I am scared. I am scared all the time now. It is a good family I think, but so many changes, all the time changes" Jenny blurted everything out in one sentence.

"Merry Christmas, Jenny. I will come and see you soon. We can talk about it if you want. Did you get my Christmas basket this morning?" I asked

"I did. I knew it was you. I knew it. They said Santa left it for me. I knew it was you." We chuckled over the notion of Santa.

"You know that it is ok to let people love you, right?"

"I do not know what that feels like, since my Mom died. I don't know what it feels like," she said quietly.

"I want you to do something for me. I gave you that journal in your basket. Today is Christmas day. I want you to write your best love memory of your mom in that journal. Take your time with it and write it like a thank you letter to her. Remember everything you loved about those moments with her. I want you to think of it as your Christmas present to you and your mom. Can you do that for me?" I asked.

There was silence at the other end. Then I heard a deep sigh. "I know which one it is, but I am always afraid to think about it," she said.

"It might hurt, but thinking about loving her as much as I know you do. Love her in this memory that you write about. Write about loving her and how you did that and how she did that. I think you will be surprised at how much better you feel." I said.

I heard some rustling of paper and there was a brief silence. "I have the journal now. I will do it Miss Emily. I will do it right now," she said.

"Merry Christmas again and good luck. I am going to hang up now," I said.

I thought about the conversation. I was puzzled at her reaction. Only because I know what the journaling did for me in reconnecting with Alfalfa girl, did I understand what the exercise might do for her. But I was out of my element. I am not a psychologist or professional in the mental health field. I wondered if I had overstepped here. Yet, she seemed so upbeat about writing in the journal. I had to toss aside my misgivings and believe that her own introspection would help reconnect her with her ability to love and trust again. Time would tell. There would be no fast answers for this little girl.

There was a knock at my door. On Christmas? I was not expecting anyone. I opened the door to see a young man and woman and two children.

"Merry Christmas," the pretty young woman said. Her two children echoed the sentiment from behind her legs.

"We live just down the block and are unable to go home for Christmas. We have this basket of fruit that we bought for our Mother. It will not keep until we see her, so we decided to give it to you," she said with a big smile on her face. The young man offered a lovely ribboned basket of oranges, apples and other fruits to me.

"This is so generous of you. Can you come in?" They stepped into my home. "I have some hot chocolate and Christmas treats if you would like," I offered.

They looked at each other and nodded. I took their coats, seated them and brought my candy cane decorated mugs of hot chocolate and some of the date bread.

"I wasn't expecting Santa today," I said almost jokingly.

The young woman pursed her lips and responded. "Oh this gift is not from Santa. It is from our Lord Jesus Christ," she said emphatically.

I was taken aback for a moment and then found my voice. "Then I have all of you and him to thank," I said politely.

They nodded in approval and we finished our snack together. They were a pleasant family. The children were on their best behavior. We chatted about the neighborhood and recent changes to its front entrance. The children talked excitedly about going out to play in the snow later in the day. It was a pleasant forty minutes or so and then they excused themselves to go home and make phone calls to family. We said our farewells and promised to connect again sometime in the future. I hoped we would.

I unwrapped the cellophane and huge bow from the basket and picked out a couple of grapes to pop into my mouth. I set the basket under the tree.

I took out my planner and reviewed my back to work schedule. I felt stronger now and the notion of returning was not as daunting as it had been. Tomorrow I would confirm my return date with my supervisor. She was a nice woman, a great friend, and I respected her greatly. She had experienced some bumps in her life and understood all that had happened. She sent me a note just before Christmas with a Starbucks card. We always joked that Starbucks was our home away from home. Staff there knew me by my order of café latte skim milk, one Splenda very well stirred. A couple of them could finish the order for me.

The day passed much more quickly than I expected. I jumped into a bubble bath for a good long soak and went to bed early. My Christmas day felt cheerful and memorable to me. I allowed the precious solitude to embrace me and my soul for Alfalfa girl.

I slept in late the next day. It was a cloudy Monday. I disposed of the wrappings from the day before and loaded the Keurig for my morning coffee. I put the fruit basket in my refrigerator. It would only be another day or so before I headed back to work and I wanted to relish the rest of my down time. I chose a plump grapefruit from the fruit basket and a couple of prunes and finished them off in no time.

Chapter Five

CALLY

My cell rang. It was Connie.

"Are you available at noon for a meeting with Dr. Cleveland and me at the pancake house?" she asked.

"I am feeling much stronger now, so I will say yes, that will work. What's up?"

"She has information about some great new research about trust building with children and child molestation. It might be helpful for Jenny. Dr. Bennington will meet with us too. He wants us to form a team of people. You are the only one Jenny trusts right now, so he would like you to meet with us. Sonya from the hospital may attend as well, but she never knows her schedule so will have to play that by ear," she said.

I felt hope rising in my heart. I did not know what the information was, but I felt excited for anything that could help Jenny. I wondered how she was doing, but I focused on getting dressed, warming my car up and getting to the meeting. It felt good to move forward with some purpose. I was surprised at how ready I felt to do that.

The temperature warmed up to 15 degrees above zero, so my car would not take so long to warm up. But the snow was knee deep to the garage. I put on some warm, wool slacks and a sweater and my tall snow boots. I grabbed the shovel. It was too far to shovel but I could spike the shovel in the snow like a cane to keep myself from falling over in a snow bank.

The city plowed out the streets and travel was not a big problem for careful drivers. You have to respect snow and ice on a roadway or you will find yourself wrapped around a telephone pole. My dad said that to me many times when I was learning how to drive.

Dr. Cleveland and Connie were already seated when I arrived. She introduced me.

Dr. Cleveland was about my age with lovely silver hair shaped around her lovely face. She wore blue jeans with a classy leather jacket and a stunning designer necklace. "Connie has told me a lot about you. The fact that Jenny trusts you is important to the process I will talk about," Dr. Cleveland said.

We ordered our food. I ordered the small chef salad. Dr. Bennington was running late and might still join us. Sonya cancelled due to an emergency at the hospital. Dr. Cleveland turned to me and spoke.

"This new research we are working on has to do with using a dog as an intervention tool for these kids who suffer the trauma of molestation. I belong to a group called Lamplighters. We work with some of the more severely traumatized children and adults. It is a healing program and a trust building process. For those who cannot trust another human being, research is finding they can make an attachment to a gentle dog. We also work with the dogs much the way police departments work with theirs except ours are trained to be very gentle and responsive to the victim. Most dogs already have that capacity but occasionally, like people, you have the brat or the wild one. So we screen the animals carefully. Connie was telling me about your Jenny and it seemed like a good idea to see if a dog might help with her trust issues. We think introducing the dog with you in her hospital setting might be a good strategy. Also, Sonya and the hospital staff are looking into what the hospital staff can do about having the dog brought up to the ward. It is unprecedented, so do not know how it will go. It might be a good transition for her. Also, we need to talk with her adoptive family. After I worked with the

149

grandma and learned more about how devastating her abuse was we need to do everything we can for Jenny. Treatment at the hands of the boyfriend was dehumanizing for both of them, but especially Jenny, " Dr. Cleveland said.

"Did her grandma know what was really going on?" I asked.

"My professional opinion is yes. However, I am convinced that grandma never realized the enabling role she played in the whole thing. Her recovery if she chooses to go that route will take years," she answered.

I was already excited about the prospect of this new recovery opportunity for Jenny. "I thought the dog approach was used mostly for victims when they testified against an abuser," I said.

"That is where it started but in our Lamplighters group we did some trials with kids who couldn't even talk. All the measurements show a good response. We are encouraged about it. There is no hard data yet, but that is coming. I have some grad students researching other programs in the infancy stages of this kind of approach," Dr. Cleveland added.

"Do you know if the hospital and the family will go along with it?' I asked.

"I don't think it will be a difficult sell. The hospital already uses pets with the elderly in their nursing home setting. We also know of success with wounded veterans. The challenge is to keep ourselves on top of what we know works and what we know doesn't and get it into useable data." she said.

"How do you see Emily's role in this plan? Connie asked.

I was about to ask the same question.

"Jenny already trusts her. We think that she introduces the idea to her and then we go from there," Bryn said.

"I got her started on journaling yesterday. She was excited about it and it was the first flicker of interest in her own life that I have heard in a very long time," I offered.

Dr. Cleveland smiled broadly and said, "I like everything I am hearing. I am going to officially put this team together and introduce it to the Lamplighters Project Board. Research is one of the legs of their mission. I think they will like it. We will ask them for a small grant for the dog expenses. There is no money for salaries, but do we agree that no one is getting a paycheck out of this?" she asked.

We all agreed. At that moment Dr. Bennington arrived and apologized for his delay. He explained he also had an emergency call from center. "I ate a protein bar on the way over. I knew you would be finishing up. But I would buy coffee and dessert," he offered.

He was a tall man, about six feet or so. He was in his late sixties with attractive graying along his sideburns and neck. He dressed very casually in jeans and a sweater. He wore plain round glasses and always walked at a brisk pace. Benningon was a leader in his field and his work with children and teenagers. He was highly respected in the professional world and accomplished significant research and papers in abusive issues. He won many awards for his work over a thirty-year career. We graciously declined the offer for dessert.

Dr. Cleveland summarized our discussion to him and drew a rough organizational chart of our team and how it would operate. Connie's involvement would be data methodology development and a connection to the training center for possible partnerships down the road.

I finished the last ounces of my diet Coke and we parted company.

I headed home, but the snowplows were out again, so I proceeded with caution. Once home, I took out my planner and looked at my schedule for work. There was only one more day off after today. I took a moment to ponder how I felt about that.

My other students had been neglected far too long and I needed to catch up on each of their job shadows and experiences. Ms. Renee had been keeping my office moving in my absence. I had done that for her once when she was ill.

She was a valued colleague and I never had a worry about how the job and the duties would be handled. I gave her a call and reminded her I would be back Wednesday at 8 a.m. Efficient woman that she was, she already had it on her calendar. I no sooner hung up from that call than the hospital called saying that Jenny wanted to see me.

The nurse said she had been writing in her journal and was excited to share it with me. They put her on the phone.

"Miss Emily, can you come over here and let me read my journal to you?" The girl actually had a bit of brightness in her voice that delighted my heart.

I agreed. "I need to do a couple of things so how would about an hour be?" I asked.

I picked up a few groceries on the way home and needed to get them put away. I hated coming home to a mess and did everything to avoid it.

It was far too early to talk to her about the dog, so I would have to be sure I kept that out of the conversation. It would be hard.

The sun was out now. The temperature was still well below zero. My car dash gauge read zero. Not much wind though and that made all of the difference.

I arrived at Jenny's room exactly the time I promised her. She had a big smile on her face. I could not remember the last time I had seen her smile. I had forgotten how pretty she really was in the girl next door kind of way.

I sat down. She reached for her journal and said, "I have never done this before."

"It doesn't matter. It is your heart that is speaking for you," I said.

She began.

"I don't remember all of my Christmases with my mommy, especially the ones when I was real little.

But she had pictures and we always looked at the pictures together on Christmas Eve. I loved every one of them. She explained what we were doing when the pictures were taken. I loved her stories. We would laugh together about them.

I had an ornament with my name on it for every year. I loved those ornaments, but he broke them all one year when he was drunk. I only have one left. It is an angel with my name on it.

Mommy and I used to make paper snowflakes. You fold and fold the paper and cut it with a scissors and when you shake them out they are beautiful paper snowflakes. We taped them in our windows. At the same time we put my name ornaments on the Christmas tree. It was special to do only on Christmas Eve. She said we put them there for the baby Jesus to see. She hugged me and said my name and then handed each ornament to me and I put it on the tree. Age one, Jenny with her Christmas stocking. Jenny Age two with chocolate on her face and a Christmas bear. Jenny, age three in her Christmas dress and a gold star. Jenny, age four with her puppy and a candy cane. Jenny, age five with her new hair cut. I asked to have my head shaved when mommy lost hers to the cancer. She took a picture each time we added an ornament to our tree. There were five altogether. I was five when she died. I always felt special with her. I always felt loved with her. I knew her heart and she knew mine. Once I stepped on a glass ball when we were trimming the tree it and broke it. She just told me that she knew I didn't mean to do it. It was an accident and everyone makes mistakes.

Jenny's voice grew softer and softer with each line. She focused on the words intently, but her hand reached up and she was holding it over her heart. She paused.

I wanted her to speak first, but she looked at me intently for a response. I knew that what I said next could be crucial to her and I winced inside.

I put my hand over hers on her heart. "Look where your hand is," I said.

She looked down at our hands. "I know. It has been like that since I started writing," she said.

'Let's give the little girl in your story a name" I suggested. If it worked for me maybe it would work for Jenny. "What name do you want to give that little girl?"

It took her no time at all to reply. "I think I should call her Rose, for my mom's drawing," she said.

I felt uplifted. It said to me that she had found her Alfalfa girl down under all of the hurt and scars.

"What do you think Rose is feeling right now? Just close your eyes and see her in your mind."

Jenny did that. "She is happy. But that is not the most important thing. She is not afraid. Mommy loves her just because she is Rose. It is enough for my mommy," she said.

I tried to suppress the tears, but I could not. Neither could Jenny.

"I like Rose," she said, "but I don't know her very well."

"I understand." I patted her hand reassuringly. "I know you don't. You don't have to right now. You see Rose wants you to come back and visit her. The journal is to write whenever you are feeling things that you remember or afraid about or confused about. Rose wants you to come back and visit her again and again. What do you think?"

"I think she does and I think mommy does too, so I am going to do that," she said with an innocent resolve.

We sat together once again in simple silence as we had so long ago in my office. Her breathing was calm and relaxed. Once again, I wanted her to take the lead. She whisked the curl back from her face. She moved closer to me. "I don't know what it is," she said.

"What do you mean?"

"I feel something, but I don't know what it is," she said.

It had likely been so long since Jenny felt anything but anger and fear that anything beyond really was a mystery to her. I accepted that she owned it, it was ok and she was right about it for herself and her feelings in her own time.

"You don't have to name it, Jenny. Does it feel bad?"

"No it is not bad at all. It feels like clean underwear."

"And how does clean underwear feel?"

"I think it feels fresh," she said.

'Well let's start there. Tonight before you go to bed, you should write to Rose about clean underwear. She might be able to help you with that," I reassured her.

She nodded. I was prepared to stay longer, but Jenny said she needed a nap. I respected that she might need some time alone now. I was glad for her that she felt that self-assuredness and a small step in regaining some ownership of her life.

"Thank you for the nice Christmas present. I didn't get you anything," she half apologized.

"You sure did. First you gave me Jenny and then you gave me Rose. No one could have given me anything better," I reassured her.

I kissed her on the forehead and headed out into the cold North Dakota winter. I sucked in all I could think about in the past hour with Jenny. I decided to follow my own advice and not analyze it right now. As my dad used to say from time to time I had to hit the ground running the next day. I wanted my clothing washed and ready for Wednesday when I would go back to work.

I always hung my clean clothing together for each day including socks and underwear. Nothing irritated me more that digging around to find stuff. That is how I grew up and I wanted none of it.

My cell rang and it was Jerry from the hospital. He called to ask if I had been watching the news. I had not. "This is not an official call. This is a friend telling a friend some information. Jenny's perpetrator went on trial last week. The verdict was handed down today. He was convicted of a Felony Class AA Continuous Child Abuse. He got a life sentence. Part of it was that they were able to also introduce his coercive abuse of the grandmother. He is headed to the state pen. I heard it through my sources. It should be in the paper in the morning. We sure are relieved around here with Jenny still in the mental health ward," he said.

"That seemed like pretty fast processing through the system," I said.

"They were causing so much trouble everywhere, I think they wanted to expedite the case," he said.

I thanked Jerry and sat down on my bed. Relief flooded over my body. It would be up to professionals to let Jenny know when they deemed it the right time.

I portioned out some leftovers into five containers to take to work for lunch. Food at the center cafeteria was excellent, but on my budget, supplementing lunch from home was a sound idea. I put four in the freezer and left one out for tomorrow.

I dug out my briefcase. It seemed such a long time since I used it. I sorted the paperwork and took out my date book. I added a couple of Jenny related numbers in my phone in case something came up. I shifted my focus to my job.

I felt strangely disconnected after two weeks and two days off.

I dug out my wool winter coat. My goose down was just a bit too worn to wear for work. The blue wool one was dressier too. I found my long scarf and dress gloves as well.

I chucked a pizza into the oven for supper. I opened the only can of beer in my refrigerator. I liked Pizza and beer, just did not indulge in it very often. I made arrangements for my friend's son to come over and shovel a narrow path to my garage. Spinal stenosis prevented me from taking on such a large task even though I really did not mind shoveling snow. My brothers and I made a game out of it as kids to see who could shovel the most snow in the least amount of time.

Bailey came by and shoveled a path clear in under an hour. I paid him and gave him a ten dollar tip. He was college bound after his senior year and could use the money. I headed to bed early.

I arrived at work a few minutes early. I anticipated a desk full of paperwork and a sorting ordeal. I opened door to my office. I saw a huge helium balloon bouquet on my desk. I knew who was behind that. Just at that moment she walked up behind me. "Welcome back," she said and gave me a big hug. Renee had grown very dear to me over the years. "Your papers are in organized piles on your desk. Each is marked."

I felt overwhelmed by her consideration for me. "You are so kind," I said.

"I remember who did that for me once," she said and winked at me.

She was an average framed woman with dark brown hair. She was in her early fifties. She wore a suit most of the time and always presented as the true professional she was. Like me she had to meet with the public a lot. She had an endearing smile you could fall in to.

I brushed the swaying helium balloons aside a bit and looked at the piles. They were in order of importance. On the job student files, new students, worksite proposals, new forms from corporate and others less important paperwork were neatly piled for my perusal. She brought in two cups of coffee for us.

"So tell me what I need to do first," I said.

"We have a situation over at the ice plant. The student working there keeps disappearing and they find him loafing around the plant. My vote is to bring him back in. He obviously is not workplace ready yet."

"I agree," I said. I wrote a note to myself to follow up. "Did you meet with my other mentees?"

She nodded. "Darren is gone. He kept pushing the envelope until he finally got himself dismissed from the program. He just could not keep his hands to himself. He was always swatting someone or taking pretend swings. He did that once too often and security caught him in the act after several warnings. He is asking to come back, but I do not know what is going on with that."

I could not resist my snide remark. "How do we expect kids to keep their hands to themselves when grown men and national leaders don't know how to do it? What do we say to kids?"

"I'm with you but let's have lunch and talk about this one. You have a new mentee as of last week. His folder is in the pile," she said and slipped out the door.

Our offices were in an older building on center with a classic stairway leading up to them. I loved the old building and my office always felt like home to me.

The day was a flurry of activity from checking messages to catching up on each file. I took my time with it so I would get a good grasp on things. I called the ice plant and rescinded the work experience for the student who was dishonoring his opportunity. I would have to speak with him. Just as with Jenny and other kids, we worked hard to help them develop work readiness.

I worked most of the day, but exhaustion caught up with me about four p.m. and I asked to go home an hour early.

Each day was better and better and my work, which was so important to me, got easier and easier. Our students came to us from so many different backgrounds, most of which did not enable them to gain self-efficiency without help.

Renee and I met for lunch the next week. There was a lot of political smack being talked during the election cycle and we had not had time to catch up. We met in the cafeteria. We liked the east end, which was a quiet area.

"Did you get a chance to meet your new mentee yet?" she asked.

"Not yet. I went to meet him and he was taking a test, so I did not get to meet him. The nursing instructor said he is very motivated and is taking English classes at the adult learning center and working on his citizenship. Where is he from?" I asked.

"He is from Somalia. He is an immigrant and he lost everything, his village was burned, his family murdered and his mother and sisters brutally raped. He is so motivated. He wants to go back eventually and help his country," she said.

"My other students from Somalia have all done very well here. Most of them went on to college from our program. One of them was a registered nurse when I was in the hospital. I look forward to meeting him next week," I said.

"How is Jenny doing?" Renee asked.

"I haven't seen her lately, but Dr. Bennington said she is working through some tough issues right now. Social services and he have worked it out so that no HIPAA violations happen if he talks to me. I have been focused on getting back in the saddle here. I sent her a card last week. But that is all I know. I plan to visit her this weekend if she is up to having company. Do you know anything about the Lamplighter project?"

"Actually I do. We have a mentally disabled niece in her forties who was brutally raped a year ago and she is a part of that group for her recovery. Her name is Dorothy and she did not even want to live anymore after the rape. They do good work there. Dr. Cleveland is the best. She puts in way more hours than she ever gets paid for," Renee said.

"What do you think about our election?" I asked.

Renee just shook her head. "I don't get it. I don't get it. What do we say to our kids when adults act like this?" she said.

"I asked that same question. Where are the churches, where are the evangelicals who got all bent out of shape when our last first lady wore short sleeves?"

"I get really bent at the national discussion about laziness and people on food stamps. Hell I was on food stamps once after my divorce. When the political talking heads loosely throw around the word lazy, I want to smack them. My experience over my 30-year career has been that the number who fit that description is statistically quite small. If you are born rich and born into all of the advantages maybe your golden highway is easy. For many of us it has not been. And I pay my taxes faithfully like most Americans do. My personal philosophy is that if you are not doing anything to uplift people from where they are at then get the hell out of the way. You are a roadblock to progress and a shameful one at that," she said.

I looked at my watch. "Look at the time. I have to meet with a business in town to see if we can partner with them to place students there, so I better get going," I said.

"Hey, Emily, It is so good to have you back. Just don't overdo things. These kids need you. Jenny needs you," she said and smiled that smile of hers. She grabbed my hand and gave me a little squeeze to emphasize her words. Renee was dear to me. We spent many travels and hours of work together over the years. We actually met in college the first time. I was off to the new employer. The name of the company was Joe's Welding. Joe Johnson owned the small welding shop. As I walked into his office he stepped out of the shop area to greet me. He wiped some grease of his hand and shook mine.

"I am happy to meet you," I said.

We talked about the program and the requirements for becoming a partner in it. He was a little surprised about us conducting an inspection of his business. I informed him we required both our trade instructor and our security director to inspect every worksite where we place students. I could tell by his demeanor that he did not like that idea.

"Our center is responsible for the health and safety of every student we place on a worksite. Currently my program has 24 students out working in eight different training programs.

"But I heard we could get free labor out of them," he said.

"May I sit down?" I said.

He motioned for me to take a nearby chair. I knew the discussion was going to take some time.

"This program really is not about providing free labor to the business community. The partners we have at Rutledge Training Center understand that our goal is to enable students to gain experience and strengthen employability potential. Many come from unfortunate backgrounds of education or life circumstance where they have not arrived at adulthood or near adulthood in any position to support themselves. Our job is to help them with that. Our partners help with that goal by providing them an opportunity to get hands on experience at first without pay and then follow with paid work experiences. We have experienced a great deal of success with that approach. Each partner has strengths and opportunities of their own to contribute. It's one of the things I like most about my job," I finished.

"What strengths do you think Joe's welding has to offer our students?" I asked

Joe hesitated and stumbled a bit. "Well I am not sure what to say about that," he said.

"What do you tell your customers?" I asked.

"We are the best quality welders around. I hire good quality people with experience. Our welding jobs rarely ever have to be redone. We are a fairly new business, so I offer a money back guarantee that if it is our workmanship that fails, we will make good on it," he said confidently.

I smiled at him. "See you do know the answer. I just needed to ask the right question, I said.

"But what kind of kids are these? I had a brother who worked for a manufacturing business in town and he said he had a kid from there who was just plain lazy and did not know how to weld properly."

"We do our best to ensure that students are workplace ready, but it sometimes happens that students slide into old behaviors. In a case like that we would bring the student back in for more training. I know the kid and the worksite you are talking about. I guess your brother forgot to tell you we removed that student and replaced him with a kid that that worked out so well they hired him there," I said.

He looked down at his shoes and shuffled his feet. "I guess that's right, too," he rather grudgingly admitted.

"Our students come from everywhere. They come from family farms in North Dakota because their parents could not afford to pay for college or vocational training. Some are immigrants working on their citizenship and others who took a wrong road in life and are trying to find the right pathway. They are teens to some who are in their early twenties. They are looking for a chance," I added.

I went on to explain how the program and diligent weekly reporting works. "If you don't think this partnership will work we can stop the process now. It is up to you," I said. "Your business must pass the inspection first. Nothing happens until that is done."

I could tell he did not like the idea, but reticently he agreed. I said I would be in touch with him when we can arrange the inspection. We shook hands and I left.

That exchange took a lot out of me. I did not hold out much hope for the inspection or the partnership. I had done this job for so long, I could get a feel for straightforward interest or other agendas.

When I encountered attitudes like that, the employer rarely brought our student's best interest to the table. I did not trust it and went back to center to arrange the inspection.

There was a message in my office from Dr. Bennington. "Jenny would like to see you. She knows you are back at work because you are feeling better now. She is feeling better these days. She would like to visit with you."

"I put aside some time this weekend to see her. What is the progress with the dog strategy?" I asked.

"We have a lot of hurdles crossed. Dr. Cleveland is writing up the plan for her board of directors. We are asking for a couple of thousand dollars to help cover the cost of the dog. We also talked with the family and they already have all kinds of pets including a goat, so they are in favor of the approach," he said.

"Does Jenny know about the dog yet?" I asked.

"No the team agrees that we want you to be the one to introduce that to her. We think trust can build more trust and we think it would come better from you."

"You know, Doc, I just do not know how it became me? I do not know how she came to trust me?"

"I know the answer to that, Emily," he said. "During one of our sessions, she told me that you are the only one who treated her like a real person and that she did not know what that really felt like until you came along," he said.

His response weighed heavy on me as I thought about the countless times in my life that I must not have been there for someone in the way Jenny described. I could even remember a few of those times, sadly. *Not going there*, I scolded myself.

I felt unusually tired after work and stopped by the new health food market to pick up something for supper. I did not feel like cooking this night. I chose a spinach salad with almonds, cranberries and quinoa.

I was excited about seeing Jenny the next day. I never visit anyone in the hospital "bare handed," as I called it. I needed to figure out what to bring her. I decided on a stuffed dog and some anise mints.

I knocked on Jenny's door and it popped open right away. She hugged me as hard as she could. We let that happen for a few moments. I sat down to find out how things had been going for her. My gift basket sat on her table with its contents strewn about. She saw me look at it.

"I don't like putting everything away. I like to look at the gifts and hold them sometimes," she said.

I smiled. She was taking ownership of her life and it felt like progress to me.

She retrieved the journal from her basket and handed it to me. "Rose likes me to write," she said.

"I know," I said. I have a journal with a little girl named Alfalfa Girl. She likes me to write in my journal as well. What does Rose feel when you write?" I asked.

She frowned at me as if the question might be an intrusion.

"If you don't want to answer that, you don't have to," I said.

She brightened. "No, I want to." she said. She wanted to share a page with me.

"Are you sure?"

She nodded her head and began to read. "It's about the clean underwear," she said.

Rose found blood in her panties one day. She did not remember him touching her there. There was usually blood after that, but he had been away for a few days and she could not understand the blood. I did not ask grandma about it. She hated it when I had blood in my panties. She blamed me for it. Rose always hurt in her heart when there was blood. She hurt in her heart again when grandma blamed her for the blood. "Damn little bitch," she would say to Rose. "That is for my panties, not yours. Stay away from him,"

My throat tightened. So a little girl's onset of her menses became entangled with her molestation and rape and we wonder why she struggles with her recovery. I felt myself gasp out loud. Jenny was not crying so I fought my tears back.

"Who taught you about your period?" I asked.

"No one really," she said far too matter of fact. "I learned some things in health class in school, but I didn't always understand some of it. Grandma was really mad that they showed us the video in class. She went to the school and complained to them. She was mad that she had to buy me pads. She refused to buy tampons. She said only whores wore tampons," Jenny said.

"That's not true, you know don't you?"

"I know. I found out. But then there were questions about blood in my panties, so we just didn't talk about it anymore," she said.

She closed up her journal which indicated to me she was done with the conversation.

I still had my gift for her in my bag. I did not want to interrupt her when we first started talking, so it was still sitting by my chair. "I have something for you," I said. I watched her smile from ear to ear as I handed her the bag.

She pulled out the stuffed animal. "It's a dog!" she exclaimed more gleefully than I expected.

"There is a tag on the dog that says his name is Goldie," I said

"Oh, no. Her name is not Goldie. Her name is Cally," Jenny said.

I sat in wonder as she went on. I had no idea what she was talking about. But she was taking command of her life and that was a welcoming sign to me. I smiled.

"Tell me about Cally," I said.

"I could never have a dog. He and grandma would not let me have one. But I had one when my mommy was alive. It was tan and it had a letter C shaped white marking on its back. I did not know how to spell very well, so I thought Sally, but we named it Cally. My mommy could not take good care of Cally any more when she was on chemo, so we had to give her away. Mommy took a picture of Cally for me to always keep, but my Dad burned up all of our photo albums once when he was drunk. I am so happy to have Cally back," she said.

This time a tear did slip down her cheek. She hugged the plush animal with a ferocity that stunned me.

"You might want you and Rose to write about it in your journal," I said. "She will want to share this story with you." Jenny nodded at the suggestion.

Food service knocked at her door to bring her supper tray in. It seemed like a good time for me to leave.

"I have to go now," I said and gave her a hug. She was still hanging on to the plush dog securely under her arm. She jumped back on her bed as I turned to leave. My heartfelt full. I felt nearly gleeful. Hope was in the air. So many victims never find hope again. I was overjoyed that Jenny might.

The next week at work was very busy. We had one more work partner applicant, my meeting with a kid named Barry for his behavior at the worksite, and a staff meeting and the chance to meet my new mentee. So far, all I knew about him was that he immigrated to the U.S. from Somalia as a refugee. He was 20 years old and enrolled in our Certified Nursing Assistant program. It was a great career starting move.

It was mentee time and with Jenny gone, I only had two mentees again. Darla was the first to arrive. She was her chipper self. She dropped into the chair closest to me.

"We have a new kid," she said.

"I heard. I haven't met him yet."

"He is a foreigner," she said rather smugly.

"No, he is an immigrant. That means he had a dream like it says on the Statue of Liberty. He left his country to find a better life in this country like my great grandfather did and probably your great-grandfather. He is taking classes to improve his English and get his citizenship," I explained. I spent my professional life tearing down walls, not building them. I did not know where her perceptions came from. I thought more information might help her a bit with her attitude.

There was a light knock on my door. My new mentee entered the room timidly. He looked at me politely and moved toward me. I took a couple of steps forward and politely offered his hand.

"My name is Omar Amadayo," he said while making intense eye contact.

I smiled at him and motioned for him to take the soft chair nearby. He seated himself.

Darla offered a quick "Hi" and a wave of her hand at him.

"We always spend some time getting to know our new group members. Please tell us a little bit about yourself, "I said.

"I came here from Somalia. My family was killed in the civil war there. Our village was burned by one of the tribes and I am here because I was off visiting some relatives. My uncle came to the U.S. to go to college after that and he looked for a way for me to come. He saved up some money. I lived with my cousins in a village outside of Mogadishu until then." he said.

Omar spoke in somewhat broken English, but his language was easily intelligible despite that fact.

"I came to Fargo in the church-based social services program. They gave me housing and my goal is to get an education and go back to Somalia to help my people there," he said. "I want to be a family doctor."

I smiled at him broadly. "You speak English very well. I certainly wish you the best of luck in your education. You know that here at center we will help you as much as we can with that.

He nodded and said, "My cousins spoke English in Somalia and I learned some there. I know you will help me. Everyone here has been so great."

"I am your mentor, so feel free to call on me any time if you need help with something."

"What do you mean?" he asked.

"If you have a problem that education or the dorm or someone else does not help you with, be sure to call me." I gave him my card with my office number on it. All my students had my business card. We did not give out our personal cell numbers to students.

"What program are you in?" I asked.

"The nursing program. I want to go to college when I am done here and become a doctor and go back to my country to help my people there," he said. His repetition of his goals was heartwarming to me and his sincerity was evident. It was important he feel empowered to tell me his own story. I was impressed with Omar's forward thinking. His motivation was written all over him.

"Do you and Darla have classes together?"

She was glad to answer the question with more than a little one upsmanship. "I started before him and I am way ahead of him," she said.

Renee knocked at the door. "There is a mandatory student meeting in the gym. We are to release our mentees now," she said.

They slipped out the door around her. I had more questions for both Darla and Omar, but they would have to wait now.

"What is going on?"

"I think the police and security are doing a general search of the dorms and our buildings. They have the drug dogs here and we do it randomly now. It helps to have the students all in one place. The K9 handlers are going to do a brief demonstration for the students first. All students must attend," she said.

Drug activity increased dramatically in western North Dakota since the oil boom and no one was surprised that it flowed into the surrounding cities keeping law enforcement steadily busier.

I made good use of the extra time near the end of the day.

Renee poked her head back in the door. "I want to fill you in on Omar." Renee directed the recruitment part of center and she invested herself with the details of each student when they came in. It was an effort almost always over and above because she had such a big heart for our students. I so admired her for that.

"I don't know what Omar told you about himself. He is amazing in his motivation for education. He will do well on center. I am so glad you are his mentor," she said.

I had performance reviews to do for my working students. Each business evaluated their student each week. Although the paperwork was daunting, it was a good measure of the student employability. As with many things, some students sailed effortlessly through their experiences gaining skills to put on their resumes. Others adjusted to the constant supervision of employers with much more difficulty. I put my signature and comment on the last student form and headed out of my office for the day.

I could not wait to call my Lamplighter Team members to tell them about Jenny's dog, Cally, and discuss it as a possible bridge to a real dog and rebuilding her trust. I was so excited. I grabbed a burger and coke from McDonalds.

I don't have phone conferencing capability, but Dr. Cleveland did so I only had to tell Jenny's experience once.

The team members were excited about Jenny's progress. We all felt we could step up the original timeline now. Dr. Cleveland said hospital administration approved this one time use of the dog. With so much research out there now on wellness and veterans, the disabled, and the elderly, it was an easy sell especially with support funding coming from another source. We received the grant as well.

"Now we have to find a dog," Dr. Cleveland said. "I talked to Jerry in security at the hospital and a friend of his is a retired K9 officer. He suggested that Brad Hoffer might still have some resources and be able to train a dog. We are looking into that now," she said. It sounds very promising," she added.

I went over and over in my mind how I would bring up the subject to Jenny. Every scenario in my mind involved Cally. What a stroke of luck to have picked up that stuffed dog for her.

I jumped in to my soaking tub for a long bath. I could not stop thinking about Jenny. I tried to imagine her with her soul intact. She could be anything or do anything she wanted. Rose would help her with that just as Alfalfa girl helped me. I wondered if Dr. Bennington used any of these strategies with her. I would have to ask next time. He certainly had the expertise in the field. Not me. That would be a discussion for another time.

After a couple of weeks back at work I was beginning to get my stride back. My colleagues were very helpful with that. Many times people pitched in to do things for me. Most recently, I was supposed to do noon hour duty. Staff provided another layer of security and watchfulness at the recreation center during noon when all students were out and about. Miss Betty from the health center volunteered to do it for me. I was glad as I certainly did not feel up to that much activity yet. Renee agreed to attend the corporate meeting at corporate headquarters for me. I was not up to that yet. She also taught my class that prepared students for their work experience. I just did not have the energy. Teaching was always my passion, but I simply could not do it all right now.

I was at my desk when the welding instructor and the security director knocked at my door.

I was certain they had done the inspection at the welding shop and arrived to report on their findings.

Welding instructor, Lewis Gary, took the lead and he just put it right out there.

"I would not put a student there. In fact I will not let any of my students work there. The place is dirty, unorganized and unsafe for starters," he said.

"I had a feeling," I said. "He seemed like he was out to make a fast buck off of free labor. I got that. I also sense some disrespect of our students," I added.

Bob Jones, the security director, responded first. "In aces! He told me not to send any niggers or Muslims to his worksite."

"What did you say?" I was stunned. "Oh my God! I am always horrified but not surprised given the callous and xenophobic national conversation this year," I shuddered as I responded.

"I had a hard time not throwing up in his face, but I took the cowardly way out. I said you would get back to him," Bob said jokingly. I served in Viet Nam for all Americans. All of us," he emphasized. "It pisses me off when people talk like that."

"I will get back to him. I had a feeling," I said, and flashed a huge smile. "I darn well will. I also want your evaluation sheets for a point by point reference for the safety issues," I said.

They left the paperwork with me and I began drafting the letter to Joe's Welding.

Dear Mr. Johnson, I want to thank you for your interest in our welding training program.

Because we have the moral, physical and emotional responsibility for every student we place, we must meet some very high training and education standards.

Upon inspection our welding instructor and our security manager found the following issues at your business.

Supplies were carelessly stored and in some cases may even present a fire hazard.

Used supplies were not properly disposed of.

Oil or some other unknown substance was spilled and tracked around the floor.

Safety equipment was in disrepair especially welding helmets and gloves.

Welding benches were not solidly secured and pose a safety threat.

Properly equipped welding booths were absent.

Large pieces of metal were strewn about presenting numerous trip hazards. Two employees were playfully sparring with their open flame welders. They did not even stop when our staff approached them. One of them accused another one of putting an unknown substance in his water bottle.

Such reckless disregard for employee safety does not meet the requirements of our center.

Secondly, we pride ourselves on providing excellence in education for our students without prejudice to their race, religion or gender. We do so confidently with the support of the American Constitution. Language used at your worksite suggests a business cultural climate unsuitable to the young developing minds of our students.

We cannot knowingly place them in such a pejorative environment. We would not be meeting our responsibilities to our students if we did. We respectfully decline any effort to establish a partnership with your business at this time. Should conditions and the culture at your business improve significantly, we would be happy to review an opportunity again at that time.

Thank you again for your willingness to participate. If you wish to contact me directly, my information is included below. Thank you again for your time.

I signed off with my name, phone number and email and I copied the letter to my director on center and corporate headquarters. I was confident of my decision. Many of my already established worksites provided both in principal and practice, solid workplace and safety practices. They established and demonstrated high moral leadership and standards. They recognized students as the potential workers of their industries. They wanted and encouraged the opportunity to help train and create stability in their respective industries. The findings at this workplace were a slap in the face to each one of our current partners as well as our students. The company did not exemplify or even come close to the stellar business practices in our community or state. I tucked the letter into an envelope and tossed it into the outbox.

I made a shrimp salad for supper as soon as I arrived home from work. I had some plans to make for Jenny and her dog.

It was time to introduce Jenny to her dog. I felt so much responsibility about it. I mulled it over and over in my mind. I decided I would focus her attention on Cally and get a feeling about how she would feel about a real dog. The loss of her puppy during her early childhood had been traumatic. I decided to do it in two parts. The first part would focus on Cally. If that went well, we could move on to part two. I passed the plan to the team members. They suggested that I flat out present the notion of a real dog to her. It was a good plan. If she freaked about her dog we would know our answer. I set the plan in place.

"Jenny, this is Ms. Emily. I found something really cute for Cally. Do you mind if I bring it over to the hospital?" I asked.

"Great, I want to show you something too," she said.

I arrived just after supper on Saturday night. Jenny met me at her door. When she opened it I saw her surprise immediately, but let her lead.

"Come and see what I did with the Christmas basket. They gave me a towel and I made a bed for Cally," she said. "Mommy made me a bed from an old clothes basket for my real dog. So I made one for mine too."

And there it was. A readymade opportunity from Jenny herself! I jumped at the chance.

"What if Cally was a real dog? How would you feel about that?" I asked.

"Oh, I can't think about that, she said.

My heart sank.

"I could never have a dog of my own. There is no way that can happen for me. I wish I could, but it cannot happen for me. Rose can tell you about it," she said with just enough sadness in her voice that I feared for Jenny. But I was proud of her for taking her life into what little control she had over it. Jenny was more important than the project. Her needs came first.

She took out her journal and began to read.

Mommy and Cally and I loved our play times together especially when she was a puppy. Mommy brought the basket bed with the blue blanket in it close to the couch where she always laid down. Mommy said the blanket was important because she used it for me when I was a baby and now we used it for Cally. Mommy was too weak to sit up sometimes. Cally knew about mommy dying. I know she did. I do not know how, but she did. Sometimes she licked mommy's face and hands and mommy would smile. It seemed like a little game for Cally. Lick, jump up, jump down, lick jump up, and jump down. I lay down beside mommy and Cally would jump up on both of us until we were laughing so hard our tummies hurt.

She stopped reading and studied my face again like she always did.

"How do you think Rose feels about a puppy," I asked.

"I think Rose would like to have a lot of things back. I think she would like her Mommy back and her daddy back and her Cally back. But she is smart. She knows it cannot happen."

Bingo! Her wishes were tied to the losses of the most important people in her life. I was in over my head. The information was valuable. Now the team needed to frame the dog part in a way that would be useful to Jenny's trust building.

I was exhausted and headed home for the evening. At the same time I felt some gratitude for Jenny's progress. I would have to wait to contact the team. But I needed to talk. I pressed the number into my cell phone and Dr. Wisc answered.

"Hi, I just came from Jenny. I think Jenny is ready for her dog now. I am feeling so good about it," I said.

"You sound tired, though, Emily. Are you taking care of yourself?"

"I am, but life goes on and I have to work and I cannot leave Jenny hanging out there."

"You know I would not want that either. But when we professionals work with people, there is a huge investment of ourselves. People run into trouble when they do not realize how much energy they are putting out there for others," she said.

"Is that what you think I am doing?"

"I hope not. I am not offering discouragement here, Emily, I am suggesting caution. Take care of you first. I know you have trouble doing that. Lots of us do. How will you take care of yourself this weekend?" she asked.

"I am headed for a nice long bubble bath tonight. Alfalfa Girl really has me in to that lately. I plan to have Raisin Bran and milk for supper, so no cooking. I am going to read a bit in one of my encouragement books for women and I am going to go to bed early. I have a new nightgown that feels luxurious. I am going to wear it to bed tonight. I plan to go to take myself out for a nice dinner tomorrow night and then to the concert at Minot State University. Sunday I plan to loaf all day and maybe order some valentine things online. I have several people I remember on Valentine Day That always makes me feel better."

"Don't forget to listen to your body. It will tell you when you are overdoing," she said.

I took her seriously. "I will do that," I said. "Thanks for your help. I am off to bed now."

I ate my cereal quickly not realizing how hungry I was. Fatigue hit me hard after that. I drew the bath and enjoyed a nice long soak.

I rumpled my clothes in a pile and smiled. Alfalfa girl let me do it. There was no Hilex or filthy water this time and no pain. Alfalfa girl gave me full permission to enjoy the bath or I gave her permission. She had actually been doing that for a time now.

The team met at the pancake house again. We agreed the next step should be giving Jenny the dog. Dr. Cleveland had worked out a plan with the hospital that included visits with the dog a couple times a week at first, moving to more frequent visits as Jenny adapted. The plan also included her foster family. The family overwhelmingly approved of having the dog at their home. They lovingly embraced the idea. The team hoped that process would help provide the framework for Jenny to leave the mental health ward and move in with the Crawford family. Time would tell.

My task was to set up the time when Jenny would have first contact with the dog. I was encouraged by how positively I thought it might go, but ever mindful of Jenny's need to process things the way she needed to do for her own survival.

All of the details moved into place now. Dr. Cleveland's work was so defined it within the report and even include details from Brad about training the dog to go outside to poop. I wondered about that and was relieved it had been taken care of. This first meeting was going to be a huge step in trust for Jenny.

I looked up and clasped my hands over my heart and whispered to myself, "Please let this happen." I arranged the visit to Jenny. The team wished me well and I needed their support. It was going to happen at last.

I entered Jenny's room that Saturday afternoon with a small gift. We greeted each other with a hug.

I took out a small bag from my pocket. "This is for you," I said.

She opened the bag and took out the rose colored dog collar. It included roses stamped into the leather. The dog information hung from a stainless steel tag on the front of the collar.

"Is this for Cally?" she asked and launched herself over to the Christmas basket where the plush animal was resting.

"Yes it is, but not that Cally," I said.

She looked puzzled.

"It is for another Cally." I opened the door to her room and Brad ushered a lively little spaniel into the room. Jenny was speechless.

"The collar is for this Cally," I said.

Jenny dropped to her knees on the floor and put her arms out to the cute little spaniel. It jumped right into her arms so forcefully she let it gently knock her over. She rolled on the floor with the dog in her arms and seemed to hang on for dear life. Tears were running down her face and mine. "Whose dog is this?" she asked pulling herself up with the dog in her lap yet.

"This is your dog, Jenny," I said.

I knew she was processing as fast as she could in her brain and trying to sort all of it out. I decided to add some information to help her. "You see, Jenny, there are people who want to help you get a new start in life. Rose helped you remember Cally. I know you thought you could never have a dog again, but you can and you do. Can you put your very own Rose collar on Cally?"

She eagerly pulled the collar forward and tried to put it on the energetic small puppy in front of her. I had to help her put the collar on. It was a teachable moment.

"See, Jenny, sometimes it takes a team to get things done. We don't always have to do things alone. Sometimes we need help. We are a good team, right?"

My teachable moment I guess. She was too busy hugging the dog to respond. She shook her head. It was all I expected now. That was a good thing. Brad stepped forward and I introduced him. This is the trainer who trained the real Cally.

"What do you think?" I asked her.

"Are you going to take her away?" she asked.

"That is up to you. We have some choices and we can talk about this more. I know you have questions, but we can talk about that later. Right now you just need to get to know her. That is your only job right now."

Cally stole the show. She had made off from Jenny's lap and darted around the room sniffing it out. She chewed away at the shoestring on Jenny's sneaker. Jenny took control. She marched herself over, uttered a "no no," and lovingly picked up the dog.

"Come here, Cally. I want you to sit with me right now," she said. She took some control of her life at that moment.

The puppy barked a couple of times and nuzzled back down into Jenny's lap. I stood up and looked at Brad, who had been patiently waiting by the door. "I wanted to see how this went. It is a gentle dog and very loving. I made sure of it. I raised her myself," he said.

I hugged him. I did not know him well, but I could tell he had a huge heart. He smiled at me and looked down at our charges playfully engaged on the floor right now.

"I will just wait outside," he said.

"You are welcome to stay if you like," I said.

He took me up on it and closed the door. I planned the whole afternoon to stay with Jenny. I wanted to see how it all went. I sat back down on the floor. Brad did too. That was where the action was right now. Brad pulled a small dog dish out of a sack he was carrying. "Do you want to give her some water?" he asked Jenny.

She jumped at the chance and scooted to the sink in her room and quickly filled the dish. She grabbed a towel on her way back.

"She will make a mess, I know," Jenny said, throwing the towel down first and putting the dish on top of it. I marveled at her recall about her puppy so many years ago. She had retained all of that. My hope for her surged If she could recall other positives as easily as this, it would be so helpful for her.

I made a mental note for Dr. Cleveland.

Brad had another surprise up his sleeve. "She really likes these. Do you want to give her these treats?" he asked Jenny.

She reached over to take them. She nodded with a delighted smile on her face. Her eyes sparkled. I had not ever seen that before from her. I studied her face now making mental notes as we went along. Jenny and Cally made a game out of everything. She threw a rolled up sock and the puppy went after it. Jenny lifted Cally up on the bed and then challenged Cally to jump into her arms. The puppy eyed all of this warily at first. Trust building of all kinds filled the room at that moment.

"I won't drop you," Jenny promised.

The dog whined a bit and then leaped into Jenny's arms.

Brad and I smiled at each other. Our part was almost over it seemed. Brad had one last trick up his sleeve. "Here, see what she does with this," he said and threw a chew toy to Jenny.

The result was predictable. The puppy went after the toy and chewed and chewed on it. Cally growled and growled and Jenny reached in from time to time to challenge her by gently tugging on the toy. Jenny lay down beside her and petted her as she enjoyed the playful antics of the puppy. The afternoon went by quickly. It came time for Brad to leave with Cally. I looked at Brad. He was one step ahead of me. "I have to take Cally outdoors now. She needs to find a place to do her business. Then I need to take her back home," he said.

Jenny understood that part and the transition to leave was easier for her knowing that. "Is she really my dog?" Jenny asked.

I nodded.

"Can I keep her here?" she asked. I could tell she had so many questions.

"When can she come back?"

I could tell from the question that Jenny knew Cally would not be a roommate.

"It is up to you," I said.

"Tomorrow?"

I looked at Brad. He nodded.

"I will go to church in the morning and I can bring her up after lunch tomorrow. I will not be able to stay the whole afternoon, but you and Miss Emily can if you like and I can come up and get her. How about 2 p.m.? Will that work for you Jenny?"

Jenny nodded and hugged Cally even more tightly. She knew the goodbye was coming. Brad picked up the dog gently. I reached over and put the stuffed toy in Jenny's arms. "Now you can think of the real Cally every time you hold this one," I said.

"No, I will think of mommy and Cally every time," she said.

I rejoiced in my heart at the emotional leap forward she was making.

Sunday morning I grabbed a bagel and some raspberry jelly and coffee. Brad agreed to meet me at the hospital. Since he was not staying the whole time, I would stay. I saw myself with less investment this time and more as a custodial visitor. The real work would be done with Jenny and Cally.

I arrived when Brad did and we watched as Cally and Jenny joyfully reunite. They behaved like a couple of old friends together. "I had a good feeling about this puppy. She has a good heart and just wants to be loved," Brad said.

"Jenny is not much different. She does too," I said.

"You need to take her outside on the leash in about an hour or so. I brought along a couple more toys for them. I have a lot of these things at home and need to get rid of some of it. Jenny can have them," Brad offered. He handed the toys to Jenny and within minutes the puppy also recognized them and the two of them were off with their games.

I needed to document some of the progress, so I mentioned it. "Jenny, Do you mind if I do some paperwork while you play with Cally?"

She was so absorbed with the puppy she threw her head back in a playful nod. I documented while they played. I finished my notes and called for the ward nurse. We agreed if someone went with us, Jenny could go outdoors for the poop break. I asked Jenny if she wanted to go.

"Oh, can I? Can I?" she asked excitedly.

I put my coat on and headed toward the door.

"Grab that bag in the corner. It has a pooper scooper in it. We do not leave Cally's messes behind for anyone else to pick up. It is our responsibility," I said.

Jenny nodded and tucked the bag into her coat pocket. She put the leash on Cally and we made our way out to a back courtyard of the hospital. It was beautifully appointed with outdoor furnishings most of which were now covered with snow banks. We trudged through the deep snow and, just as trained, Cally scooted off to poop. Jenny scooped it up and put it in the disposable bag.

The charge nurse took the time to grab a quick smoke break. I moved down from her as I did not want to inhale the smoke.

Cally loved the snow and made a game of rooting some of it up and tossing it about. Jenny picked up a mitten full of snow and launched it toward Cally. The puppy was all in for the game. She leaped in the air and chased the falling snow that was now airborne. The afternoon shadows lowered the temperature and we made our way inside again.

In the weeks to come I turned in all of my notes to the Lamplighter Team. It included many more successful visits between Jenny and her puppy. It was amazing how fast the pup was growing, but Brad was a good caretaker and the dog was healthy on every level. Jenny seemed to be moving in that direction as well.

The team met at the pancake house again.

Dr. Bennington, Dr. Cleveland, Sonya from the hospital and I were all present. That did not happen very often. We kept up with the project by email or conference calls as needed. Dr. Bennington took the lead with our conversation.

"I have to say that this trust project with Jenny is one of the most successful of its kind I have ever seen. With your consent I would like to start a paper about it. It is my privilege to work with such dedicated people," he said and made eye contact with each of us.

"Sonya, what are you hearing from the hospital perspective?"

"I am hearing all good things. In fact the mental health department director is wondering if this approach might work for other types of patients," Sonya said. She was dressed in the most amazing yellow pantsuit I had ever seen. With her dark hair and features she looked stunning. Her generous smile was always a treat to experience.

"I anticipated that, but we need to keep our focus in one direction for now. The research, our careful notes from Emily and the solid data Connie is building will give other projects plenty of good material to replicate our work here," Dr. Cleveland said. She posed the question we were probably all thinking.

"We have given the bonding and trust period between Jenny and the puppy a good amount of time."

"Emily and Dr. Bennington, do you think it is time to include the family now?" Dr. Cleveland asked.

Dr. Bennington responded first. "I think so. Jenny has worked hard on her issues. I was visiting her one day when the food services people brought her tray up. She noted that the juice had spilled all over her napkin. 'I would have put a clean napkin on that tray,' Jenny remarked at the time. I saw that as such growth with her very short training experience. A couple of months ago she would not have been capable of making an observation like that. I have to commend you Emily. You have brought her a long way," he complimented me.

"I never think of it as my accomplishment. Jenny is the one doing all of the hard recovery work, and her counselors do the heavy lifting," I said.

"My vote is that we discuss not if but how we design the transition of the puppy to the family and their home," Dr. Bennington said.

Everyone agreed it was time.

"I will say that like before, we need to be cautious. As much progress as we have seen, we do not want to jeopardize it now. I think we should design the first couple of meetings with the family in the hospital," I offered and continued, "Here is why. Remember that it was the death of Jenny's mother that led to getting rid of the dog. Tie that into the burning of the pictures of the dog after her father suffered his breakdown and we have some fragile emotional dog experiences in Jenny's background," I said.

"Maybe we replicate what already worked before. We could introduce the family with the plush toy Cally before we actually introduce all of the changes." Dr. Bennington said.

We agreed to the process and left our meeting with cordial goodbyes and our individual tasks. Mine would be to talk to Jenny about the family and start the ball rolling with that step.

Jenny was receptive to the idea immediately. She seemed so much stronger these days. In one of the many conversations I had with her she agreed to meet with the family and catch up on her missed Christmas with them.

"Can I tell them about Cally?" she asked the last time.

I was thrilled that she thought of it before I said anything. "Do you mean your toy Cally or your real Cally?" I asked.

"Both. I want them to know about this one and my puppy," she said.

I sucked air and asked her more about what was on her mind. "Do you see Cally living with you and the family?"

She paused a moment to think about it. I let the silence support her thinking. "When I am ready for that, I think that would be great. Maybe they could take Cally to their home so it would not be so strange for her then," Jenny said.

I was stunned Jenny invested herself into Cally to the extent that she put the puppy out there first. I felt on safe enough ground to ask the obvious question. "What about you at the family home?" I asked.

"If Cally is ok there then I will be too," she said in pure innocence and newly forming trust inside herself.

I hugged Jenny tightly. Do you want me to check on those things for you?" I asked.

"Can't I do it too?" she asked.

"You can and you should," I said.

Jenny and I talked another hour or so about how she wanted to talk with the family. She wanted to talk to all three of them face to face and make sure they knew all about Cally before they could take her home. She decided she wanted Cally to go live there before she moved into the home with them.

Dr. Cleveland and Dr. Bennington did the heavy lifting and made all of the arrangements for the hospital meetings together and the home transitions. They worked with the Crawford family. They had the expertise and could gauge the situation better than any of the rest of us on the team.

Sonya and I made all of the hospital arrangements and scheduled the meeting with Jenny. Sonya suggested the ward family room would be bigger and a better fit for this activity than Jenny's room.

We all received an email from Dr. Cleveland saying the Crawford family was overjoyed about getting both the puppy and Jenny. The family had been doing foster care for years. They were unable to have another child of their own but had wanted to expand their family. Their only child, Kimberly, needed a sibling according to them. They lived about an hour drive south of Minot. They were well settled into the community where the father and United Church of Christ minister, David Crawford, oversaw his parishioners. Kimberly was a Senior at the high school there. They had already checked into the possibility of Jenny returning to high school to complete. She had enough credits to enter as a Junior at that school. The Crawfords had already checked out all of those things, but it was a lot for Jenny to handle at one time. The team would cross those bridges down the road.

I scheduled the first session with the Crawford family. Ellen Crawford, the mother wanted to bring a basket lunch for the occasion for everyone. She did not want hospital food to be the basis of this first meeting. She was adamant about it, which worked for all of us. The team agreed and we moved forward with the plan.

Chapter Six

THE CRAWFORD FAMILY

We met on a Saturday to fit everyone's schedules. I was the first one to arrive. I wanted to be early and collect my thoughts. Staff set up the larger family room with a table and chairs for lunch. Comfortable chairs and a couch with big fluffy pillows flanked it on either side. I chose a big soft chair.

The family arrived next and Ellen Crawford spread out a checkered tablecloth and napkins. She put the ham and cheese sandwiches, chips, potato salad and brownies in the middle of the table. She had a bright spray of daisies in the middle. It looked so festive. I admired her attention to detail. Pastor Crawford and Kimberly came in and sat near me. We greeted each other. We all seemed to feel the same excitement.

Jenny came in the door. She carried her plush dog with her and squired it around the room proudly showing it off to the family. Kimberly asked if she could hold the dog and I drew a deep breath waiting for this test of trust to unfold. Jenny took it in stride and handed over the dog. She stayed close to Kimberly and eyed the situation closely before taking her seat next to the other teen.

Pastor Crawford called everyone to the table and we sat down for our lunch together.

Jenny took her seat between Ellen and Kimberly. I watched carefully.

Her decision to sit apart from me was positive. I saw it as a willingness to trust more than she probably had in a very long time. The buzz of the conversation at the table was encouraging. The family welcomed every exchange made with Jenny. Then it seemed Jenny could not contain herself any longer.

"My real dog, Cally, is coming in a few minutes. I want you to meet her because she can go with us, right?" she half said and half asked the family. It was like she could not contain her excitement.

The statement included a lot of information. At some point Jenny accepted her move to a new family. None of us knew she had actually made that emotional leap of acceptance. It was huge for her. I sat down in my chair with my coffee. I wanted to hug her but it was not the time.

Brad knocked at the door and ushered a playful Cally into the room. Everyone responded with jubilance.

The family gathered around her and they were highly engaged in their discussions of the puppy.

Brad and I chatted on our own. He reminded me that the puppy was fast outgrowing the puppy stage and that he would be training it into permanent behaviors. It was ok just now to jump in her lap, but the larger the dog would need to behave much differently. I had not thought of any of that. He was so competent. We were lucky to have his volunteer services. We were lucky he was willing to share his time from the nursing home in their dog program.

Our team met at the pancake house again. Dr. Bennington could not come. I filed a full report on the trust issues gained with the dog and the family. He emailed that he read all of the notes. I carefully detailed each step of the trust building for research purposes. Connie collected and organized the data. Most recently I gave them the report about the family meeting.

The purpose of today's meeting was to discuss a transition for Jenny to her foster home. The Crawford family was very excited to set a start date. We included them on a speakerphone in relevant parts of our discussions. They assured us they had everything ready for her including her own bedroom if she wanted. But she would be given the option to share a room with Kimberly If she preferred. It was clear they understood the needs of foster children very well. They also seemed to understand the responsibilities in meeting those needs.

Pastor Crawford told us something that I did not know about their meeting at the hospital. Jenny brought up two memories from her childhood to them. One was about picnics. Her mother often took her on picnics as a child before her illness. The basket and table setting that day reinforce to her that many picnics were ahead in her life.

She was also curious about Kimberly's goat. She wanted to know more about it. She had never seen one before. Kimberly had a photo of it in her purse that day Kimberly shared with Jenny that the goat won a superior purple ribbon at the county 4H event.

Pastor and Ellen Crawford engaged Jenny in her favorite foods and what she liked to do for fun. Jenny shared that she liked to ride bicycle, but that her dad ran over hers and she never got a new one. The Crawfords were avid cyclists and they had several bicycles. They even participated in the North Dakota Can Am cycling event held every year in the fall in North Dakota. All of the information was outstanding and we came away from our meeting with positive feelings about the transition for Jenny.

As always Dr. Bennington and Dr. Cleveland took the lead with all of the foster home arrangements. Everyone agreed that March would be far enough and soon enough for the transition. March 10 was Jenny's birthday and it was perfect to plan a birthday party for her in their home. They suggested the idea.

I began planning for my part. I would meet with Jenny to get her ready for the transition. We agreed that Brad would need to be part of it to transition with Cally. He was more than excited about it. He was also glad the family lived in the country with plenty of space for the dog to run. He also said he would work with Cally to adapt to that type of setting. "I have seen some dogs go very crazy when confronted with so much open space. I will work with them on how to adapt to that. I don't mind getting out of town once in awhile," he said.

I felt a little regret start building. Jenny had been such a large part of my focus for so long that it started to feel like a loss. I called Dr. Wisc and met with her in her office. I had not been there for such a long time.

"How are you feeling about Jenny's move?"

I shrugged. "Overjoyed, relieved and maybe a bit regretful about her leaving," I said.

"How do you want to handle that?"

"I always knew this day would come." She needs to bond with them and maybe I visit once and awhile. I don't really know. I know it would be self destructive to try to hang on to her emotionally. Not good for me and not good for her. I am satisfied that my role in her life has been a positive for her. I believe in the process and I believe she is far better off than when she came to center," I said.

"When is that move expected?" she asked.

"The family wants to have her birthday in their home on March 10. They invited me to the birthday party and Brad, the dog handler is going out a couple of times to train Cally out there. He asked if I wanted to go along and I accepted if it worked out."

I wanted to take part in the Million Women March to stand up against the misogynic atmosphere created around our country after the election. Fargo held a march and it would not be that far for me to travel. I wanted to stand up for the Jenny's and Alfalfa girls of the world to say we do not accept the outright discrimination and hate talk against women. I was never able to shake the horrific language out of my mind. I thought it over for days, but decided it would not be in my best interest to go. I could watch it on television and I also contributed money to a local women's group so that others could go to it.

I sat by my television the day of the March and shook with laughter and tears as 690 events worldwide unfolded and numbers in the 4 million turned out to show women are a strong and relevant part of all levels of society and government. The report in Fargo was that over 2,000 people showed up that day. I saw it on a video my friend took while she was there. It filled me with hope for all of the Jenny's, Alfalfa girls and Miss Universe contestants everywhere.

Work never seemed to slow down much back on center. I enjoyed my duties with the students immensely. It was gratifying to help some of our students move from unfortunate circumstances to a better life.

My mentee, Darla, was blazing right along in her program. She was ready for her work experience. We talked about it and she had a total change of heart since our earlier discussions. She had several work site day experiences in her classes at two different nursing homes. She fell in love with the work and was leaning toward a nursing career by taking classes at Minot State University. I was gratified to hear that. Sometimes experience has a leveling impact with our pre-conceived notions. Darla's initial distaste with old people who pee themselves seemed resolved in her mind enough for her to adjust her career decisions. It was a plus in my mind.

Omar joined us to visit with me about his work experience. He was not complete enough with his training to go out but he wanted to talk about it, which is a good sign with students. "I am ready to go on my work experience. I know you have places. I want to finish my training here and go on to Minot State to get my full nursing degree. Then I want to work on becoming a doctor. I want every step to go toward my goal," he said.

"I actually do have one place in mind for you," I said. "We have a University clinic here in town. It is a University of North Dakota clinic. Doctors there come from all over the world. I would love to have you work with them. My guess is that they would have valuable career suggestions and experience to share also. I can arrange for a day shadow for you when you get far enough along to do that. You can see how you like it," I said.

"That would be great," he said. He took notes as I spoke. That demonstrated his serious interest. Students rarely took notes on what I said. He shook my hand and departed. I finished up my report for Omar's file.

Renee stopped by my office. "How is Jenny doing?" she asked.

"She has come a long way. She will be transitioning in March to her foster home," I said.

"How do you feel about that?" she asked.

"I am very excited for her. The puppy trust rebuilding process with her was an overwhelming success. It looks like a very good family and she may have some renewed educational options open to her there. There are no guarantees, of course. Time will tell. I am encouraged by all of it and I have to say the people on our team are the best. Everyone one of them has the heart and soul to help people," I replied, happy to have good things to share.

Renee nodded in agreement. Her cell beeped and she stepped out of the room to take the call.

I headed off to my worksite training class. I was excited about it, as I had not taught it for a long time. I loved teaching and this gave me a chance to keep one foot engaged in it. Most of my duties were administrative by design even though it seemed like lessons popped up in most situations with our students all the time.

The day ended and I headed home. February can bring storms and serious winter or it can start peeling back below zero temperatures to get us ready for spring. Today Mother Nature treated us to mild temperatures. The warm up created slippery conditions and I practiced all of my skills for ice driving.

I was crossing the Broadway bridge when an ambulance and lights seemed to appear out of nowhere behind me. I moved over as far as I could, but the bridge and the snow piles made it quite difficult. The car in front of me did not move over at all. The ambulance hit the siren to get by the rude driver.

I loved preparing for my trip to see Jenny and her new family. The plan for Brad and I to share the drive did not work out due to his family commitment that came up.

It was a beautiful and comfortable hour or so drive to the country. The North Dakota landscape sparkled with new fallen snow. Luckily today it wasn't blowing across the road like it can and often does. Shrubs and trees dotted the countryside adding their own ochre drama. Fences defined boundaries and the occasional farm popped into view now and again to remind drivers that this was, indeed, people country even if the vast, unfolding rural landscapes did not make it seem so.

I arrived at the small hobby farm at lunchtime. The family planned a noon lunch and sixteenth birthday party for Jenny. From their description, it sounded fun and I was looking forward to it.

I pulled into the short driveway that was now piled with several feet of snow on either side. It allowed me to drive up very close to the front stairs of the attractive two story farm house with its sprawling front porch. I could already see Ellen Crawford's attention to detail with its vintage rocking chairs and antique pitcher with winter greens and a ribbon around it. There were flower pots and a black pot bellied stove to complete the welcoming porch entry. A hunter green striped rug helped to frame the door and its appealing oval window.

There was a low red barn off to the side of the home. Another small steel building with split wood fences completed the backdrop to the small country setting. The family did not farm, but enjoyed the simplicity and lifestyle of the country just the same.

I parked my car and walked up the stairs toward the door. Just as I was about to knock, I heard barking and a commotion coming from the end of the railed porch. Suddenly, Cally rushed around the corner and headed right toward me. Jenny and Kimberly trailed as fast as they could right behind her. They gathered quickly around me and Jenny had a stern word for Cally.

"No jumping! No Jumping," she wagged her finger at Cally. The dog settled into place and looked at me. I was an outsider just now and she knew it. Jenny wrapped her arms around me and I offered another hug to Kimberly as well. By this time, David and Ellen Crawford joined us on the porch.

"Come in, come in," Pastor Crawford invited. Cally did not waste any time scooting ahead of the humans. Her basket sat beside the fireplace in the combination dining and living room. The home smelled heavenly with some kind of roast in the oven I guessed.

The girls deposited their coats and hats on the coat rack by the door. The family ushered all of us toward the dining room. Just that quick, Ellen Crawford and the girls brought bowls of steaming corn chowder to the table. We sat down at the table. Pastor Crawford offered a prayer of thanks for food but also included thanks for the girls and Cally and me.

The girls were excited about sharing Jenny's transition to the family. The team asked for them to keep a journal of the transition. Jenny went first.

"Cally got so excited she peed on the floor the first night. And look, her basket is getting too small for her. David is looking for a new one for her. She sleeps right there by the fireplace. She wanted to sleep with me the first night, but we talked about it and we all decided that was not a good idea," Jenny said.

"Cally likes the goat too. I wondered about that, but they are good friends now," Kimberly added.

I was waiting for more information about Jenny's adjustment when Jenny brought it up. "I decided to have my own bedroom at first," she said. I nodded and she volunteered to show it to me later in the day.

We ate our way through a pot roast and vegetables very quickly amid a buzz of conversation about all of the adjustments and experiences for the family.

"We have some surprises for your birthday, Jenny," Ellen said. She disappeared into the kitchen and returned with a beautifully decorated birthday cake and candles.

Pastor Crawford lit all the candles and we sang a rousing birthday song to Jenny. She looked almost shy at all of the attention.

"Make a wish," make a wish," Kimberly encouraged with all the excitement she could muster.

Jenny closed her eyes and I could not help wondering what she wished for. She blew the candles and they were trick candles that kept relighting themselves. She laughed heartily. I stepped back in my mind to try to assess the family setting. Jenny looked like she fit perfectly into the Crawford household. I know from previous work experience that does not always happen.

Ellen cut large slices of cake, added ice cream and passed them around the table. Everyone dived into the delicious chocolate cake with vanilla ice cream. The conversation tapered off now as we finished our dessert. Ellen offered coffee and I was glad to have a cup. We always had coffee with sweets when I grew up and it stayed with me as I aged.

David Crawford stood up with a bit of ceremony, an abnormal departure in behavior for him.

"Close your eyes, Jenny," he said.

She put her hands over her eyes and only her smile peeked out now.

David rolled a brand new Schwinn bicycle into the room. "Open them," he said.

Her first look at the shiny new bicycle elicited disbelief from her at first glance. "Is it mine? Is it mine?" she half shrieked with glee. "Mine got run over," she said like it happened yesterday. "I love it, I love it," she gushed with excitement. She hugged the bike and then steered it around the small room offering hugs to each of the Crawford family members as she steered her new possession merrily along.

By this time, Cally joined the excitement and was jumping and yipping around Jenny to get in on the party. Jenny patted the dog on the head and she healed beside her as she moved around the room.

Kimberly held on to Jenny's hand as she passed by her and said, "I have something for you too!"

She reached under the table and withdrew a gift bag. Jenny looked at it in amazement. She opened the gift to find a lovely, hand-knit winter cap. It was a rose color with a rose knitted on the side of it. Jenny placed it on her head immediately.

"I knitted it myself," Kimberly said.

"Can you teach me?" Jenny asked. And then in a split second she strutted around the room.

"How does it look?" she asked everyone.

Everyone cheered and applauded.

"I have something for you too," I said.

I produced the gift sack from behind my chair.

"Oh, Miss Emily, you did not have to do that,"

"Of course not. I just wanted to."

She pulled the journal from the gift bag with some bit of playful ceremony. "Oh look, it has my name on it. And a rose just like the one mommy drew me!" she exclaimed.

"Brad made the cover for you. I asked him to do it. He does leatherwork as a hobby and I think it turned out fine. Open the front cover," I suggested to her.

I had placed a hundred dollar bill inside a plastic pouch with a zipper. "This money is for an emergency only. If you don't have an emergency you can keep adding to the money as you get some. I call it a stash. Every woman needs a stash," I said.

Jenny danced around with her journal singing, "I have a stash, I have a stash."

I wasn't sure Jenny had completely wrapped her head around the concept of a stash, but for now it was important that she understood how much control she owned. It would serve her well down the road.

Dave Crawford offered advice. "In this home, we keep our money in savings accounts. Next week we can go to the bank and open one for you," he said.

Then he looked over at me and added, "We have done that with all of our foster children. That keeps money accounted for and traceable," he said. His integrity and wisdom presented themselves in his statement.

The afternoon passed very quickly. I needed to head for home.

"You haven't seen the goat yet," Jenny bubbled. "Come on Miss Emily, Come on! Let's go see the goat!" Now this would not be the first time I saw a goat, my grandparents raised goats and I visited them one time in California. They milked them, sold the milk but kept enough milk for their own use including making butter. They did not put coloring in it, so I was turned off the first time I saw a clump of what looked like Crisco in a bowl on the table. I turned my nose up at it, but my grandma Sorenson spread some on a bit of bread and gave it to me to taste. It was not like ours at home but good in a sharp way. It was the only time in my life I ate goat butter.

When I was a kid we used to get the white margarine packages with the Orange button of color in it. We kids fought over who should get to squeeze the orange button. The downside was the longer time it took to squeeze the food coloring into the rest of the package to create the yellow margarine and do it evenly.

The entire Crawford family bundled up to make the short trek in the snow to the barn. It was not far away but a snow trail made getting there easier.

The goat, Esmeralda, was munching away on her feed as we arrived. She was obviously used to visitors, and did not move when we walked up to the fence. She looked up at us and Jenny reached out to pet her. Esmeralda walked closer to the fence.

"She likes me," Jenny announced.

Cally ran up behind Jenny. She seemed a bit jealous and nuzzled Jenny's knees. Jenny reached down to affectionately stroke Cally on the head. The dog barked a couple times and seemed to want to engage in some play. That pretty much took care of the goat visit. The goat moved away from us. She did not seem to like the noisy yipping from the playful dog. Cally and Jenny chased about in the snow. Jenny formed a small snowball and tossed it Cally's way. Cally jumped to catch it and the bite sent small chunks of snow flying in every direction.

I caught Jenny on her way by me and told her I needed to leave.

She frowned but accepted the decision readily. I was grateful.

"I know. I miss you. When can I see you again?" she asked.

I pulled my business card out of my pocket. "Here is my information. We can write or call or stay in touch like friends and family do for each other. I do not know when I will see you again. It may be awhile, so let's stay in touch. Walk with me back to my car."

The family walked with us. There were hugs all around and they gathered on the lovely porch to offer farewells. I let my car warm a bit. I never took a cold vehicle out on the roads during the winter.

The snapshot in my mind of Jenny so solidly bonding with her family filled my heart. I offered a sweeping wave and blew a kiss to all of them. My Sebring kept me toasty warm despite the fact is a convertible. I headed back to Minot to get ready for work the next week. It felt like a mini vacation to me as I drove.

In the weeks and months to follow, Jenny and I kept in touch as much as we could, but over time the frequency of our connection faded. Jenny was finding her stride. Once she found safety with a loving family she also found human freedoms to fulfill her own destiny and chose her place within it. The Crawford family continued to supply her with a nurturing environment for her growth. Not every kid gets to grow up in such a supportive environment, as I knew so well. This opportunity was a gift for her and the Crawford family as well.

Jenny wrote me a letter to let me know that she planned to return to high school. She had already started taking sessions online to catch up. She also bubbled about having her own laptop now. The Crawfords provided it for her. Kimberly had one, so they felt Jenny should have one too. I wrote back to her and gave her an email account I kept for students only.

Jenny's grandmother, a heavy smoker for many years, developed lung cancer and was treated for it. She completed her mental health assessments and treatments and permanently located in Fargo where she continued work with some mental health support groups. I was out of the loop on whether she knew anything about Jenny's relocation. I doubted it.

"It is odd that Jenny's grandmother is conspicuously absent in any of Jenny's memories of her own mother's cancer and death," I said to Dr. Cleveland at one point.

"Oh, I am not surprised at that at all. Grandma was a somewhat unwilling custodial parent to Jenny. When we were working together, she told me that she thought having Jenny around would be a problem for her hooking up with a husband or a man. She pretty much stayed out of the situation by choice. I am not at all surprised," Dr. Cleveland said.

I asked Dr. Cleveland about keeping Jenny's location secret from Grandma. I was afraid she might stalk Jenny and undo all the excellent progress she had made.

Dr. Cleveland doubted grandma would ever live on her own again. Her mental challenges were many and with the difficulty in breathing, she did not see a threat from her again. Dr. Cleveland also believed with the boyfriend locked away behind bars and out of influence with her that the whole motivation for going after Jenny was a moot issue now. She did have one new development.

"We learned just recently that his name came up on a porn site for human trafficking. It is called Backdoor and state law enforcement has shut it down. They investigated the participants on the website and found his name all over it. Thank God that Jenny did not go through being sold into prostitution or being trafficked for sex. Thank God for our work to get her into a good home."

I took a deep breath. My Lord, this could have been so much worse for Jenny. It certainly has been for girls and women around the world in the age we live in.

Jenny and I gradually drifted farther and farther apart. I attended her birthday parties and we always made time for each other at Christmas. I attended Jenny's high school graduation. Through those years, the Crawfords continued to be a wholesome and inspirational influence in Jenny's life. Jenny played high school sports, took part in drama and even went to Girl's State. She made many friends. She rode in several of the Can Am bicycle rides with the Crawfords. She even liked the camping trips with them.

I invited Jenny to camp with me at my favorite North Dakota park, Cross Ranch. She joined me on several occasions and I introduced her to my friend, Richard, the ranger there. We attended his presentations in the evenings. We made smores and cooked over my tiny camp stove and enjoyed our walks through the forest. She liked to make chili and it was her thing at least once on every camping trip.

Ellen and David Crawford kept me posted on all of her accomplishments. They were overjoyed at what good friends the girls had become. In her last card to me, Jenny included a picture of them with Cally and the goats. Jenny had her own goat now and even showed it at the local 4-H event.

The girls were very active in their high school, taking part in many extracurricular events. The Crawfords purchased a car for the girls to make logistics a little easier on the family. Jenny now had a drivers license. She sent me a copy of it and I posted it next to her cards in my office.

Jenny told me that she saved all of her birthday and prize money. Both girls worked part time at a local café and babysat whenever they could to earn extra money. Jenny told me she saved every penny and she had a tidy little bank account "stash" now. The Crawfords pitched in an allowance for completing chores for the girls as well.

Jenny's first day of college was treated as celebration in the Crawford family. The girls enrolled at Minot State University. The Crawfords planned a lunch date at the college and my invitation to it was kept as a surprise for Jenny.

I threaded my way through campus to the cafeteria, which had changed drastically in the nearly 50 years since I attended. I only hoped college would be the game changer for Jenny that it was for me. I loved all the improvements I found there.

We met in a quiet corner of the cafeteria. Jenny was standing with her back to me, which was perfect. I walked up behind her and spoke her name. She turned around flashed me a joyous smile and hugged me tightly.

The beautiful, confident young woman I saw in front of me nearly made me weep. She looked so grown up compared to the tortured little waif I first met.

The human spirit can be a fragile thing. It can be delicate and easily beaten down. But there is no mistaking what happens to it when a little caring is spread around. It is a lesson too often lost on many people. The opportunity to soar is kindled sometimes by even small gestures it seemed to me. My thoughts must have betrayed me because I could hear my name and realized that Ellen Crawford had been calling it for a few moments now. I was lost in my own thoughts.

"Miss Emily, would you sit here next to Jenny, please?" We all sat down. Pastor Crawford was already over at the counter bringing back burgers and fries for everyone. College students filed in and out of the cafeteria all around us. I remembered my college days and the brief reprieve from reading and assignments. Sometimes the English majors gathered at a table on the far end to discuss the newest assignments or other issues.

"How are you feeling about college?" I asked Jenny.

"I am nervous. But we have a friend, Carole, who is a sophomore here and she says we will get over that," she answered.

Kimberly nodded and added, "We are going to major in Psychology. I want to double major in music and Jenny wants to double major in Psychology and Nursing," she said.

"That was going to be my next question," I said. "It is good you are going right out of high school. I married first and then went to college. I commuted 120 miles a day for five years to get my degrees. It is so much easier to do it the way you are doing it. I was an older than average student and had a lot of catching up to do. I am so glad you have this opportunity," I said.

"I am going to work, too. We both have grants and scholarships and we will get loans if we have to, but I would like to pay for as much as we can in work study," Jenny said.

I smiled. The Crawfords did not miss a beat. The girls already saved money in the bank and all of their options were fully explored.

"I have some cards for both of you," I said. I gave each girl a good luck card with the sentiment spelled out in several languages. I signed it "Bonne Chance" in French. The girls asked what it meant and I explained my French Major and two summers of study in Paris. Their eyes opened wide at the information.

"You studied in Paris?" they practically chimed in together. I guess I never mentioned it before. Most of my discussions focused on Jenny, of course.

"I did! And at that time terrorists were just starting to kick up their deeds. There were twenty-one acts of terrorism in the city that summer. One occurred only two blocks from where my class was having lunch at a bistro. My family begged me to come home. I just refuse to live in fear anywhere. If we are afraid they win, is my philosophy then and now. I refuse to let them win," I said.

The family looked at me as though they were seeing me for the very first time. I felt the need to go on. "I was on the front steps of the capitol in Bismarck to support the Equal Rights Amendment too. An opponents of the movement arrived by the busload. A sitting member of the North Dakota legislature walked up to me, looked at my ERA button and said, "Why don't you just stay in your own town!" An amendment that would have delivered equal pay for equal work was spun and spun into things like men would not have to open a car door for women if it passed, etc.

"I remember that," Ellen said and nodded in agreement.

"I don't remember anything like this," Jenny said.

"Life was giving you a pretty rough ride then. I wouldn't think you would remember. However, we all have a chance to stand up for what is right."

"We have some surprises for you," Pastor Crawford announced to the girls.

The Crawfords gave each girl a lovely card with a gift certificate from the college book store to pay for books. My cards also had gift certificates from the book store. I knew books tripled in price since my college days.

We finished our lunch, the girls hugged us and I chose an extra long walk back to my car. Minot State University was a game changer for me in my life and I wanted to enjoy some of the changes. I had not taken the time to do that.

College opened doors that would never have been open to me otherwise. It would for them too. Despite the cold temperature, I chose a longer walk back to my car. I just wanted to savor my beloved college. Much had changed there over the years, but I hold it profoundly in my heart to this day. As I walked I remember a comment one of my professors told me: "We know we've done a good job here when our students are able to function independently in their careers and remember their time here with fondness," he said.

Dr. Cleveland introduced Jenny and the Crawfords to the Lamplighters survival group in case she hit those bumps of memory down the road, she would have a soft place to land with people who understood

Jenny and I never lost touch with each other over the years. She and I and Rose and Alfalfa girl saw each other as often as we could for lunches and other quick catch ups. We rejoiced each time and fondly parted each time.

Jenny completed her studies at Minot State University. I attended her graduation from MSU. At our lunch that day, she surprised me."I have been accepted to North Dakota State University to work on my Masters Degree.

"NDSU was where I attained my Masters Degree," I said.

"I know. I want it to be my graduate school too," she said.

Her decision nearly brought me to tears. I did not even recall much about our discussions of it. But we must have at some point.

"I learned a lot in college and I want to help change things. I plan to get my degree in Political Science. I want to run for public office. I want to see that women are better represented than we are now," she said.

This little girl, now all grown up, was ready to take on problems much bigger than herself and do it to unselfishly help others as well. She had all she needed to do that. I stared at her poise and self-assuredness and recalled a time when she had all she could do to serve a roast pork dinner. But she did not give up on herself, ever.

My heart rejoiced! I smiled. Alfalfa girl's heart rejoiced! Alfalfa girl smiled.

THE END

CPSIA information can be obtained
at www.ICGtesting.com
Printed in the USA
LVHW031753190919
631610LV00003B/353

9 781984 544919